Y0-BZA-260

Please kiss me

Merry lifted her face, closed her eyes. An act of faith. Faith that Lucas was the guy she'd known, from boy to man. Bossy, infuriating, even arrogant. But not a man who would let her down.

She felt the whisper of a breath, then firm lips pressed to hers.

Thank you.

Lucas smelled of soap and spice and salt air. For that fraction of a second, she was warm, despite the brisk northerly wind coming down off the hills behind.

Then he pulled back. Merry's focus cleared from the odd haze in front of her eyes—*must be sea spray*—and she saw her father beaming from ear to ear.

That's why we're doing it. We're giving Dad peace of mind. It was all worthwhile.

Dear Reader,

Marriage is never straightforward, even when two people love each other and are committed "till death do us part." If you're married, you'll already have figured out that while love is a wonderful thing, a lasting marriage also requires patience, forgiveness, generosity, kindness...and much more!

I love marriage-of-convenience stories, where a couple ties the knot for reasons that don't include love, often under the delusion that it will be simple. As a writer and a reader, I love that moment where they realize marriage isn't a toy you can pick up and put down, and ignore when not in use.

Like a real marriage, a marriage of convenience tests the participants in ways they'd never imagined, forcing them to draw on all those qualities I mentioned earlier...and it's when those other things are being practiced that love has a chance to grow.

In *The Wedding Plan,* Merry Wyatt hatches a scheme to make her dying father happy—a noble goal. Unfortunately, it involves marrying Lucas Calder, the man who rejected her (and the brother of Garrett Calder from *That New York Minute*). The situation soon grows way more complicated than Merry or Lucas anticipated. I hope you enjoy the story of how these two independent people learn what real love is all about.

To share your thoughts about *The Wedding Plan*, or any of my books, please email abby@abbygaines.com. To read an After-the-End scene, visit the For Readers page at www.abbygaines.com.

Sincerely,

Abby Gaines

The Wedding Plan

ABBY GAINES

HARLEQUIN®
entertain, enrich, inspire™

If you purchased this book without a cover you should be aware that this book is stolen property. It was reported as "unsold and destroyed" to the publisher, and neither the author nor the publisher has received any payment for this "stripped book."

Recycling programs
for this product may
not exist in your area.

ISBN-13: 978-0-373-71814-6

THE WEDDING PLAN

Copyright © 2012 by Abby Gaines

All rights reserved. Except for use in any review, the reproduction or utilization of this work in whole or in part in any form by any electronic, mechanical or other means, now known or hereafter invented, including xerography, photocopying and recording, or in any information storage or retrieval system, is forbidden without the written permission of the publisher, Harlequin Enterprises Limited, 225 Duncan Mill Road, Don Mills, Ontario, Canada M3B 3K9.

This is a work of fiction. Names, characters, places and incidents are either the product of the author's imagination or are used fictitiously, and any resemblance to actual persons, living or dead, business establishments, events or locales is entirely coincidental.

This edition published by arrangement with Harlequin Books S.A.

For questions and comments about the quality of this book, please contact us at CustomerService@Harlequin.com.

® and TM are trademarks of Harlequin Enterprises Limited or its corporate affiliates. Trademarks indicated with ® are registered in the United States Patent and Trademark Office, the Canadian Trade Marks Office and in other countries.

www.Harlequin.com

Printed in U.S.A.

ABOUT THE AUTHOR

Abby Gaines writes contemporary romances for the Harlequin Superromance line, and Regency romances for the Love Inspired Historical line. Those might sound like two completely different genres, but Abby likes to say she writes "stories that leave you smiling"—wherever and whenever they are set. Her Harlequin Superromance novel *The Groom Came Back* won the 2010 Readers Crown Award, and her novella *One in a Million* won the 2011 Readers Crown. *The Wedding Plan* is Abby Gaines's twentieth book for Harlequin Books.

Abby loves cooking, reading, skiing and traveling...though not all at once! She lives with her husband and children—and a Labradoodle and a cat—in a house with enough stairs to keep her semi-fit and a sun-filled office whose sea view provides inspiration for her writing. Visit her at www.abbygaines.com.

Books by Abby Gaines

Other titles by this author available in ebook format.

For Irene Francis,

who still loves Russian literature and still hates
conversational lulls,

who is always true to herself and to those she loves.

CHAPTER ONE

LUCAS CALDER HAD SPENT the past eight years flying his chopper in places where no one spoke a language he recognized. But the hand signals and facial expressions of Afghani kids had been easier to understand than the scene he was witnessing now.

His father, Admiral Dwight Calder—famously rigid, gimlet-eyed and about as warm as a midnight watch on an aircraft carrier in the Arctic—blew a raspberry on the tummy of his baby daughter, Lucas's half sister, who was lying on her changing table.

Incomprehensible. And right now, damn inconvenient.

Lucas glanced at his watch: 3:00 p.m. Ten at night in the Gulf. He should be sitting at the tiny desk in his cabin, processing the next day's minesweeping flight plan, imprinting it on his memory.

"Who's a smelly girl?" Dwight teased. Mia shrieked with delight, apparently undisturbed by the stench emanating from her diaper.

"Dad, can we talk?" Lucas tried again to drag his father's attention to more serious matters. Such as Lucas's down-the-toilet military career.

"Of course we can." Dwight untaped the diaper.

Lucas took a hasty step backward. "Man, she stinks."

"Don't talk about your sister like that." Dwight wielded a wet wipe with surprising efficiency. It went without saying that he hadn't done any diaper changing when Lucas and his older brother, Garrett, were babies. Their father's metamorphosis to doting dad was very new. For Mia's sake, Lucas was pleased.

He just wished it was possible to have a conversation with his father that wasn't about feeding or potty time.

As Dwight tossed the diaper in the trash, Mia wriggled, a flurry of pudgy arms and legs. Lucas surged forward to block the side of the changing table.

Dwight held her in place with a hand on her chest. "I wouldn't let her fall," he growled.

Lucas hadn't come back to New London, Connecticut, to argue with his dad. He stepped away.

"Pass me a new diaper," his father ordered. The return to something approaching military style was so welcome that Lucas obeyed.

When Mia was dressed again, Dwight picked her up. "Would you like to hold her?" he asked Lucas.

"Uh, no. I'm good, thanks."

Mia nestled against Dwight's shoulder, eyelids at half-mast.

"She'll nod off soon," he predicted. "Let's talk downstairs in my study."

As they reached the bottom of the staircase, the glass-paned front door opened. Stephanie, Lucas's stepmom, came in and set her purse on the hall console. She gave a squeal of pleasure. "Lucas! When did you get here? Come give me a hug, you adorable boy."

He squeezed her tightly. "I don't need to ask how you are. You look great."

She smacked his shoulder. "Liar. Do you know how hard it is for a woman in her mid-forties to lose baby weight? But I love you for saying it." She pulled away to address Dwight. "Darling, you know very well Mia should be in bed."

"She kept calling to me over the baby monitor," he protested.

Lucas noted with some discomfort that his father sounded *sheepish*. Great. The country had benefited for decades from Admiral Calder's unrelenting sense of mission, but the one time Lucas needed his dad operating at full aggression… What had happened to Admiral Cold-ass, as he'd been irreverently known to his crew?

Stephanie took the baby from Dwight. "I'll put her to bed. Sorry, sweetie," she crooned to Mia, "but Mean Mommy's back."

Mia babbled something that may or may not have been an attempt at words. Her parents cooed as if she'd just recited Shakespeare.

Lucas couldn't help noticing that Dwight caressed his wife's bottom as she passed. Things really *had* changed.

Was his dad even capable of focusing on Lucas's problem?

Lucas reminded himself that Dwight had been a navy man far longer than he'd been a family man. If he could just recall his "pre-enlightened" state, he would understand why Lucas needed his help.

"It's good to have you home," Dwight said as he settled into the burgundy leather chair behind his oak desk. The desk had once graced the captain's stateroom on a nineteenth-century sailing ship. "How's the hand?"

"Fine," Lucas said. "Great. Fully recovered." Sixteen months ago, his minesweeping chopper had been shot down in the Persian Gulf. Lucas had been medevaced to the U.S.A. for treatment—on the day Mia was born, as it turned out. Getting over the concussion, broken ribs and ankle and punctured lung had proved easy. Or so he'd thought at the time.

The surgery on his shattered hand had been more complex, the rehabilitation endless. Partly because Lucas had insisted on doing it all in one long stretch, relocating to Baltimore to be closer to the rehab center.

"Shame about your eyes." Someone must have reported the details of Lucas's latest physical to Dwight. Shouldn't happen, of course, but Admiral Calder had so many friends in high places, there was always someone keen to fill him in about his son. Even though Dwight would have been too honorable to ask.

"The only problem was my depth perception," Lucas said. "Everything else was fine." He'd had no idea that, after working so hard to restore his hand, he would fail his back-to-duty physical because of his eyesight. The doctor had attributed the change in his vision to the deep concussion he'd sustained in the crash.

The skeptical pursing of Dwight's lips said his father wasn't fooled by the words *the only problem*.

It was an insurmountable problem.

Nothing is insurmountable.

"You've heard they're discharging me, as of December 31," Lucas guessed. "I'm on leave until then."

Dwight nodded. "I understand you turned down a desk job."

"I want to fly." They'd told him that couldn't happen. He should have known better than to issue an ultimatum to the U.S. Navy. But no way did he want to sit at a desk while, out there, men risked their lives to protect others.

Thanks to his ultimatum—*send me back or discharge me*—he'd be out at the end of the year. A man without a mission. He couldn't get his head around the idea.

Hopefully, he wouldn't have to.

"You failed the physical, you can't fly," Dwight said.

Usually, Lucas considered having his father so high up in the navy to be a disadvantage. Today, he hoped that for the first time in his life, it would help.

"That's what I want to talk to you about," he said. "I need to see a different doctor, get a retest and a second opinion. I figured you'd know someone."

Someone who would understand his need to get back out there.

"We don't do retests," Dwight said. "Besides, if you failed it once, you'll fail again."

"There are exercises I can do to improve my depth perception," Lucas replied. He hoped what he'd read on the internet was true, not some urban myth. "If I'd known I had a problem, I would have done them already. As it is, I want to spend a month strengthening my vision, then sit the test again."

Another pilot had been assigned to Lucas's chopper on a temporary basis, on the assumption that he'd be back. Now that he was out, his C.O. wanted to appoint the other guy permanently. At Lucas's request, he'd agreed to hold off for a few more weeks. Seemed he had more faith in Lucas's ability to swing a retest than his dad did.

"I'm not sure I like the idea of you going back after what you went through," Dwight said. "You're lucky to be alive. You've done your duty to your country, and then some."

"It's not about duty," Lucas said. "It's about…" *No one*

in my unit is better than I am at undersea mine detection and destruction. No one is better at protecting our ships and their crews. They need me. He wasn't about to argue with his father about the numbers of lives and ships that were at stake every day over there. "This is who I am, Dad."

"Maybe this is a time to reevaluate *who you are.*" Dwight's emphasis recognized the irony of a man like himself talking such postmodern jargon. "The navy isn't everything—I almost lost what really mattered before I figured that out."

He and Stephanie had split up briefly before Mia's birth. Lucas wasn't sure what happened during their time apart, but Stephanie had said his father had come through it a changed man. His dad hadn't seemed much different when he'd visited Lucas in Baltimore, but here at home...

Change wasn't always a good thing.

"I'm a bit young for a midlife crisis, Dad," Lucas said evenly. "I know who I am, and I know what matters. Will you help me or not?"

His father picked up a fat, cigar-shaped gold pen and flipped it between his fingers. "What does Merry think you should do?"

"We haven't talked lately, and I haven't seen her since I got into town. I came straight to you."

Merry Wyatt was the daughter of John Wyatt, retired navy lieutenant and Dwight's best friend. John and Dwight had served in Vietnam together, on a submarine, back when they were practically kids. John had saved Dwight's life. Which Lucas assumed was why his unsentimental father had always shared John's desire to see Lucas and Merry's childhood friendship evolve into a romantic attachment.

He and Merry had humored their dads by dating once a year for the past, what, nine years? Yeah, nine, starting right after Merry graduated from high school. That first date had been a disaster, but some of the others had been…interesting. Over the years, each of them had used their on-again, off-again "romance" to their own advantage. Such as the year Lucas had claimed a back-home girlfriend as an excuse to refuse the attentions of his captain's daughter without offending the captain.

Their last date, six months ago in Baltimore, was responsible for the recent radio silence he and Merry had been observing.

"You should ask her what she thinks," his dad urged. "Merry's a sensible girl."

Sensible wasn't the word Lucas would use. But if talking to Merry would help bring Dwight around…

"Sure," he said. "I'll go see her now."

Sooner or later, they would have to meet up again. Might as well be now.

Merry was the forgiving type…wasn't she?

She's a romantic. An idealist. Idealists are quick to forgive.

Dwight beamed in approval of the plan. Since his father wasn't the beaming type, Lucas found it creepy. Still, he took advantage of that approbation to push his luck. "Dad, you didn't say if you'll help me get a retest."

An appeal against medical disqualification would require Dwight to pull strings. Something he had an aversion to.

Dwight steepled his fingers on his desk. "I'll think about it. How long are you staying?"

"Until you've thought about it," Lucas said.

LUCAS SLID OPEN THE double-wide, yellow-painted iron door of Wyatt Yachts' waterfront workshop. The track needed oiling; Lucas despised the effort the movement took.

A year of rehab on his right hand and it still felt as if muscle and sinew could turn to water at any moment. Part of his rehabilitation had been schooling his expression to not show pain.

He stepped into the workshop. The familiar smells of wood, mineral oil and polyurethane overlaid with salt hit him. High above his head, light filtered through salt-crusted windows, set below the roof trusses. The scale of the building dwarfed the overturned wooden hull in the middle of the floor, and dwarfed the man who was buffing it with sandpaper even more. Not for John Wyatt the electric sander, not once he got beyond the first stages. Wyatt Yachts created handcrafted wooden yachts, and it had a waiting list a mile long—even with Merry running the admin side so that John would be free to do what he loved most.

The older man must have heard the clank and rattle of the sliding door, but he didn't look around. He wouldn't, until he'd finished the line he was sanding. Back in high school, Lucas used to work here over the summer, so he knew John's methods. The place hadn't changed a bit.

Lucas veered right, toward the end of the workshop that had been closed off to make an office and kitchen.

A large window allowed people in the office to look out, and vice versa.

No sign of Merry.

Relief mingled with irritation. Now that he'd decided to clear the air, and to ask for her help, he didn't want to delay. Of course, he might have ensured a better response if he'd called her in the past six months. Or emailed. Or texted. He should probably have told her he was coming, at least.

He'd hoped it might all blow over if they didn't speak for a while.

At last John straightened, one hand pressed to the small of his back. "Lucas, when did you get in?" He came over and clasped Lucas's hand in both of his. "How're you doing? Your dad tells me you'll be out by year-end. Must be disappointed."

That was more like it. John knew how Lucas felt.

"I am," he said, returning the handshake. "But how are you?" John had always had a spare build, but today he looked almost skinny, and his grip was bony.

John rubbed his back again. "My kidneys are giving me trouble. I'm on the blasted dialysis twice a day now. At least the hospital has set me up so I can do it here, or at home." It was a cheerful grumble, the way a guy might complain when someone drinks the last of the two-percent, forcing him to pour skim milk over his cereal.

Or when he's being pursued by an enemy aircraft, faster than him and with more firepower, and he doesn't want his buddies to know he's terrified.

Lucas had seen a flash of terror in John's eyes.

"Your blood pressure still bad?" he asked. It was the

older man's hypertension that had damaged his kidneys in the first place. "You seen the doctor lately?"

"The doctor can't do a thing to knock my BP down." John chuckled, as if it was all a joke. "Though Merry has me on egg-white omelets." His heavy sigh suggested his only daughter had devised a particularly cruel form of torture.

"Tell it to Amnesty International," Merry said from behind Lucas.

When he turned around, she was crossing the workshop. She must have squeezed through the sliding door he hadn't managed to open very far. She wore skinny jeans and a pale green T-shirt that crossed over in front, creating a deep V. With her shoulder-length, light brown hair pulled back in a loose ponytail, she looked more or less the way he remembered her at twelve years old.

She'd been eyeing her dad with loving exasperation, but when she turned to Lucas, the loving disappeared.

To be replaced with an entirely adult glitter in her gray eyes. A woman-scorned kind of glitter.

I should have called.

"Lucas, I didn't realize you were coming home." Which was more or less the same as *you should have called,* uttered in a cool, distant voice that didn't suit her at all.

"Surprise," he said, forcing a smile. He stepped closer.

John would think it odd if he didn't at least kiss her cheek. No need to broadcast their rift to her dad, and therefore to his own father.

Lucas pressed his lips to Merry's cheek.

And was startled by a rush of sensation, of memory that he'd thought he'd put behind him, provoked by the scent of her skin. It was sweet, like the wild strawberries they used to pick at the start of summer. If he moved an inch or two to his right, to her lips...and if she opened her mouth...he knew she would taste of wild strawberries, too.

No, no, no. Not going there.

Merry took a step backward, away from his lips. Her face was stony.

With disconcerting slowness, Lucas's brain resumed normal service. That concussion must have done even more damage than the doctors knew.

John chuckled as he looked from Merry to Lucas. "Have you two had another tiff?" he said indulgently. "Why don't you go to dinner tonight, clear the air?"

Merry transferred her full attention to him, and her face softened. "Sorry to disappoint you, Dad," she said. "But Lucas isn't back in town to see me."

Lucas's eyes narrowed. She seemed mighty sure about that. "Actually, Merry, I do want to see you," he said.

Her father chuffed with satisfaction. "You two have your ups and downs, but you always come back to each other. One day, you'll sort yourselves out for good."

Not the most helpful observation, after Baltimore.

"I'm busy," Merry said. "I have a ton of supplier payments lined up this afternoon."

"How about I come back when you're done, and we go for a drink?" Lucas suggested. Not as big a commitment as dinner, but still in a public place. No room for misinterpretation.

She lifted her chin. "I have a date tonight."

Lucas felt a niggle of irritation. He wanted to *apologize,* for goodness' sake.

"Not with that Patrick again," her dad said disapprovingly. "I thought you broke up."

"He's been away the past week or so," she said. "That's all."

Who was Patrick?

Behind Merry, a collie dog rounded the sliding door and padded across the concrete floor.

"You have a visitor," Lucas said.

"That's Boo. My new dog." She snapped her fingers. "Come on, boy, come to Mommy."

Her voice went all gooey, much the way Dwight's had when he talked to Mia. Even if it was only about the dog, Lucas figured any sign of softening had to be good.

"You dog-napped Lassie," he said too heartily. "Way to go, Merry."

Pointing out the resemblance was a nod to Merry's favorite movie, a reminder of how well Lucas knew her. But it wasn't without risk. Merry had insisted they see *Lassie* on their very first date; Lucas had never been so bored in his life. She'd decried his bluntly voiced opinion as a sign of a lack of emotional depth. He'd accused her of being out of touch with reality.

And there ended Date Number One.

The dog lurched from side to side like a drunken sailor.

"Why is he walking funny?" Lucas asked.

"Shh, he'll hear you," she said. "Boo can't go."

"Can't go where?" Lucas asked. Her irises were flecked with gold…he'd never noticed that before.

"Can't *go*. He's constipated. Big-time, long-term. I've tried everything."

"She sure has," her dad said. "Not even the animal hypnotist could convince that thing to poop."

The dog's rolling gait suddenly looked less drunken sailor and more accident-waiting-to-happen.

"Have you tried feeding him whatever my baby sister's eating?" Lucas asked. "That'll fix it."

"Patrick thinks it's psychological," Merry said. "Boo's owner, Ruby, died of a heart attack late last year."

Boo perked up at his owner's name, his head swiveling between Merry and Lucas.

As if Lucas cared what her boyfriend thought.

"Patrick is Boo's vet," Merry explained. "Boo was boarding with him while Ruby was away on a cruise. After she died, her family didn't want him, so Patrick offered him to me. He's the sweetest thing."

"Boo or Patrick?" Lucas asked.

"Boo—well, both. Though I wouldn't say Boo's entirely accepted me as his owner."

The collie's long nose nudged Lucas's knee, as if to say *she's right*.

Lucas ignored the dog's purported emotional distress and homed on the most alarming aspect. "Are you saying this animal hasn't *gone* in six months?"

"Of course not." She tsked. "He'd be dead. But he doesn't go very often, and it's not comfortable when he—"

Lucas held up a hand. "I get the picture." Baby diapers and a constipated collie. Such were the challenges of life in New London.

"How long are you here for, Lucas?" John asked. "What are your plans for life after the navy?"

He glanced at Merry. Since she didn't look surprised,

she must have heard the news, too. "Actually, I have some ideas for how I might be able to get back to the Gulf."

"Maybe your eye trouble is a message that you should stay home," Merry said. Unlike the women he dated—the ones he dated for real—she'd never been impressed by his military career.

Sometimes it rankled.

"A message from who?" Lucas demanded. "Al Qaeda? Because that sounds like a damn good reason to go out there again."

"My hero," she murmured.

It wasn't a compliment.

She'd started calling him that back when they were kids, playing war games. Sometimes just the two of them, or sometimes he'd invite her to join him and his buddies. Lucas would set up a scenario that involved rescuing Merry from dire peril, but invariably she'd screw it up. He'd explain to her that the Viet Cong had covered her in honey and staked her to a fire ant mound, but don't worry, he would trek through the jungle to save her. Simple, right?

Wrong. You could bet that when he turned up at the "anthill," she would clasp her hands and say, "My hero," in gratifying tones. *Then* she'd inform him she'd freed herself by using a magnifying glass and the sun to set fire to the ropes that bound her, and had destroyed the ants by, say, playing music at a deadly pitch only ants could hear. In other words, she didn't need a hero.

Back then, Lucas never had high hopes for a *girl* in his platoon. Merry had managed to fall short of even his modest expectations.

He couldn't think why he'd kept asking her to play.

"You can't blame Merry for worrying about your safety," John said happily. He tweaked his daughter's ponytail. "Looks like your dog wants to go, Merry-Berry."

Boo was circling around, sniffing the ground.

"I just took him, and he didn't do anything—but I guess I'll try again," she grumbled.

Lucas seized the opportunity. "I'll come with you."

She glanced at her father, then pressed her lips together.

"Take your time," John said archly, as if he imagined they were headed outside for some nookie. He started back toward his work, but after a couple of steps, halted abruptly. Lucas couldn't see his expression, but recognized the clenching of hands at the older man's sides, and the way John deliberately loosened the fingers, one by one.

Pain.

Lucas took a step toward him.

Merry pushed past Lucas. "Dad, are you okay?"

Boo whined.

"Fine, Merry-Berry." John's smile was obviously forced. "Just some stomach cramping." He paused, as if counting silently. Then his smile grew more natural; the spasm must have passed. He made a shooing motion. "Off you go."

She hesitated.

A guy didn't want a bunch of people nosing around when he was in pain. Lucas jerked his head, indicating Merry should follow him.

Her reluctance was evident, but she came anyway.

Which could be a positive sign. On the other hand, her demeanor didn't exactly scream forgiveness.

I should have called.

CHAPTER TWO

ACT COOL, MERRY INSTRUCTED herself as she and Lucas walked with Boo toward the shingle cove that butted up against the wharf area, which in turn butted up against the marina. She sneaked a sidelong glance at Lucas, to find his handsome face angled down, his hands shoved in his pockets. *Pretend that night never happened.*

"I owe you an apology," he said.

Ugh.

"What for?" She injected surprise into her tone. Then she muttered, "Don't answer that." Because she really didn't want him to elaborate.

"It seemed a good idea at the time," he said.

Did he mean having sex or not having sex?

Boo headed for the rock pools, his usual silent, stoic, constipated self. He liked to sniff at the baby crabs, but didn't have the enthusiasm for an actual attack.

"It was one crazy moment," she said. "You were understandably upset, and I happened to be there...." *I happened to launch myself at you, taking advantage of your vulnerability.*

"You agree," he said, "that we were right to stop?"

"Absolutely." She did *now,* after what he'd done.

"It would have been for all the wrong reasons."

"Wrong," she agreed, wishing he would shut up.

She'd gone to visit him in Baltimore because their

fathers had been nagging, asking when she and Lucas would see each other again. The visit had been as much about getting their dads off their backs as about their fluctuating friendship.

She'd arrived a few hours after Lucas had learned that two men from his unit had been killed during a minesweeping operation. An operation Lucas would have been involved in, if he'd still been in the Gulf. He'd been a mess—he'd seemed to think he could have saved his friends.

Fueled by a couple of whiskeys that he shouldn't have drunk while on pain meds, he'd poured out guilt and self-recrimination with a depth of feeling Merry hadn't known he was capable of. Naturally, she'd wanted to comfort him. When he slung an arm across her shoulders, she'd snuggled into him on the couch. And was reminded of Date Number Eight, in December last year. Lucas's brother's wedding. When for the first time ever, they'd given in to the sexual chemistry that had arced between them on and off for years, and had kissed.

That's all. Kissed.

But it had been *H-O-T.*

So hot, they'd both pulled back. Yeah, there was chemistry, but they wanted different things out of life, and getting involved would be too…involved.

But in Baltimore, with Lucas all vulnerable and upset beside her, Merry had forgotten the complications and remembered the heat. In the next minute, she'd been on his lap, her mouth pressed to his.

He hadn't objected in the slightest. In record time, he'd had her out of her clothes.

And then…

Then he'd looked down at her naked body, which, admittedly, was nothing great. She didn't have legs up to here, or high, bouncing breasts—she was short, and had hardly any breasts at all. Lucas had paused and looked down at her for a long time, and then he'd said, "Let's not do this."

Merry had dressed in mortified silence. She'd left while he was in the bathroom. They hadn't spoken since.

Boo trotted up, carrying a stick of driftwood. Merry busied herself, patting his head, cooing at him. When the sting in her eyes had gone, she straightened and threw the stick. Boo watched its trajectory, but didn't bother to pursue it.

"So, are we okay?" Lucas was eyeing her with concern. As if she was a problem he needed to fix.

"Of course," she said. "I'd hate to be held to one stupid moment, and so would you. Sex is one thing, but relationshipwise, I want what my parents had. You're the last person in the world for that."

He looked taken aback at being "the last person in the world." But it was true. Lucas was pragmatic, protective and, in his own way, caring. But she knew from the debates—purely theoretical—they'd had over the years that he didn't believe in the kind of soul-mate love her parents had had. He would never love a woman the way Merry wanted to be loved. Her mom had died twenty-three years ago, when Merry was three years old, and her dad still grieved.

Lucas's mom had died when he was twelve, and Dwight had remarried in less than six months. Merry could easily imagine Lucas doing the same.

"If anything, I'm the one who should apologize," she

said. "Frankly, Lucas, given how upset you were, my behavior was predatory."

His shout of laughter startled her.

"Merry Wyatt, sexual predator," he mused, and she felt a sliver of relief at the release of tension.

"At the very least, I was exploitative." She scuffed her sneaker in the sand.

"Don't talk dumb," he said. "I'm pretty sure I started it."

He hadn't, but she didn't argue.

If only he'd turned her down *before* she was naked. Then she could have accepted the "too complicated" excuse without a qualm. As it was, for weeks she'd wondered, *Was it something specific? My breasts, or my legs? Or did I just not turn you on?*

They'd reached the stick she'd thrown for Boo. Lucas bent to pick it up with his left hand. He was right-handed.

"How's your injury?" she asked to change the subject.

"Never better." He let his hand swing freely at his side. Which, judging by the tightening of his jaw, caused him pain.

Stupid hero complex.

What kind of guy would want to go back to the place where he'd suffered such horrible injuries? A guy like Lucas, who couldn't help jumping in and saving the world.

Boo nudged Merry's thigh. She noogied his head, the way he loved. He rewarded her with a rasp of his tongue on her wrist.

"Your dad doesn't seem too well," Lucas said. His turn to change the subject, it seemed.

"He gets tired more easily," she agreed. "Anyone would find five years of dialysis wearing."

"You should get him to a doctor."

Oh, honestly. Did he think no one was monitoring the dialysis? "Dad has regular checkups." Before Lucas could ask, she said, "I'm not sure when the next one is."

"Merry, your dad's in pain. Severe pain. I know the signs."

A chill swept her, borne on the fall breeze. "No, he's— It's just the doctors can't manage his kidney condition when his blood pressure's so high." A sudden prickle behind her eyes made it hard to continue. "But they can't seem to get his blood pressure down. His doctor thinks it's emotional stress."

"What emotional stress would he have?"

"Dad's not the kind to talk about his worries," she admitted. "But the past six months, I've caught him several times just sitting in a kind of trance."

All she had to do was speak, and he'd snap out of his private thoughts, but still, those moments worried her. She wasn't used to him not telling her everything. But she didn't want to discuss this with Lucas. Didn't want him to see how scared she was. *Dad's got through everything else. He'll get through this, too.*

"We've had a really mild fall," she commented.

"So, what's with this guy you're dating?" Lucas asked. "This Patrick?" He whistled to Boo, who was nosing a pile of rotting seaweed. With one last sniff, the collie abandoned his find.

"He's great," she enthused. She wanted to say, *He can't get enough of my body. He thinks small boobs are gorgeous. He's crazy about me.* But that might sound a tad defensive. "He's very romantic." Despite it being true, Lucas didn't look impressed. But then, he wouldn't. "He's a vet," she added, babbling now.

"I already got that," he said.

So he did.

"I think it might be serious," she said.

His head snapped around. "Really?"

"Um, yes." Patrick certainly talked as if it was. "Yes," she said with more certainty. "It might be."

"But your dad doesn't like him, right?"

"That's the one drawback," she agreed.

"What's wrong with the guy?" Lucas asked.

"He's…" For one moment she wished Patrick was a different kind of guy. "Um, you know that Shakespeare quotation, 'Cry havoc, and let slip the dogs of war?'"

"One of my favorites," Lucas deadpanned.

Entirely possible, given his penchant for rushing to the rescue. Merry sighed. "Patrick's the founder of the Dogs of Peace."

"The *what?*"

"It's a peace protest group."

Lucas snorted a laugh.

Merry was all in favor of the laying down of arms and everyone loving their fellow man, et cetera. Truly. But it would be a lot handier if Patrick could devote himself to a different cause. Saving trees, for example. Trees needed protestors, too.

Her father might not have much respect for tree huggers, but he didn't despise them.

"Patrick thinks the military is evil." She ignored Lucas's exaggerated gasp. "He believes he has a right to say so, and he likes to exercise that right. Often. Turns out Dad doesn't appreciate free speech, not all the time."

"Where did you meet this flake?" Lucas asked.

In the interest of winning the war, rather than every tiny battle, Merry bit down on the urge to extol Patrick's wonderful, manly qualities. "He was protesting outside the submarine base in Groton."

"With…the Dogs of Peace." Lucas said the name as if it were a rat's carcass that Boo had dragged in.

"Right," Merry said. "Patrick's a veterinarian. *Dogs of Peace,* get it?"

"Oh, brother," Lucas muttered. "How long have you been seeing him?"

"Several months." Since soon after that night in Baltimore, but that was sheer coincidence.

Lucas's forehead cleared. "So, if you and Patrick are serious, you really are fine about that night we…"

"Totally." Ugh, her voice went too high.

"That's great, Merry, because I want us to stay friends." His sudden smile was oddly boyish. It tugged at the same part of her that had been attracted to Vulnerable Lucas six months ago.

"I bet you do," she said. "I probably know more of your faults than any other woman, and I'm still willing to talk to you." *Yes, remember his faults. That'll help.*

He grinned. "That goes both ways. Does Patrick know how bad you are at letting a guy look after you?"

She used to enjoy infuriating him during their childhood games. He would turn up to rescue her, claiming to have boarded the submarine where she was being held hostage. She would claim to have overpowered her captor, escaped the sub, then grabbed on to a passing dolphin that delivered her to shore. A scenario no dumber than his, which involved him sneaking into a submerged submarine.

It wasn't that she didn't like being looked after, it was more that she'd never liked Lucas's reasons for wanting to protect her and everyone else in his path. It was nothing personal…and that was the problem.

"Patrick doesn't need to save the world to feel good about himself," she said. Wonderful though he was with animals, there wasn't much chance of Patrick overdoing the rescuer instinct.

Lucas opened his mouth as if to argue. Then he paused, and said, "Since we're okay, can I ask you a favor? I just came from my parents' place."

"Did you see Mia?" Merry asked. "Isn't she adorable?"

He blinked. "Yeah, sure. Dad wants me to talk to you about whether I should be trying to get back to the Gulf." Lucas sounded as if he couldn't quite believe his father was relying on any opinion other than his own.

They'd reached the end of the beach; they turned and started back.

"Your dad's a changed man," she said. "I like him a lot better these days."

Lucas didn't look excited. "Could you tell him you think I should get a retest on the physical?"

"What if I don't think that? What if I think it's time you accepted reality and figured out what matters?"

He rolled his eyes. "You sound like Dad. But it's not like you're big on reality yourself, with your romantic ideals." He must have sensed her imminent objection, because he hurried on. "And it's not like I haven't helped you in the past. You used the fact we were 'dating' to make your father feel better about you turning down a full ride to Berkeley."

Lucas had been hopping mad with her about that. But she'd wanted to stay with her father. They were each other's only family, and family was important. But Dad wouldn't have wanted to "hold her back," so Lucas had grudgingly let her claim a closeness they didn't have. While her dad had been disappointed she wasn't going on to further study, he'd been happy that she and Lucas were together.

"I've already done my share of helping you out," she said. "I was your decoy for six months when that captain's daughter was after you. We didn't 'break up' until you were assigned to the ship you wanted."

"I know, but—"

"And what about when you were worried Dwight might use his influence to keep you out of a war zone? I gushed for three months about how thrilled I was that you were fighting tyranny on foreign shores. I did a great job."

Their strategy had been simple, but effective. Since Lucas and his dad had a weird don't ask, don't tell policy on any number of subjects, Dwight would never discuss Lucas's love life with him. Instead, Merry informed her own father of their latest status, knowing that he would pass it to Dwight over their weekly game of pool, or while they tended meat on the grill.

"In hindsight," Lucas said, "I don't think Dad would have intervened. So that one doesn't count."

"It counts," she retorted. "Then there was that ex-girlfriend's wedding I had to attend as your date." Lucas had wanted to make it clear to the groom he wasn't pining for the bride.

"You've been a trouper," he said insincerely. "One more time, Merry, that's all I'm asking. Then you and Patrick can ride off into the sunset spouting poetry or whatever it is you romantic types like to do."

She smacked his arm before she remembered that touching him wasn't a good idea. Too much room for confusion.

Boo yipped, as if questioning her intent; his Lassie face had lengthened in anxiety.

"Fine," Merry said.

He stopped. "You'll do it? You'll ask my dad to request a retest?"

"Yes, I'll do it," she said. "What are friends for?" He was right; they did help each other out when they could. And if he went back to the Gulf, she wouldn't see him for another year, by which time there was a faint chance they would both have forgotten Baltimore.

Not.

"Thanks, Merry," he said.

For one horrendous moment, she thought he might kiss her.

Then he said, "I'll ask your dad to put in a good word, too. I need all the help I can get." Mission accomplished, he strode toward the workshop, distancing himself from her with every step.

He wrenched the iron door along its track, pausing halfway, then finishing the job with renewed vigor. He disappeared inside.

Ten seconds later, Merry heard a shout. And despite

all the denials she'd issued to Lucas, in that instant, she *knew.*

She sprinted after him.

Her dad was lying on the floor of the workshop, next to the hull of the half-formed yacht. Lucas had one hand on his pulse, the other wrapped around his cell phone.

CHAPTER THREE

"WHEN WILL THEY TELL ME what's going on?" Merry gripped the edge of her plastic chair in the ICU waiting room that the hospital had assigned to "Family of John Wyatt."

"As soon as they know something." Lucas was doing a good job of acting as if she hadn't asked that question twenty times already. She wondered if the U.S. Naval Academy ran classes in Maintaining a Rocklike Calm in a Crisis. Lucas would have aced it.

"I called my dad," he said. "He and Stephanie are waiting for a sitter for Mia, then they'll be right here."

"They don't need to come." Her father and Lucas's had been there for each other at all the most important events of their lives. She wanted this to be a little glitch, not a defining moment.

She and Lucas lapsed into silence again. When a nurse stuck her head around the door, they both jumped.

"A doctor will be out to see you in about ten minutes, Ms. Wyatt." Her gaze drifted sideways to Lucas. Her eyes widened and she smiled. "Thank you for your patience." She left the room with a lingering glance over her shoulder. Not at Merry.

"If you're looking for a date, you could be in luck," Merry said.

"Not interested." Lucas stretched back in his chair.

"I didn't ask," she said. "Are you seeing anyone at the moment? Other than me?"

It wasn't much of a joke. Still, he smiled. "Currently single. There was someone last year, before I was shot down—a nurse on my aircraft carrier. She married another guy. Lucky for you, I wasn't invited to the wedding, so I didn't need a date."

Merry forced herself to keep talking so she wouldn't fall into a panic about her father. "That seems to be a recurring theme. Girlfriend breaks up with you, then marries someone else six months later. Do you think the adrenaline rush of getting away from you makes them crazy?"

"She proposed to me, and I turned her down. She found a man who wanted the fairy-tale wedding. End of story."

Lucas stood and crossed to a poster of CPR instructions on the wall. He began reading, though Merry suspected he knew the details inside out from his military training. Her dad had still had a pulse when they'd found him, so CPR hadn't been necessary. Maybe she should take a refresher course, so that next time...

She shied away from the thought. Yeah, Dad was sick, but the dialysis was working. Whatever this episode was, he'd get past it. *They'd* get past it. "Why didn't you want to marry her? What was wrong with her?" Easier to analyze Lucas's patchy dating history than her father's health.

Lucas leaned against the wall, obscuring useful advice about clearing the airway before commencing CPR. "Nothing. She checked all the boxes."

"Loves the navy, built like a Victoria's Secret model..." Merry counted points off on her fingers.

He grinned. "Pretty much."

So Merry's small breasts *had* turned him off. The only kind of Victoria's Secret model she could be was for one of those bras that transformed nonexistent boobs into almost-cleavage. "She sounds perfect."

"She was turning thirty," Lucas said.

Merry gasped. "An old hag!"

His mouth quirked. "Her biological clock was ticking. When I said I wasn't ready for marriage, she asked me to be a sperm donor."

"And you didn't want to?"

"If I was going to procreate, I'd want to raise the kid myself." He sat down again, this time several seats away from Merry.

Of course he'd want to do it himself. He would never shirk a responsibility. But there was more to parenting than that, or there should be.

"Being a dad is a big deal," she limited herself to saying. John Wyatt was the only parent she knew. He'd not only been a wonderful father, he'd kept alive the mother she didn't remember. If she lost him...

"Snap out of it, Merry," Lucas said. "Don't assume the worst."

"Quit ordering me around." Her reflexive reaction.

"You never could do as you were told." He shook his head with mock disappointment.

"*You* never could explain why I had to be the petty officer third class, while you always got to be the captain."

He blinked at the reference to that childhood resentment. But she *felt* suddenly like a child. Vulnerable to loss.

"It was for your own good," he said. "I couldn't promote you until you learned not to be insubordinate. You were even worse when you were the enemy—you could never accept that prisoner of war meant you were the loser."

"You could never understand that I might have cooperated if you didn't insist on being in command," she retorted.

Though today had proved that a tendency to take charge wasn't always a bad thing. While Merry had been paralyzed with shock, Lucas had found a blanket in the office, put it over her father, continued monitoring his pulse. He'd stayed so calm as they'd waited for the ambulance.

"You were great today," she blurted.

"I didn't do anything." He folded his arms across his chest.

The door to the waiting room opened. A woman wearing scrubs came in. "Ms. Wyatt?"

Merry stood on legs that were suddenly leaden. "That's me."

"I'm Dr. Randall. Your father is stable in ICU."

"Stable." Merry clutched the word.

"I'm afraid that's a temporary state," the doctor said. "We're still running tests, but we believe your father has dialysis-associated peritonitis."

He'd had that before, though not so badly that he'd collapsed. Infection was a constant risk for peritoneal dialysis patients, usually resulting from a lapse in hygiene during the process. Merry made sure everything occurred in a sterile fashion during his lunchtime session, but she could imagine her dad "not bothering" in the evening.

"I'll supervise him every time from now on," she vowed. "I'll move in with him—I'll hold a gun to his head until he scrubs every last speck of sawdust from under his fingernails."

Dr. Randall looked startled. Lucas grinned.

"I'm afraid it's not that simple," the doctor said. "If the infection's as severe as we believe, Mr. Wyatt can't continue on peritoneal dialysis…and the reason he switched to PD two years ago was because hemodialysis was no longer a possibility for him."

Lucas's smile vanished. "How long does he have?"

What did he mean, *how long?* That was the kind of question you asked about people who…

"We expect his kidney failure to become fatal in the next ten days," Dr. Randall said.

"Dad's going to *die?*" Merry's knees sagged. Before she could keel over, Lucas's arm came around her shoulders, held her up. Impersonal, but strong. "In *ten days?*"

"Given his current condition, I'd say more likely in the next four or five days. I'm sorry, Ms. Wyatt, not to have better news." The doctor fingered the stethoscope protruding from her trouser pocket. "I know this won't make you feel better right now, but kidney failure is considered one of the gentler forms of death. Very peaceful. Many medical personnel say it's the way they'd like to go."

Merry started to laugh. She knew she was becoming hysterical, but couldn't stop it.

The doctor took a step backward.

Lucas tightened his hold on Merry's shoulder. "There must be something we can do."

"There's still the possibility of a donor kidney becoming available," the doctor said. "I know you're not a match, Ms. Wyatt, but are there any other relatives or friends who might agree to being tested?"

"I will," Lucas said.

Merry caught her breath. "You'd do that? For Dad?"

"Your dad saved my dad's life. Time the Calders returned the favor."

The doctor looked confused. "So…this isn't your husband?"

"No!" They spoke almost in unison, with Merry just a tad faster.

"What blood type are you?" Dr. Randall asked Lucas. "That's the first thing to consider before we move ahead to any tests."

"I'm A positive. What do you need?" As if he could change his blood type to suit.

"I'm sorry." The doctor told him what Merry already knew. "Mr. Wyatt is type O, so we need an O donor."

"Maybe my father's a match." Lucas offered up one of Dwight's kidneys without hesitation.

"Your dad already got tested back when Dad had to move off hemodialysis," Merry said. "And Dwight made such a fuss about Stephanie doing it, she backed down. I think we've exhausted our pool of related donors," she told the doctor. "Has Dad moved up the general transplant list?"

"It's not a list, as such," the doctor said. "Patients are assigned points based on several criteria. But, yes, your father has more points than he did yesterday." She scrubbed at her eyes with her hands, looking exhausted. Merry almost forgave her the comment about a "gentle" death.

After the physician left, Merry realized Lucas's arm was still around her. She moved away. "Lucas, thank you for offering to get tested. That was—" Her throat clogged.

"A safe bet," he said with a shrug. "What were the odds I'd end up a match?"

But she knew he'd meant it. Merry found herself scrubbing her eyes the same way the doctor had. "Where am I going to get a kidney?" she said. "Could I buy one on eBay?" She was joking, but only just.

"Too Third World," he said. "Better to stake out the blood donor clinic, figure out who's a match, then run them over in the parking lot."

She managed a watery smile. "Great idea."

"The challenge is not to kill them," he mused, "but to get them into the hospital close enough to death for the kidney to be available stat."

"Okay, now you're scaring me."

The nurse stuck her head around the door again. "Ms. Wyatt, you can see your father now. Ten minutes, just one of you." She spoke to Merry, but looked at Lucas.

Merry jumped to her feet. "At last. Thank you."

Lucas put a hand on her arm, stalling her. "Merry... if the doctor's right, and your father doesn't have much time, you probably need to tell some people. Folks who want to say goodbye. I could leave now, go make some calls."

The room swam for a moment and she grasped the back of the chair she'd just vacated. "His friends," she murmured. "Old navy buddies. If we ask your father and a couple of others to pass the word along… Dad will tell me who to speak to. I'll text you."

"Family?"

She shook her head. "He has cousins in England, but it's only the younger generation left. We're not in touch."

It sounded so lonely. So sad. Yet it hadn't been, not when there'd been the two of them.

But in a few days, it would be only Merry.

MERRY'S FATHER'S ROOM was a hive of monitors, wires, tubes. He took up most of the length of the bed, but little of the width. His eyes were open, unblinking, and for a horrified moment she thought he—

"Merry-Berry," he rasped.

She rushed forward, looking for some part of him she could hold on to without ripping out a tube, or hurting him. There was nothing, no part of him untouched, except for the callused fingers of his right hand.

She sandwiched them between her palms. "Dad, you…" *Slow down, don't upset him.* "You gave me a scare."

His chuckle sounded like air leaking out of a balloon…but at least it was there. Maybe the doctor was wrong.

"When you get out of here, I'm going to monitor every dialysis session, whether you like it or not," she vowed.

"Yes, dear," he said with a faint smile. But his eyes said he knew he wouldn't be getting out of here.

To her horror, a tear leaked out of the corner of his right eye and ran onto the pillow. "Dad, please…"

His fingers twitched between hers. "Merry...the lawyer has a copy of my will."

"The doctor says you've moved up in the transplant points," Merry said. "You could get a new kidney any minute."

"It's pretty straightforward. Everything to you, except for a small bequest to the VVA." Her dad was a longtime supporter of the Vietnam Veterans of America.

"We'll get you through this," she said. "I'm not letting you go, Dad."

"I'm not worried about you financially," he persisted. "You'll do nicely by selling the business. But...Merry-Berry, I think I made a mistake."

She blinked away tears. "Dad, it's so hard to avoid infection when you're on dialysis, anyone could—"

"Not that," he said. "After your mother died, I should have— Maybe I should have married again."

Merry straightened, shocked. "No, Dad. You always said you could never love anyone else."

"Maybe I should have tried. Then I wouldn't be leaving you alone." John tipped his head back and stared at the ceiling. "I wish I *had* met someone else, like Dwight did. But I didn't even try."

"I never wanted a stepmother," Merry said. She thought about Lucas's brother, Garrett, who until recently had considered Stephanie his enemy. A stepmother she hated would have been far worse than no one at all. "I've loved it being just you and me. And I love your stories about Mom, and about how you two met and fell in love."

Her father's chin quivered. Barely noticeable, but it was there. Amazing that the memory of her mother still had the power to affect him like that.

"I hate the thought of you being alone," he said. His fingers fluttered in her grip. "Merry, this has been on my mind for a while."

If he'd been thinking about it, he'd obviously sensed he was sicker than he'd let on. Was his worry about her future the cause of those "trances" she occasionally found him in? The reason for the stress that had sent his high blood pressure over the edge?

"I'll be just fine." Her attempt at reassurance came out thin and unconvincing. Her dad was everything, everyone, to her. She had friends, boyfriends…but no one who put her first in their life. "I—I love you, Dad. So much." She dug in her pocket for a tissue, blew her nose. "Please, don't worry about me, just concentrate on getting better."

A stupid thing to say.

He nodded. But another tear leaked onto his pillow, and then another. And now her tissue was all snotty.

"You've been wonderful, the way you've looked after me," he said. "Never interfering or pushy, but making sure I was doing my dialysis, getting regular checkups."

"I haven't done anything," she said. "You wouldn't let me."

He smiled, and it felt like a gift. "I was mad when you wouldn't go away to college, but I've been so grateful to have you here with me. A lot of parents, their kids go away to school, they meet some guy or girl on the other side of the country, and that's it. Gone."

"I couldn't leave you, Dad."

"Instead, I'm leaving you," he said. "Who'll look after you, Merry, if you get sick? Who'll fix your car when that starter motor plays up again?"

"My doctor and my mechanic," she said, and this time she managed the necessary lightness.

"Who's going to comfort you when I'm gone?" he asked. "Be at your side, through good times and bad? Not just next week, but for the rest of your life."

It struck her that during all that time in the waiting room, she hadn't once thought of calling Patrick.

"There'll be someone." She tried to sound confident. "Dad, I don't want you worrying about me. Think of something that makes you happy."

"I'll tell you what would make me happy," he said with a surge of energy that sent her hopes soaring. "It'd stop me worrying, too."

"Whatever it is, I'll make it happen," she said instantly. "Uh, I don't have to 'hang, draw and quarter those idiots who made Fisher Street one-way,' do I?"

Her father gave a raspy chuckle at one of his favorite threats. "Nothing so drastic, Merry-Berry." He patted her hand. "I'd like you to get married."

She laughed, louder than the joke deserved, but if he felt well enough to kid around…

Wait a minute.

He wasn't smiling.

He was giving her the same look he had when he'd said, "I'd like you to promise me you'll never get in a car with a boy who's been drinking." And, "I'd like you to never smoke marijuana." No problem with the second, but she couldn't say she'd obeyed the first a hundred percent. As for this one…

"Dad, no! I can't just get married out of the blue."

"What happened to 'whatever it is, I'll make it happen'?" He lifted his tubed-and-wired left hand a few inches off the blanket, agitated.

"I can't work miracles," she said. "Patrick and I have only been dating for—"

"Patrick!" John's face turned red. "I don't want my daughter ending up with that lemon. You need to marry Lucas."

Merry's chair scraped harshly against the linoleum as she jerked backward. "Dad, that's crazy."

"Think about it," he said. "You've dated on and off for years, so there's obviously something strong between you."

A strong desire to shut their fathers up. "More off than on," she said. "Dad, we're not—"

"You both know that Dwight and I always hoped you two… But that's not a good reason," he said. "What *is* a good reason is that you suit each other. It's obvious to everyone."

"Dad, Lucas and I aren't that close." Damn those stupid exaggerations she'd fed their fathers. "Let alone *soul mates,* which is what you've always said I should look for."

"How do you know you're not soul mates?" John said. "You've never given each other a serious chance."

"You and Mom knew instantly," she reminded him.

"We met when we were in our twenties. Chances are, if I'd known her since I was three years old, like you've known Lucas, it might have taken me a little longer to see the treasure right before my eyes."

"Dad, I'm not Lucas's treasure, and he's not mine."

"I think you are," he said obstinately. "Lucas told me when he was ten years old that he planned to marry you."

Her jaw dropped. "No way."

John managed a grin. "Where do you think Dwight and I got the idea?"

"You can hardly hold Lucas to a ten-year-old's crush." She wondered if he remembered. Reminding him could be fun....

An alarm beeped on one of her father's monitors, and she jumped. "What's that? Dad, are you okay?"

A nurse, older than the one from the waiting room, bustled in, just in time to stop Merry hitting the panic button. "Time for a top-up, Mr. Wyatt." With deft movements she removed an empty IV bag from its hanger and replaced it with a full one.

Merry didn't speak until the monitor was chugging along in what she assumed was a normal fashion. Then she said, "Dad, it's sweet that you're worried about me...."

"It's not sweet," he growled. "It's hell."

That silenced her. Momentarily. "Even if I was willing, Lucas doesn't want to marry me."

"Have you even asked him?" her dad demanded.

"Of course not."

"Merry..." Her father briefly closed his eyes. "We both know I'm not going to make it. It would mean more than I can say to know you're married to Lucas. A man who'll look after you."

"He wants to go back to active duty," she reminded her father.

"That's his job. The navy will take care of him. And of you, when he's away."

Men like her dad and Dwight—and Lucas—

considered arguments about the mortality rates in the services irrelevant.

"I know Lucas cares for you," John said. "If it's at all possible, please, could you ask him if—if he cares enough to marry you?"

Not in a million years.

Another monitor started beeping. This time, Merry didn't panic. But this time it was serious. Two nurses ran in, followed by a doctor. Merry found herself out in the hallway, the door closed in her face.

She leaned her forehead against it and prayed for her father's survival. For a miracle cure.

What if there is no miracle? Would she let her father die worrying about her, deprived of the peace a man should have in his final moments? When just maybe, she had the power to give him that peace?

CHAPTER FOUR

MERRY PUSHED OPEN THE DOOR to Pete's Burger Shack. She couldn't have been thinking clearly, to have suggested this place to Patrick when he'd texted to confirm their date. *Of course I wasn't thinking clearly.* The only thought in her head had been how she might ease her dad's fears.

Pete's might be a New London institution, but it wasn't the setting for important occasions. It had been the venue for Merry's second annual Date With Lucas.

At first glance, she couldn't see Patrick in the happy-hour crowd. She was about to text to ask if he was here when her cell phone buzzed. A message from Lucas: WHERE ARE U?

She texted back: PETE'S

He probably wanted contact information for the people he should notify about her dad. But since she hadn't been allowed back into his room, she didn't have it. Ah, there was Patrick, waving to her from the back corner booth.

She pushed her way through the happy drinkers. Patrick already had a glass of red wine and a bowl of peanuts in front of him; he stood as she arrived.

"Hi, sweetheart." One hand settled on her hip as he leaned to kiss her. "I missed you."

"I missed you, too." She slid into the seat opposite.

Patrick had the kind of looks any woman would like.

His brown hair was slightly long and flopped over his forehead. He was slim but well-proportioned with a ready smile. His two passions—animals and peace—seemed to Merry the ultimate in caring. She felt a rush of affection for him.

Most parents would be thrilled to have their daughter bring him home…so long as those parents weren't navy personnel and committed militarists.

Merline, Pete's wife and longtime waitress, came over. "Merry, honey, I'm gonna need to see some ID." She still made Merry do this every single time. Merry's second date with Lucas had been her first visit to Pete's; she must have been eighteen going on nineteen, with him twenty-one. She'd produced a fake ID to buy a drink, and he'd told Merline that Merry was underage. For her own safety, he'd announced sanctimoniously.

Now, she handed over her driver's license for Merline to hold up to the light, align the photo next to Merry's face and generally make a production out of inspecting it. At last, she consented to take her order for a glass of chardonnay. She was chuckling as she walked away.

"What was that about?" Patrick asked.

"Old joke, long story." Merry leaned her head back against the booth and gathered her energy.

"How's Boo?" Patrick asked. He was convinced Boo's constipation was the result of emotional trauma and would ease as soon as the dog accepted Merry as his new owner.

"No change," she said.

Patrick filled the time until her drink arrived with an entertaining account of the conference he'd attended in Denver.

Merline reappeared with the chardonnay and a much larger bowl of nuts, which she set in front of Merry. Her apology for the driver's license trick.

"Thanks, Merline," Merry slid the bowl sideways to cover up a beer ring on the table. Every table at Pete's had multiple such rings, and had for as long as she could remember. Shouldn't Lucas have taken her someplace fancier on that second date?

As soon as Merline left, Merry leaned forward. "Patrick, something awful happened today. My dad's in the hospital—he's really sick." She managed to tell him the situation without actually using the word *dying,* but her voice shook all the same.

"Sweetheart, that's terrible." He grasped her hands across the table, his eyes filled with tender concern. "You should have called me. I would have come to the hospital with you."

She didn't say, *I never thought of it.* "I know it's hard for you to leave your patients. Besides, Lucas was there. Lucas Calder. He's this guy, the son of—"

"—your dad's best friend. The hero chopper pilot you always talk about," Patrick said.

Merry blinked. "I don't always talk about him. I never even mention him."

"He's the guy who got shot down last year," Patrick said.

Okay, she might have mentioned *that.* Getting shot down was a big deal.

"The guy you played with as a kid, the 'bossy jerk with an overactive rescuer gene,'" Patrick continued, clearly quoting her. The words did sound kind of familiar.

Weirdly, she had the impulse to defend Lucas. To say

he wasn't entirely a jerk. Even though he'd behaved like a massive one that night in Baltimore. *Not thinking about that.*

"The thing is," she said tightly, "I do need your help now."

Patrick shut up about Lucas, all concerned about her. "Anything," he said. "Let me be here for you, Merry. I want to help." His charming, boyish smile came out. "I love you."

Phew, this is going to be okay. "Thank you," she said.

When he blinked, she realized he'd been waiting for a reciprocal declaration. Time for that later.

"Dad's worried about me being alone after he— In the future," she said. "He asked me to get married."

Patrick froze, wineglass halfway to his mouth. "I thought your dad didn't like me. Now he wants me for a son-in-law?"

Merry noticed he wasn't cheering at the prospect of matrimony. "Actually," she admitted, "he asked me to marry Lucas."

"Why would your father want you to marry a guy you've always said is a creep?" Patrick swigged his merlot. "Hasn't he heard you go on about how Lucas doesn't know the first thing about relationships?"

She wanted to dispute *always* and *go on,* and she was pretty sure she'd never said *creep*...but now wasn't the time to split hairs. She managed a shrug. "It's a family friend thing, that's all."

"You always say Lucas doesn't like New London," Patrick accused. "How come he's even here?"

Could he stop with the *always?* "He came back to see his family." Merry squeezed Patrick's fingers. "Of course

I'm not going to marry Lucas." Now would be a good time to say "I love you." "I'm not going to marry anyone at all, not right now. But if you truly want to help me... would you mind pretending to be engaged?"

Patrick's fingers jerked; she tightened her grasp.

"Not for long," she said quickly. "Just until Dad... Just for a few days."

Patrick took another drink of his wine and swallowed hard before setting down his glass. "How would that help, when it's Lucas he wants for you?"

"He might have a preference for Lucas, but his main concern is seeing me happy," she assured him. "If we tell Dad we're getting married, and I convince him I'm blissfully happy, I'm sure he'll be delighted."

She just couldn't ask Lucas, not after Baltimore. If she asked him, and he turned her down again...or worse, if he thought she still wanted him... *Ugh.* She could make this work with Patrick, even if he wasn't Dad's number one choice. Her father was the ultimate romantic, if she convinced him she adored Patrick, he would be satisfied. Maybe she could persuade Patrick to say something nice about the navy.

"But we'd be lying," Patrick said. "Getting engaged isn't a game, Merry. You can't devalue marriage like that."

"You said you love me," she snapped. She drew a calming breath. "Sorry, I'm under a bit of stress here. We won't make a public announcement," she promised. She might have to tell Dad they'd put a notice in the *Day,* but that would be a minor lie compared with the "we're engaged" one. "It'll be just between us and Dad, for a few days, maybe a week. Or so."

That was another advantage Patrick had over Lucas. Lucas's family would have to be lied to; Patrick's parents in Colorado would know nothing about it.

Patrick was looking at her as if she was some kind of monster. She was starting to *feel* like a monster.

"Patrick, I know it's not honest—" she reminded herself she *liked* his idealism "—but it's for a good cause. The…the *best* cause." Her voice cracked. She pushed the peanuts toward him as if they might serve as an incentive to get engaged to her.

Reflexively, he grabbed a handful of nuts and tipped them into his mouth. Which gave her more time to talk, to persuade him.

"It's not as if you and I don't care for each other a lot," she said. "Maybe we could look at this as a trial run for a real engagement." When he didn't argue, she figured she was making progress. "Do you remember, on our very first date, you said you knew for sure I was going to be important in your life? And I said I felt the same? Maybe this is—" She stopped.

Patrick's color had deepened. His hand was pressed to his throat; his eyes bulged.

"Uh, Patrick…are you choking?"

Stupid question. Of course he was.

Merry jumped to her feet, knocking over her chair. "Help!" she called. "He's choking." She dashed around the table. *Heimlich maneuver.* She'd seen it performed in countless movies.

For a moment it seemed no one had heard her over the happy hour hubbub. Then Merline rushed up. "What can I do?" Now other people turned to look, started to move, but in what seemed like slow motion.

"Just help me shift him...." Merry had her arms around Patrick from behind, but the high seat back made it impossible to get a grip. Dammit, this didn't happen in the movies. "If we get him off the chair..."

Next moment, the chair was gone, Merry had been shoved aside and Lucas—*where did he come from?*—had his arms around Patrick, hands positioned beneath his rib cage. Two sharp heaves, and a nut flew from Patrick's mouth, landing in his wine.

Patrick sucked in great gasps of air, his color quickly returning to normal.

"Are you okay?" Merry asked, as the other drinkers applauded.

He nodded, rubbing his throat. "Yeah." It came out as a croak. He glanced around. "I thought it was all over. Who...?"

Lucas stepped forward, hand outstretched, as relaxed as if he regularly performed the Heimlich maneuver ten times before breakfast. "You must be Patrick. I'm Lucas Calder."

Patrick's handshake looked disappointingly limp, but, heck, the guy had almost died. *Lucas saved his life.*

"What are you doing here?" Merry asked Lucas.

"You said you were here. I was worried you might be drowning your sorrows alone." His gaze flicked over Patrick. "I should have known better."

Patrick was looking him up and down, suspicion blooming on his face. Maybe Lucas didn't seem quite like the creep Merry had apparently called him. In fact, even in worn jeans and a plain, long-sleeved dark T-shirt, he looked...gorgeous.

If you liked that kind of thing.

Merry realized Patrick was pocketing the wallet and keys he'd left on the table. "Patrick, wait, we haven't finished our conversation." *I need a fake fiancé.*

"I think we have," he said, his voice still croaky. "If it takes desperation for you to suggest we take our relationship to the next level, Merry, I don't think we have much going for us. I've suspected for a while that only one of us was actually committed to this relationship."

She pressed a hand to her chest. "You're breaking up with me?"

"Hey, buddy," Lucas said. "What kind of guy dumps a woman when her dad's in the hospital?"

Patrick flushed. "You'd better ask Merry that question."

"Don't go," Merry pleaded. "We can work this out."

"You…" Patrick stopped, mouth open, an arrested expression on his face.

"One thing you ought to know, Merry," Lucas said.

Patrick leaned forward and barfed. All over her.

"The Heimlich maneuver can cause vomiting," Lucas said helpfully.

AS THE BUSSER CLEANED UP the floor, Lucas stood aside, then ordered a fresh glass of wine for Merry, plus a beer for himself. Just as the drinks arrived, along with a fresh bowl of nuts, Merry emerged from the bathroom wearing a red-white-and-blue Pete's Burger Shack polo. Merline's, going by its generous sizing. The rolled-up black pants weren't her own, either. Lucas guessed her clothes were in the plastic grocery bag she set under the table.

"I ordered you a chardonnay," he said. "Thought I'd

save you the hassle of having to show Merline your ID again."

"A ritual for which I have you to thank." Merry sat down with a little whoosh of breath. She dug into the bowl of peanuts on the table and crammed a handful into her mouth.

"Careful," Lucas murmured.

"I'm sure you'll save my life if I choke," she said around the nuts. She waited until she'd swallowed before continuing. "Besides, I haven't eaten since breakfast."

"I stopped by the hospital again this afternoon," Lucas told her, "but they still wouldn't let me see your dad."

"Thanks for trying," Merry said. "And thanks again for what you did at the boatyard. You're not bad in a crisis."

"You should see me in a war." He took a swig from his longneck. "So, how's he doing?"

"Nothing's changed from what the doctor said when you were there." She wrapped her fingers tightly around the stem of her wineglass. "He's dying."

From the sudden widening of her eyes, Lucas guessed she hadn't truly admitted it to herself before. Saying the word—*dying*—left her opening and closing her mouth like a goldfish.

"Take a drink," Lucas said.

She glugged too big a mouthful and coughed.

"I'm sorry, Merry," Lucas said. "Maybe he'll get a donor kidney."

"Maybe." Blinking hard, she took a more moderate sip of her wine.

A waitress, one-third Merline's age and three times prettier, struck a pose next to their table—hip cocked, shoulders thrown back to accentuate her breasts in her low-cut T-shirt. "You guys, like, need anything else?" She batted her eyelashes at Lucas.

"Gosh, yes, thanks so much," Merry gushed. "Some privacy would be wonderful."

The girl scowled, dropped the pose and walked off.

Lucas laughed.

"Okay, that was rude of me," Merry admitted. "But I'm not in the mood." She propped her chin on one hand, the picture of moroseness. Was that only about her dad? Or...

"I wouldn't worry about losing Patrick Peacenik if I were you," Lucas advised.

She glowered. "Thanks for the tip."

"If the guy's not willing to stand by you in a crisis..." He didn't mean to sound quite so contemptuous. But, hey. There were some things a man should do without question. Lucas's instincts had proved right—from first sight, he'd been irritated by Patrick with his floppy, pretty-boy hair and his bug eyes. Admittedly, the bug eyes were caused by nearly choking to death.

"I might have made it hard for him to be supportive," Merry confessed. "I asked him for a pretty big favor."

"You wanted him to run over a potential kidney donor?"

She smiled reluctantly. "That might have been easier. Dad's got it into his head that he wants to see me safely married before he...you know."

"You asked Patrick to *marry* you?" Lucas said, appalled.

"Hey, he supposedly loved me," she retorted. "Besides, he didn't have to actually marry me. Just pretend to be engaged for a few days."

"Is that all?" Lucas set down his beer. "And he said no?"

"He said marriage is too special to devalue in that way," she muttered.

Lucas snickered. "Poor Merry. No way could you disagree with that." He knew exactly how she felt about love and marriage.

"Ordinarily, no." She sipped her wine. "Actually, Dad wanted me to marry *you*."

Lucas snorted. "Those must be some drugs they're giving him."

"He's drugged, but lucid. He's just very worried about me being left alone."

"Poor guy." Lucas tried to imagine John saying such a thing. It was an indication of how keenly the man must be feeling his mortality. Even trapped in a sand hole in the desert, Lucas had never doubted his ability to survive. Never found himself coming up with crazy ideas for the people he'd leave behind.

But John was right to be worried. His closeness to Merry and the lack of any other family meant his death would be extra hard on her.

Looking at her, biting her lower lip, just slightly to the left side, the way she always did when she was anxious. That lower lip of hers was remarkably full.... He shifted his focus to his beer, brought the bottle to his mouth.

"What am I going to do?" Merry said. "I can't bear to see Dad so distressed."

She appeared so bleak, so hopeless, Lucas felt a tug

of response in that deep part of him that compelled him to action in a crisis. Lucas Calder to the rescue.

"Any reason I can't be your fake fiancé?" he asked. "It's just for a few days, right? And I'm your dad's preferred candidate."

She swallowed some more wine. "I appreciate the offer, but…"

"Are you saying no because of Baltimore?" he demanded. The memory of that night gave him a mental pause, too, but they were both adults.

"Of course not. Doing it with you—" her cheeks colored at the poor choice of words "—is too complicated. Patrick's family live in Colorado and would never need to know. Your parents are right here."

Okay, that was a problem.

Lucas thought about it. His father had an almost fanatical regard for the truth. "Dad would never lie to John, or let someone else get away with lying to him."

"Exactly."

"So we wouldn't tell them it was fake until later." Lucas warmed to the idea. "Merry, if it wasn't for your dad saving my father's life, I wouldn't exist. If I can help give John some peace in his last days, for the price of an engagement that'll mean nothing to either you or me, and will soon be forgotten… It's a no-brainer."

There weren't enough good reasons *not* to do it.

She pressed her hands to her cheeks. "When you put it like that…Lucas, thank you. I can't tell you how much it would mean to me to be able to reassure Dad."

"All in the line of duty." His mind raced ahead, scoping out the mission, the critical path. He was surprised to feel a faint buzz of adrenaline. Yeah, he wanted to do this—support her, make her dad happy.

"We'll be doing pretty much what we'd be doing over the next few days anyway," he said. "I'd want to help you and your dad out while he's sick. Now I'll be doing it as your fiancé." Lucas drummed his fingers on the table. "Maybe calling you honeybun every now and then." He added casually, "I'd probably have to kiss you once or twice, too."

His gaze had got hung up on her mouth again. He wrenched it away.

"No honeybun," she said firmly. "No kissing. No... no hanky-panky at all."

Her edict naturally made him immediately want *hanky-panky*—dumb, old-fashioned word—and lots of it. But...

"You're right," he said, and meant it. "We should avoid complications. This needs to be easy to unravel afterward. The best missions are the simplest."

She rolled her eyes at the military analogy.

He sensed the situation wasn't without risk, though he hadn't had time to quantify it. But whatever it was, Lucas was an expert at risk management. "We'll make it work," he said confidently. "No problem."

CHAPTER FIVE

MERRY'S FATHER WAS ASLEEP when she arrived in his room at seven the next morning. Now that he was stable, he'd been moved out of ICU, and even with all his tubes and monitors, he looked peaceful. More peaceful than she felt.

She'd had a third glass of wine with Lucas last night—it seemed they'd both felt the need of some liquid courage—and now she was paying for it with the thumping in her temples.

She sat with her eyes closed, waiting for her dad to stir. Lucas had said he'd meet her at the hospital this morning so they could announce their "engagement" together. She had to admit she was pleased not to be doing it alone.

By the time John woke, soon after eight, she felt a little less seedy.

"Merry-Berry," he said sleepily.

She sprang to her feet. "How are you feeling? Can I get you something?"

"I feel good," he murmured, sounding surprised.

The words sent a chill through her. Dr. Randall had described kidney failure as a "peaceful death."

A nurse came into the room then. Merry wondered if one of her father's monitors had alerted the nursing station that he was awake.

"Good morning, Mr. Wyatt. Think you can manage some breakfast?" The nurse's tone was brisk, practical.

"I'll have the pancakes with extra syrup," John joked.

His courage brought tears to Merry's eyes.

The nurse's expression didn't flicker. "You'll have oatmeal."

Merry gave her a look that asked her to lighten up. The woman—the name badge pinned to her pale pink tunic top said Cathy Martin—met it with indifference. She checked her patient's blood pressure, tutted a little, then left.

"Are all the nurses that unpleasant?" Merry asked, feeling disturbed.

"They're fine. That particular one seems grumpy." Her dad sounded tired.

"Hi," Lucas said from the doorway.

She spun to face him. Embarrassment and nerves—and maybe a slight hangover—made her clumsy, and she knocked her dad's IV stand. Somehow, that set off an alarm.

"Damn." Flustered, Merry gazed at the three screens that monitored goodness knows what, trying to figure out what she'd done. "Damn, damn, damn."

Lucas sauntered over, as unflappable as a guy who'd aced the Rocklike Calm class would be. "If it's important, someone will be here soon."

Before he'd finished speaking, Nurse Cathy Martin was back. She bustled to the displays, then hit a button on one of the devices hooked up to Merry's dad. The beeping stopped. She turned to Merry. "Who set that off?"

"It might have been me," she admitted.

"Be more careful next time." The nurse left.

Lucas raised his eyebrows at Merry. "Dad and Stephanie are parking the car. They'll be here shortly."

Merry glanced at her watch. Not even eight-thirty. "That's an early visit."

"I told them our news," he said, too quietly for John to hear. "They insisted on coming."

She stared at him, aghast. So there was no going back. Not that she wanted to…much.

Sure enough, Dwight and Stephanie arrived a minute later. Stephanie, pushing Mia in a stroller, was smiling brightly enough to light up a Christmas tree, and even Dwight looked almost jolly.

"Did you tell him?" Stephanie asked.

John lifted his head. "Tell me what?"

Merry gulped. Drew a breath. Before she could speak, Lucas said, "Merry and I got engaged last night."

Any doubts Merry might have had evaporated in the burst of elation that came over her father's face. "Merry, that's…" He stopped, choked by emotion. His jaw worked. "That's wonderful." He stretched his arms out; carefully, she went in for a hug. He kept his left arm around her while he shook Lucas's hand. "Smart decision, Lucas. You won't regret it."

"I know," Lucas said with such sincerity that she stared. Then she realized he meant he wouldn't regret faking an engagement for a few days.

Nor will I. Not now that I see how happy it's made Dad.

Her father chuckled. "To think that all you two needed was a little push from me. Dwight, didn't we always know they were destined to be together?"

Lucas's dad was more about logic than destiny, but he nodded.

"We should have pressured them years ago," John continued.

"We should have," Dwight agreed. "If you recall, Stephanie wouldn't let us."

His wife swatted his arm, and he caught her hand and kissed it.

"So, where's the ring?" John asked.

"We haven't had time—" Merry began.

"Right here." Lucas pulled a dark blue velvet box from his pocket.

What the heck? Merry held her breath as he opened the box. Nestled on the plush white lining was a ring. A square-cut emerald flanked by two diamonds. *Where did this come from?*

"You going to put it on, honeybun?" Lucas asked.

Hadn't she said no honeybun?

Lucas placed a finger beneath her chin and lifted. Ugh, she'd been standing there with her mouth open.

"No, she is *not* going to put it on," Stephanie said.

Merry turned to her gratefully.

"Not even you could be so unromantic, Lucas," his stepmom scolded. "You're going to put it on her."

Lucas paused. "Of course I am." Next moment, he had the ring out of the box and was advancing on Merry.

He took her fingers in his. For a long moment, he examined her hand, as if weighing his options. *Don't you dare back out now.*

He must have read her thoughts, because he slipped the ring on swiftly, decisively. Slightly too large, it glided over her knuckle.

Stephanie applauded; little Mia clapped her hands in imitation.

John gestured to Merry that he wanted to inspect the ring. She moved closer, relieved to get away from Lucas.

The bad-tempered nurse came in with John's breakfast. "Very nice," she said about the ring, though no one had asked her. She plunked the tray down on his table and marched out again.

"I gave your mother an emerald," John said, his voice heavy with emotion. He closed his other hand over Merry's. "Nice job, Lucas."

"Thanks, John."

"So, when's the wedding?"

From the jerk of Lucas's chin, Merry guessed he hadn't anticipated the question. Lucky for him, she had.

"It'll take us a couple of months to get organized," she said.

Her father's face fell. "I was hoping it would be before…"

He seriously expected her to go from single to engaged to married in just a few days?

"There's nothing we'd like better, John," Lucas said. "Unfortunately, blood tests and waiting times and the like mean it can't be done. We figured we might as well wait a little longer and do it properly."

Nice work. Merry telegraphed the message with her eyes.

He gave her a smug look that said, *What do you expect from a guy with a degree in Rocklike Calm?*

"There's no blood test in Connecticut," Stephanie said, sounding confused. "No waiting time, either. Don't you remember, Dwight, you rushed to get our license, thinking it would take forever? And it turned out you could just roll up, pick up a license and get married five minutes later."

"That's right," Dwight said. "Lucas, where did you get your information?"

Oh, heck. Merry held her breath.

"It's been a while since you and Stephanie tied the knot," Lucas said. "Things have changed."

Good, she congratulated him mentally. *Good thinking.*

To her horror, Dwight pulled out his iPhone.

"Let's see," he said. He typed surprisingly fast for an old guy typing with his thumbs on a virtual keyboard.

Dread pooled in Merry's stomach. *Let Lucas be right. Let the rules have changed.*

"Ha," Dwight said with a note of triumph that sent her hopes plummeting. "You're right, darling." *Darling* being Stephanie. "No waiting period in Connecticut and no blood test. You can apply for a license Monday to Friday between eight-thirty and four, and get married five minutes later."

Lucas looked faintly green.

"Today's Wednesday," John said. "Isn't it?"

Merry nodded.

"Well, then. Nothing to stop you." Uh-oh, he was looking teary again. "To see my little girl get married… a man could die happy."

"I—I don't have a dress," Merry blurted. As if that mattered.

"You can wear mine," Stephanie said. "It's not new, but it's Vera Wang. Great design doesn't date."

Merry whimpered.

"Merry," Lucas said calmly, "could I see you for a moment?"

In the hallway, he dragged her out of sight of her father's glass-walled room. "You do realize you need to tell your dad that we're not getting married?"

"Of course I do!" she hissed.

"Then stop talking about your damn dress, and get back in there and do it."

Immediately, her hackles rose, the way they had since they were kids. "It's not that easy. You're the one who told him the blood test was all that stood in our way."

"How was I to know there's no blood test in Connecticut?"

Grouchy Nurse Martin walked by, eyeing them curiously.

Merry waited until she'd passed. "You're the one who gave me an engagement ring—no wonder he thinks we want to get married."

"I was trying to look convincing," Lucas said.

"Where did it come from, anyway?"

"Jeweler friend," he said. "Let's get back on topic. Namely, telling your dad there won't be a wedding."

She closed her eyes. "How am I supposed to do that when he said he'll die happy if I get married?"

"He'll just have to die mildly content," Lucas said.

Her eyes snapped open.

He swore. "Sorry, I didn't mean that. You know I didn't, or I wouldn't have offered to get engaged in the first place." He pinched the bridge of his nose. "There must be a way to do this. Let's think."

Merry thought.

Presumably, he was doing the same.

"We can come back tomorrow and say we got married," he said in a flash of inspiration. "We'll tell them we went to city hall."

"Dad said he wants to *see* me get married. I couldn't do that to him."

"You won't be doing it to him. You'll be pretending to. In the end, he'll just be relieved we're married."

"What if he wants to see the marriage certificate?" She could imagine her sentimental father wanting to admire the document.

"We'll say we lost it."

She rolled her eyes.

"You think of something, then," he ordered.

Silence fell again.

Lucas had the next idea, too. "We could pay someone—an actor—to be a fake celebrant."

It was a tempting possibility. But…

"Dad will want Reverend Carter from our church to do it," Merry said glumly. "And I can't just say he's not available—Reverend Carter's coming to visit him this afternoon. Plus we'd still have the marriage certificate problem."

More thinking.

"There's only one possibility," Merry said at last.

"Fire away."

"We really get married," she said. "Right here, in front of Dad. And then we get a divorce."

"Are you nuts?" His voice rose, and the security guard stationed by the elevator looked in their direction.

Merry spoke quickly, quietly. "My friend Sarah got divorced last year, and it's almost as easy as getting married. From what I remember, we can file for a no-fault divorce on grounds of irretrievable breakdown of the marriage as soon as we like. The day after the wedding. Ninety days later, we're divorced."

"No," he said firmly.

"Divorce isn't ideal," she agreed, as if the only problem with getting married would be how to end it. "It means we both end up, well, divorced. We could look into annulment."

"No," he said again.

"You were willing to give Dad a kidney," she reminded him.

"A lot less complicated," Lucas said.

He was right. But Merry was desperate. "This is your big chance to rescue me. You love to rescue."

"You hate being rescued. You *refuse* to be rescued."

"Not this time," she promised. "Do you remember when you were ten years old, telling Dad and Dwight you wanted to marry me?"

He blinked, then shook his head, as if shaking off that moment of weakness. "Yeah, and the next day you peed your pants and I changed my mind."

The heat in her cheeks told her she was blushing. "So I had the occasional 'accident.' Shoot me. Look, Lucas, Dad wants us to get married, and right now allowing him to die in peace is number one on my list. Are you going to marry me or not?"

"Not." He folded his arms across his chest and stared her down.

Merry spun on her heel and marched back into her father's room, Lucas right behind her. She narrowly missed crashing into Nurse Martin, also on her way in again.

Her father gave her an anxious, hopeful look.

Merry beamed. "Great news, Dad. We're getting married tomorrow."

CHAPTER SIX

MERRY TUGGED AT THE BODICE of her blue dress, her backup option in case Stephanie's bridal gown didn't fit. This was a bridesmaid dress; it had looked fine, though far from lovely, when she'd worn it two years ago as maid of honor for what turned out to be Sarah's short-term marriage. Now the sleeves looked ridiculously poufy. Every time she moved, the taffeta seemed to rustle accusingly.

At least the pale blue matched her complexion.

Merry rubbed her cheeks briskly with her palms, watching the effect in her bedroom mirror. She looked as if she were headed to an execution, not a wedding.

There was every chance this wedding would be followed by an execution, she thought grimly. Lucas had been so mad when she'd announced they were getting married, he'd been white with fury. She shivered at the mere recollection. But he'd been too nice, too *heroic,* to wipe the joy from her father's face. As she'd known he would be.

This is the lowest thing I've ever done in my life.

But for the best of reasons.

And Lucas really would be free and clear of her, and their marriage, after ninety days. No lasting scars.

Which was more than she could say for that night in Baltimore, which still left her mortified six months later. Really, Lucas had it easy.

She was having trouble convincing herself of that, so it was a relief when the buzzer to her apartment sounded. She glanced at her watch. Ten-thirty; Stephanie was right on time.

One hour until the wedding.

Merry pressed the buzzer to open the street door. Her apartment was above a bowling alley, the only location where she could afford loft-style, the rent being low due to the constant rumble of bowling balls beneath her feet from 11:00 a.m. to 10:00 p.m.

Stephanie maneuvered her way inside, hampered by a large, flattish carton with a small wooden chest perched on top. "I brought my sewing kit so we can make any needed adjustments." She eyed the toast crumbs on Merry's kitchen counter with misgiving and headed to the coffee table to set down the carton and the chest. "Merry, as your matron of honor, it's my duty to tell you that the blue dress isn't good."

"It's not that bad. And this isn't a white satin kind of wedding." Merry had asked Stephanie to be matron of honor on the basis that the fewer people who knew about this, the better. Though she would have asked her best friend, Sarah, if Sarah hadn't been on vacation in Mexico. Thankfully, the need for haste meant everyone readily agreed on a small celebration.

"It's still *your* wedding," Stephanie said. "Merry, I know that in the next few days you'll lose your dad, and the prospect of happiness seems distant, if not impossible. This isn't how anyone would choose to start married life." She worked the tight-fitting lid off the carton. "But at some stage you might want to look back on this day and find some reasons to smile." She lifted a dress from the box and carefully shook it out.

A confection of white silk. Stunning.

"Uh, Stephanie…" Lucas would freak out if Merry showed up in this. That is, if he even showed up himself.

"Our sizes aren't that different," Stephanie said. "And your father would love to see you looking like a bride." She began undoing the tiny pearl buttons at the back of the dress. "Merry, there's another reason this dress seems right for you. My marriage to Dwight started in less than ideal circumstances, with our wedding so soon after Michelle died. But we loved each other, and we did eventually get it right. That's what I hope you and Lucas might do—preferably a bit faster than we did." She blinked rapidly, her smile tremulous.

"You know this wedding was Dad's idea," Merry said. She didn't want Stephanie investing a whole lot of emotion in today, when by the end of the week it would prove wasted.

"Yes, but I know how much Lucas cares for you. You need to give your marriage every chance," Stephanie insisted. "The dress is one small way in which you can do it right. Now, are going to step out of that blue puffball or do I have to tear it off you?"

Merry gave up and unzipped the blue dress.

Two minutes later, she was standing in front of the mirror in the Vera Wang gown, while Stephanie pinned the hem.

"This is an amazing dress," Merry admitted. "It must have cost a fortune."

"I didn't want to look back on my photos and cringe

in years to come," Stephanie said. "You pay a lot for timeless quality."

She was right; the fitted bodice, with long, off-the-shoulder sleeves, and the stiff A-line skirt that flared out from her hips looked as contemporary now as they must have when Stephanie married.

"Your bust is bigger than mine." Merry touched the too-loose front of the dress.

"That's the biggest challenge," Stephanie agreed. "But I have a solution."

"Of course you do," she muttered.

The solution turned out to be a band of white silk that matched the dress. Stephanie wrapped it around Merry's torso, pulling in the excess fabric. "That'll work when I've tacked it into place," she said.

Merry took off the dress and waited while Stephanie put in just enough stitches to make everything fit for the duration of the ceremony.

When it was ready, Merry slipped the dress back on and stepped into her sandals. Not the usual footwear for a late-October wedding, but her dad had asked that, rather than get married at his bedside, they do it on the beach. Alongside his beloved ocean.

"It'll be the last time I see the sea," he'd said.

Dr. Randall had given her permission; an hour away from monitoring would make little difference. So how could Merry refuse?

"You look gorgeous," Stephanie said. "Just one more thing." She began unwrapping some tissue paper that Merry had assumed was filler for the excess space in the dress box.

Like a conjurer, Stephanie produced a veil, seemingly

out of nowhere. A cloud of tulle that, when she fixed it in Merry's hair, transformed the dress from beautiful to spectacular.

"Perfect." She smiled at Merry in the mirror, then glanced at her watch. "We need to go. I brought Dwight's Hummer, since it has lots of room. If we push the passenger seat back, you won't get rumpled."

"Let me just put Boo out on the balcony," Merry said.

"I'll do it—he might slobber on your dress. Come on, boy." Stephanie clapped her hands, and Boo rose from his mat in the corner.

Ten minutes later, they pulled up at the oceanside a block from the hospital. Not the prettiest beach around, but it was better not to go too far in case something went wrong. A small group waited on the sand: Merry's father in a wheelchair, wearing his only suit. The suit he'd be buried in. Merry swallowed and moved on to the other participants in this unlikely event. Nurse Martin stood to one side, in a lilac tunic today, her expression as severe as ever. Reverend Carter, the priest from her dad's church, Saint Thomas's Episcopalian, wore a suit with his dog collar.

Dwight, the best man, was holding Mia, which didn't detract from his military bearing. Then…the groom. Lucas stood next to his father. Both men were in uniform.

Merry lifted her skirt so it wouldn't trail in the sand. "They're wearing swords." Maybe Lucas would stab her instead of shoot her when this was all over.

"A sword is part of the service dress blues for officers," Stephanie said. "They look amazing, don't they?"

The swords or the men? Lucas's dark blue jacket emphasized the breadth of his shoulders; the medals on his chest gleamed in the sunlight. He took off his hat as they approached, and the breeze ruffled his dark hair. He looked like a movie hero.

Then Merry saw tears in her father's eyes, and she forgot about Lucas.

"Hi, Dad." She bent to kiss him.

"Merry-Berry, you look…" He shook his head.

She was glad she'd worn the dress.

"You look like Sally," John croaked.

Sally was her mother. Merry felt the prickle of tears in her own eyes as she gripped her dad's shoulder.

Under the weight of Lucas's stare, she lifted her gaze. "Hi," she said.

"Hi."

There was a silence while everyone waited for him to say more. He didn't. Merry was just grateful he was here. As long as he went through with the ceremony, she didn't care if he ever spoke to her again.

"She looks beautiful," Dwight said as he handed Mia over to Stephanie. "You do, Merry."

"Uh, thanks." She still wasn't used to the new, softer Dwight. Self-conscious, she rubbed her palms down her skirt. Lucas didn't pass comment on her beauty. She wondered if everyone noticed how disconnected she and Lucas were from each other. Hopefully, they'd put it down to nerves.

"Shall we get started?" Reverend Carter said.

The words of the wedding service swirled around Merry on the sea breeze. As the reverend moved on to the vows, the cry of a gull sounded like a warning overhead.

"For richer for poorer…in sickness and health…"

Merry tried not to think about her intention to immediately break the promise she would make today. *It's for Dad.*

She realized everyone was waiting; the question had been for her.

"I do," she said. Or should that be *I will?*

She focused harder as the celebrant asked Lucas for the same commitment, as though her willpower could force Lucas to give the right answer.

"I do," he said, and her shoulders relaxed slightly.

"I now pronounce you husband and wife," Reverend Carter said. Merry had asked him to leave out the part about kissing the bride.

"You may kiss the bride." Ugh, that came from her dad. Romantic to the last.

Merry dared a glance at Lucas, the first time she'd met his eyes since the ceremony started. Cool distance. Was that better than anger?

Please kiss me.

She lifted her face, closed her eyes. An act of faith. Faith that he was the guy she'd known, from boy to man. Bossy, infuriating, even arrogant. But not someone who would let her down.

She felt the whisper of a breath, then firm lips pressed to hers. *Thank you.* Lucas smelled of soap and spice and salt air. For that fraction of a second, she was warm, despite the brisk northerly wind coming down from the hills behind them.

Then he pulled back. Merry's focus cleared from the odd haze in front of her eyes—*must be sea spray*—and she saw her father beaming from ear to ear.

That's why we're doing it. We're giving Dad peace of mind. It was all worthwhile.

Stephanie snapped a few photos. Now that the ceremony was over, Merry's father looked suddenly smaller and grayer.

"Time we got you back to the hospital, Mr. Wyatt," Nurse Martin said briskly.

Merry wondered how she'd managed to push the wheelchair down the beach. Then Lucas lifted her father out of the chair, which the nurse tilted and easily dragged over the sand. Question answered. Lucas carried her dad as if he weighed no more than his navy kit bag. On the promenade, he settled John back into the chair.

"We've ordered a cake," Dwight announced. "It's waiting for us in the hospital cafeteria. Not the fanciest venue, but they've promised us a quiet corner."

This wasn't over yet.

"Lovely," Merry said.

"Nurse Martin helped us smuggle in some champagne," Dwight added.

Really? Merry opened her mouth to thank her, but the woman's scowl stopped her.

In the cafeteria, they attracted plenty of stares from staff and customers. This whole day had been so weird, Merry didn't care. She drank her champagne quickly and accepted a top-up. When her dad couldn't manage more than a sip of his, and offered the rest to her, she polished that off, as well.

Another half hour and she could get out of this dress. She'd brought an overnight bag in the Hummer, and had asked Stephanie to take Boo for a walk and feed him late. That way, Merry could spend the rest of the day with her father, maybe even the night, if he couldn't sleep. She didn't want to waste a minute of the time they had left.

"Merry, you and Lucas need to cut the cake," Stephanie said.

Goodness knows how she had managed to get hold of a wedding cake at such short notice. It even had two tiers, total overkill.

Merry lined up obediently with Lucas, his hand over hers on the knife, while Stephanie took more photos. They made a ceremonial cut, then Stephanie sliced pieces for everyone.

Dwight had taken over the camera and was scrolling through the gallery. "You were right, John," he said. "Merry looks just like Sally. Look at this one."

He held the camera out to Merry's dad. John took it, but immediately dropped it. He'd gone rigid, Merry realized. "Dad?" She stepped toward him.

Nurse Martin elbowed past her. "Mr. Wyatt?" She crouched in front of the wheelchair and grasped his wrist.

His eyes were glazed. He seemed…asleep?

"You," Nurse Martin barked at Lucas. "Take Mr. Wyatt back to the ward while I phone ahead."

Lucas snapped into action.

"What's wrong?" Merry rushed after her to the phone on the wall.

"I suspect he's slipped into a coma." Nurse Martin pressed a three-digit number.

"A *coma?*" Merry put a hand to the wall to steady herself.

The nurse issued a curt report into the phone and hung up. "Follow me," she ordered, and set off swiftly, Merry jogging in her wedding dress to keep up. "It's not unusual," she said over her shoulder, "in the end stages of kidney failure."

They reached a staff elevator; Nurse Martin pushed the call button.

"You mean this is *it?*" Merry asked. "He's dying?"

The woman's face softened, and for a second she looked like an entirely different person. "I'm sorry, Ms. Wyatt—Mrs. Calder. But, yes, this is it."

CHAPTER SEVEN

JOHN'S SUDDEN, SHOCKING collapse jolted Lucas out of his anger with Merry.

How could he hold on to his resentment after the doctors confirmed Nurse Martin's guess that John was in a coma? They predicted that although he could linger for a couple more days, he likely wouldn't regain consciousness. Which meant the last thing he'd seen was what he most wanted: Merry and Lucas married.

Viewed through the lens of John's death, Lucas's objections seemed trifling. There would be time enough later to deal with the complications of telling his parents the whole thing had been an elaborate ploy to comfort a dying man. Time enough to file for divorce.

For several hours, Merry refused to leave her father's bedside. She sat, still in her wedding dress, holding John's hand, talking to him, sometimes begging him to wake up. Not crying. Every so often her voice thinned and wobbled, but her eyes remained dry.

When Mia became restless, Dwight and Stephanie had to leave. Lucas stayed. Not because he was faking being a loving husband, but because Merry was his friend and John was like family.

At one stage, he convinced Merry to take a few minutes away to change out of her dress. Which was when they realized her overnight bag was still in Dwight's

Hummer. When his parents didn't answer their phone, Lucas offered to fetch more clothes from Merry's place, but she looked so alarmed at the thought of him leaving that he abandoned the idea.

Lucas had picked up his service dress blues from the dry cleaner this morning and changed here in John's bathroom ahead of the wedding, so he had civilian clothes—jeans and T-shirt—on hand. He'd bet he was a lot more comfortable than Merry, but that couldn't be helped.

Twice, he slipped out to buy coffee downstairs. The second time he came back with an egg salad sandwich. Merry ate a bite, but didn't want any more, so Lucas finished it.

At six o'clock, Nurse Martin came in.

"My shift is over," she announced in her abrupt style. Presumably she'd been hired for her nursing skills rather than her bedside manner.

"So, we'll see you tomorrow?" Lucas said, mainly to be polite.

She ignored him. "You should go home, get some rest," she told Merry.

"I don't want to leave Dad." Merry clutched her father's hand tighter.

"He won't die tonight," the nurse said. "Better to save your stamina for tomorrow." She straightened a corner of John's blanket that to Lucas looked perfectly neat already.

He saw that the practical, economical movement soothed Merry.

"Nurse Martin's right," he said. "I'll take you home now so you can sleep. I'll bring you back first thing tomorrow."

The thought of sleep prompted an enormous yawn from Merry, forcing her to let go of John's hand, clasped in both of hers, in order to cover her mouth. Breaking the physical connection seemed to help her make the decision.

"Okay, we'll do that. What you said." She stood with a rustle of white silk.

Lucas drove Merry to her apartment above the bowling alley. She'd moved in within the past year, so he'd never been there. Inside, the decor was just what he'd expected—cozy despite the soaring loft ceiling, with the romantic touches Merry liked: deep-pile rugs, velvet cushions on the couch, ambient lighting.

The apartment was open concept, with what he assumed was a bedroom area sectioned off by a silk screen. He went to check it out. Yep. Above the bed hung a mosquito net, presumably for decorative effect rather than because an outbreak of mosquitoes had hit New London in fall. Who knew how she'd hung it up there.

He heard barking, and when he got back into the kitchen area, Merry was letting the dog in off the balcony.

"He needs to go outside," she said. The first words she'd spoken since they left the hospital.

"I'll take him." Lucas grabbed the leash hanging on the balcony door handle. "You get changed while I deal with the dog. Do you want dinner?"

"Just a piece of toast." She sounded distant, numb.

"I'll make it." He decided to get it going while he was out with Boo. He found bread in the refrigerator. On the counter next to the kettle sat an open pack of peppermint tea bags. It seemed the right sort of drink for the occasion; he put the kettle on to boil.

When he turned around, Merry had disappeared into the bedroom.

Grabbing her keys, he took the dog for a five-minute walk. When he got back, the toast had popped up and the kettle had boiled. No sign of Merry.

She still hadn't emerged by the time he buttered the toast and made the tea, which looked disgusting, like hot pond water, and smelled almost as bad.

"Merry?" he called. "You okay?"

"Sort of." Her voice was muffled.

"You coming out soon?"

"I'm kind of…stuck."

Stuck?

"Okay, I'm coming in." Lucas headed for the screen.

"No, it's fine, don't…"

He stepped into the bedroom area. And burst out laughing.

All he could see of Merry was a pair of bare feet with pink-painted toenails, two slim calves, and one hand protruding from the top of the wedding dress, which encased her from head to knees. A narrow strip of silk—some kind of sash?—lay discarded on the bed. She'd obviously been trying to remove the dress over her head, for reasons unknown.

"It's not funny." But he could hear a smile in Merry's voice. "I can't get out of this thing, I can't move and I'm terrified I'm going to tear Stephanie's beautiful dress."

He circled her, to get a full picture of the situation. "Wouldn't it have been smarter to undo the buttons so you could just step out of it?"

"Thank you, Hero Chopper Pilot, yes, it would. But there are a million buttons and I don't have the octopus arms required for the job."

He tsked. "All you had to do was ask." He was aware she probably hadn't wanted him that close to her, not after Baltimore, so he kept his tone light. "Okay, we're going to get you out of this thing, but we'll have to pull it back down first."

"I can't get it to budge, up or down," she admitted.

"You keep still while I tug."

"Be careful," she warned.

Pulling the dress back down again without yanking it too roughly required Lucas to put his hands pretty much all over Merry. He worked the fabric around her shoulders, smoothed it down the sides of her breasts, then pulled it to her waist and hips. Then he had to go back to the beginning to repeat the entire process. He tried to imagine she was a tailor's dummy, but her skin was too warm, even through the silk, and her slight curves too soft.

When her head emerged from the top of the dress, he knew they'd made real progress. Her brown hair had gotten mussed and her cheeks were flushed, but she was free.

Then he liberated her other arm, and she was able to help. Their hands brushed and collided, until at last the gown was in more or less the right place with the bodice over her breasts. The style had left her shoulders partly, tantalizingly exposed, but with her arms out of the sleeves, the dress hung lower, leaving her shoulders and the upper slope of her chest entirely bare.

Phew. Lucas felt as if he'd run a marathon. Merry must have her heating set way up high.

"Turn around and I'll get the buttons," he said. "Then I'll leave you to it."

She was right, there were dozens of buttons, starting midway down her shoulder blades.

Lucas couldn't see too well—it was dark outside and only the bedside lamp lit the space—but he applied himself to the task, appreciating its simplicity after all that tugging and smoothing.

A dozen buttons into it, he realized Merry wasn't wearing a bra. It would have to have been the strapless kind, and…it wasn't. He found just an expanse of pale back, the skin satiny where his fingers brushed.

"Is something stuck?" Merry asked.

He met her eyes in the full-length mirror that hung on the wall next to the bathroom door, and realized he'd stopped working. "It's fine." He started again. "You'll need to hold on to the front of the dress."

She clutched the silk to her breasts, as if she'd suddenly realized, as he had, that once those buttons were undone, there'd be nothing holding it up.

Man, it was hot in here; Lucas was almost thirsty enough to drink that peppermint tea. He wiped his fingers on his jeans and persevered, slipping one button after another through its tiny silk loop.

Merry swayed.

"Have you eaten today?" Lucas asked. They hadn't got to the wedding cake, with John going into a coma, and she'd had only one bite of that sandwich. "Did you have breakfast?"

"Just coffee before the wedding," she admitted. "And three glasses of champagne afterward."

Plus those coffees he'd bought her since then. Hell, all she had in her system was caffeine and alcohol. Better get that toast into her pronto, then make her some more.

"Not hungry," she murmured as if she'd read his mind.

He ignored that, put aside his distraction and made swift work of the rest of the damn buttons. It helped that she stood so utterly still. The buttons ran all the way down past her waist, to the hollow at the base of her spine. Any lower and he'd be...

He jerked his eyes away.

And saw Merry in the mirror. Holding the dress to her chest while tears coursed silently down her cheeks. The very picture of despair.

"Merry," he said, horrified. "Don't cry, honeybun."

She shook her head, but there was no denying what they both could see.

"What—what am I going to do, Lucas?" she asked, the words hiccupping, soft, damp, broken. "Who will I have to love, and to love me?"

The answer to both questions: *I have no idea.* Not helpful. So Lucas said, "Hush, we'll work it out." Also not helpful; her tears fell harder.

Hell. He turned her around and pulled her into a hug.

At last he'd got it right. She sank against him, crying harder now that she had somewhere for the tears to land. Their wet warmth soaked his T-shirt. Lucas moved one hand up to stroke her hair. Her shuddery sigh suggested she found it comforting, so he carried on.

He had no idea how long they stood there, him taking most of her weight—she must be ready to collapse from hunger and exhaustion by now—while she cried herself out.

At last she stilled, her face pressed into his shoulder. Lucas was about to pull back, to suggest he make her some fresh tea and toast, when he realized that at some stage she'd wound her arms around his neck. Which meant she was no longer holding her dress.

In fact, the gown seemed to have slipped somewhat. His hand, the one that wasn't in her hair, was spread across her bare back. The breasts pressed against him were mostly naked. No sooner had he registered that than his body stirred. Talk about bad timing.

"Uh, Merry," he said.

She lifted her face to him, pale and tearstained. "Thank you," she said. "I really needed to be held."

"What are husbands for?" he joked. Which might not have been the smartest thing to say.

Her gray eyes widened. Then she went up on tiptoe, her breasts brushing his chest in the process, and kissed his mouth. Just one kiss, but she didn't move away again. Just stood there, her mouth against his.

"We should probably…" Lucas began. But talking involved moving his lips against hers, and then her lips were moving, too, and suddenly there was no talking, there was just kissing.

Deep, intense, hungry kissing.

He couldn't say exactly when the dress slipped to the floor, but he did remember its existence long enough not to trample it when he scooped Merry up and carried her to the bed. All without breaking the connection between their mouths.

He set her down carefully, and then had to cut the connection while he pulled his T-shirt over his head, dragged off his jeans. Merry lay staring up at him, eyes wide, lips parted. Naked except for her lace panties.

A warning clanged in Lucas's mind: *This is Merry. Pull up, pull up.* The same warning he'd heeded six months ago when, like tonight, he'd reacted on autopilot to her kiss before he'd remembered that getting it on with his oldest friend, his dad's best friend's daughter, was stupid.

Gingerly, he sat down on the edge of the bed so he wasn't looming over her. "Merry…"

The horror in her face stopped him.

"You're going to do it again, aren't you?" She scooted up the pillow, bringing her breasts right into his line of sight. "You're going to tell me you don't want me."

Yes, though "don't want" wasn't quite accurate. "It's not that."

"Is it my breasts?" she demanded. "Are they too small?"

"No!" he said, horrified.

"You always date well-endowed women." Her complexion had gone from pale to scarlet.

Guilty as charged. "It's nothing to do with that," he said. "Your body is amazing. Fantastic." He was overdoing it. Her body was nice, but not sensational… In fact, he couldn't think why he'd had so much trouble banishing it from his mind over the past six months.

But she said, "Really?" in a quavery voice. "So you're not thinking of backing out now?"

Hell. The instincts he relied on to keep him safe in a war zone told him making love to her would mess things up. But *not* making love when Merry was feeling lost and desperate for comfort would hurt her unforgivably.

"You bet I'm not backing out," he said hoarsely.

She closed her eyes, as if in relief, and when she opened them again, they held a purposeful look that he found a little unnerving.

"But I don't have protection," Lucas said on a wave of inspiration. Relief surged through him.

"My purse," she said. "On the floor. The zip pocket."

Damn. Her purse was next to the bed. In the pocket, he found two little foil packets. He tore one open, slowly. Hoping it would give her time to change her mind.

Her mind didn't change, but the mood did. Merry pulled him down to her, and when he started kissing her again, he sensed she was determined to do this. As was he.

He couldn't help thinking mutual determination wasn't a basis for great sex.

There was a kind of resoluteness to their kisses, a mechanical rhythm to the movement of his hands and hers, underscored by the soundtrack beneath them, the rumble of bowling balls and the thwack of pins.

Just when Lucas was thinking he should put a stop to this after all, Merry said, "Now. I want you now."

He hesitated. "You're not ready…."

"Now," she insisted, and he was so worried that he was about to lose all interest, which would be an even bigger disaster, he complied.

Afterward, he lay in the dark, wide-awake, while Merry slept beside him. That was the worst sex—no way could it be called lovemaking—he'd ever had.

Never again.

THE PHONE RANG AT THREE in the morning. Merry jerked awake, the blur of dreams dissipating in an instant. *The hospital. Dad.* She flung the covers aside.

"Whassup?" Lucas said next to her.

Merry yelped. He was in her bed!

As she stumbled to the kitchen, the memory of what they'd done flooded back in far too much detail.

Awful.

She shoved the images aside as she picked up the phone. "Hello?" *Please don't let Dad be dead.* But what else could it be?

"Ms. Wyatt? This is Dr. Randall."

Lucas appeared around the screen. *He's naked.* So was she, Merry realized. Her teeth started to chatter. "Is Dad…?"

"We're prepping him for surgery right now," the doctor said. "A donor kidney just became available. Ms. Wyatt, your father's getting a transplant."

CHAPTER EIGHT

WHITE LIGHT. SO BRIGHT, John could see it with his eyes closed.

At least he thought his eyes were closed. He could, he supposed, be dead.

Which would make this...heaven?

Had he been good enough? And was "good" what it was about?

Didn't feel hot enough to be the other place. That was a relief.

He realized there was noise, muted but earthly. The occasional clank of metal penetrated first, then distant voices. People. Hospital. He was still in the hospital.

Now he remembered. He'd woken, who knew how long ago, without having realized he'd been asleep, or unconscious or whatever. A doctor had introduced himself as an anesthetist and said John had woken from his coma—what coma?—just in time to be sent to sleep again. Because he was about to have a transplant.

If that hadn't been a dream, the fact he was conscious now meant he'd survived the operation.

So...he had a new kidney? Hard to tell. He twitched one hand and realized he had a monitor attached to his finger. Come to think of it, everything felt as if it had something attached.

He would see Merry again.

Didn't she get married? Yeah, to Lucas. Good.

Maybe he'd have grandkids soon. And live to see them.

Too much to hope for? He hadn't seriously hoped for a new kidney, but now look at him.

"Is he awake?" The voice was close. Merry?

"He came around down in post-op. He had some nausea," someone said. A nurse. The crabby one. "But he's drifted off again."

John didn't remember being awake after the surgery, nor the nausea.

"His eyelids are moving," Merry said.

"He could wake any moment," the nurse replied. She always sounded belligerent, as if she expected an argument. "Dr. Randall was very pleased with how the surgery went. She'll come by soon. You can ask her yourself."

Should he open his eyes? Could he? He wasn't sure he had the energy, not so much for the eye opening but for the conversations that would follow.

"It's like a miracle." Merry sounded tearful. "I thought we'd lost him. And now..."

"Another chance at life." The nurse's no-nonsense tone robbed the words of any poetry.

Another chance at life. A do-over. What would John do differently, given that chance? He'd told Merry he wished he'd remarried. But that was for her sake, not his own. There wasn't another woman who would match up to his Sally. He'd never felt with anyone else the extraordinary connection that had drawn him to Sally the moment he'd met her.

What else could this do-over life offer, if not love?

He used to paint, watercolors of the sea and the coast. He hadn't done that in a few years. It was the sort of activity that might be good for his blood pressure. *I'll work less, paint more.*

The decision afforded him some satisfaction. But only briefly.

If he was honest with himself, he'd admit he was lonely. Merry was wonderful, but she had her own life. A new life, now that she was married.

I have a new life, too, he reminded himself, and sent up a prayer of thanks for his anonymous donor.

He owed it to the donor, as well as to himself, to live this new life to the full.

A full life wasn't lived alone.

I need someone. A woman. A companion more than a lover, but maybe he wouldn't say no to the physical side. If he was still capable.

How to go about it? How did a sixty-one-year-old man who hadn't been with a woman in over twenty years start dating?

John pressed his lips together against a sudden wave of nausea.

The first time would be the hardest, as with most things in life. An idea drifted into his head. *I'll ask out the first woman I see, get it over with.* Yeah, why not?

John felt pressure against his shoulder, caught the scents of lemon and lavender. Merry had put her head against him. *My best girl.* He tried to say it, and to touch her, but his tongue felt thick, his hands like lead weights. He tried to sink back into the bed so she would feel him soften against her.

She'd said something that he didn't catch, he realized. He heard footsteps leaving. Merry or the nurse?

"You can open your eyes now," the nurse said.

He was so startled, he did.

Everything looked identical to the way it had before—the room, the nurse—and he wondered if he'd imagined the anesthetist, if he'd merely been asleep. He opened his mouth to ask, but his throat was as dry as a ship's biscuit.

He licked his lips.

"I'll pour you some water," the nurse said.

Though he couldn't focus on her badge, he remembered now that her name was Cathy Martin.

She poured water into a glass, then pressed the lever to raise the head of the bed. She leaned over him, propped him in the crook of her arm and held the glass to his lips. All her movements were efficient to the point of minimalism. John mistrusted efficiency, which too often occurred at the expense of contemplation. But she coaxed the right amount of water into him with no discomfort whatsoever, and he gave credit where it was due.

"Thanks," he said, and this time it was audible, if hoarse.

She set him back against the pillows with a gentleness completely at odds with her manner. "Feel better?" she asked. Her voice was still brusque.

He nodded. "So, it worked? The transplant?"

"As good as they get." She noted something on his chart, probably that he'd woken up and drunk some water. "You're lucky."

Her oval face was serious, and made more so by the tight bun she'd scraped her brown hair into.

"I should be celebrating," he said.

Then it clicked: *the first woman I see*. He should have realized when he had such a nutty idea that the nurse would be the first, but his brain must be in go-slow mode.

She sniffed. "Wait a few days and see if your body rejects the new kidney. Of course, you'll be on antirejection medication the rest of your life, which is no picnic."

"Bundle of joy," he said.

"I'm a pragmatist," she said. "And I'm menopausal." More than he ever wanted to know about his nurse. "If you want light and fluffy, I'm not your woman."

He knew *that*.

But she was the first woman he'd seen. She brought new meaning to the phrase *the first time's the hardest*.

"So, Nurse Cathy Martin," he said, bold with a new kidney, his voice gaining strength. "Assuming my body doesn't reject the kidney, and I don't get a superbug or fall out of bed and break my neck…"

She tapped her foot, impatient.

"You want to go out for dinner?"

"EVERYTHING LOOKS AS IT should, Mr. Wyatt," Dr. Randall said. "Assuming nothing changes overnight, I'll sign your discharge papers tomorrow. You should be out of here by noon."

"Are you sure?" Merry asked. "It's only been five days since the transplant." She couldn't wait until Dad got out of here, but she didn't want to take any risks.

"The wonders of laparoscopic surgery," the doctor said crisply. "Recovery is so much faster. Your father's had no discomfort during the times he's been up and about, and he's showing no signs of rejection. We'll give him instructions as to how to monitor for those," she added, handing the patient notes to Nurse Martin, who was standing by. "We'll schedule regular checkups, of course."

"That's wonderful," Merry said. "Dad, we're about to get our lives back." She couldn't wait. Couldn't wait for them to be a family again.

Couldn't wait to get unmarried.

Why did I sleep with Lucas? She'd never regretted anything so much.

"The doc says I could be back at work in a couple more weeks." Her dad's voice was so much stronger, just listening to him gave Merry a thrill, chased away her regrets over her wedding night. Those would come back all too soon.

"*Light* work," the doctor clarified.

"What about his blood pressure?" Merry asked her.

"That's in some ways the most encouraging news of all," Dr. Randall said. "Just now it was 160 over 100."

Numbers that would scare most people, but for John, the 160 was a slight improvement.

"I'm not sure why it's down," the doctor continued. "Could be a temporary aftereffect of surgery and inactivity, or it could be a reduction in stress. It may even be the new drug regimen we've been experimenting with." She said this last with her eyebrows raised, as if it was the most far-fetched possibility.

Merry suspected that was her idea of a joke.

"We'll have to wait and see if the improvement holds up." Dr. Randall turned to John. "I don't need to tell you, Mr. Wyatt, that if we don't control your blood pressure, there's every chance disease will develop in your new kidney."

And this nightmare would start all over again.

Dr. Randall issued a couple more dire warnings, then left.

"Lucas will be pleased to have you home," John said to Merry.

"Uh-huh." She'd slept on a cot in this room every night since Dr. Randall's call.

She didn't know where Lucas was sleeping. He'd assured her that he was looking after Boo, so he might even be staying at her place. She didn't want to know. She was just glad she hadn't been forced to have a meaningful conversation with him. Sleeping together had been a big mistake in a dozen different ways. Talking about it would only prolong the agony.

So instead, she greeted Lucas politely whenever he came to visit Dad, exchanged the pleasantries she would with anyone, then used his visits as a chance to grab some food. Too bad she couldn't go into the cafeteria without thinking of her wedding cake. Which made her think about the fiasco of her wedding night all over again.

The sooner they got divorced, the better.

"I have to tell Lucas you're coming home." She pulled out her phone and began typing a text message.

Their divorce was the one subject they'd discussed, though entirely by text. Because as wonderful as her dad's recovery was, it did complicate their marriage. If he'd died, they'd have filed for divorce by now. But they'd married to please John, and John was still around. The divorce would still happen, but would entail a few more explanations.

DAD HOME 12PM TOMORROW, she wrote, then sent it.

They'd agreed to tell their parents they were divorcing before her father's discharge from the hospital, since that was when they would go their separate ways. Merry would stay with her dad a few days, then move back into her loft, while Lucas either stayed with his parents or, hopefully, left town.

"Dwight and Stephanie have invited me to move in with them for a while," her father said.

"But I want to look after you," she protested. "I don't need to go back to work until you do, so I have the time."

"You're a newlywed," John pointed out. "That loft of yours is too small for two people, no matter how in love they are." Merry flinched. "You and Lucas can have my place while you work out where you plan to live long-term."

"Dad, there's no need—"

"I don't have to tell you, Merry-Berry, Dwight's place is a lot more comfortable than mine," he said.

Warmer, too, Merry knew. Her dad's house had heating, but the wind whistled through the aged boards in winter. In his postoperative state, Dad might be vulnerable to pneumonia, or worse.

Her phone beeped. New message from Lucas Calder. She opened it. OK SO U WILL TELL HIM RE DIVORCE NOW?

YES. She sent the reply.

"Frankly, Merry-Berry, Stephanie's a better cook than you," her dad added, only half-joking. "You and Lucas take all the time you need. Think of it as a kind of wedding present."

This was her cue.

"Dad, you know Lucas and I only got married because you were worried about my future."

"That's why you got married *now,*" her father agreed. "You would have got around to it eventually. You two are soul mates." He gave a happy sigh. "Merry-Berry, you and Lucas tying the knot has been a load off my mind like you wouldn't believe."

"Because you thought you were dying," she agreed. "But now you're well. The doctor says you might have as long as twenty years."

"Unless I have a heart attack tomorrow."

"Don't say that!" Merry's phone slipped from her grasp and clattered to the floor, landing at Nurse Martin's sensibly shod feet.

The woman bent to pick it up. She glanced down at it as she handed it to Merry, her expression neutral.

"Thanks," Merry muttered. Her smartphone displayed her text conversation with Lucas in speech bubbles, which meant Lucas's mention of divorce sat center screen.

She thumbed back to the main screen and tucked the phone in her pocket. "There's nothing wrong with your heart, is there?"

"Not yet," her dad said.

Nurse Martin made a huffing sound that eased Merry's anxiety.

"But anything could happen, anytime," he said. "Merry, I hadn't realized how afraid I've been, for some years now, of leaving you alone. Now that fear has gone."

"That'll be why your blood pressure is down," Nurse Martin said with a cool look at Merry. She'd probably read that mention of divorce. Who asked the nosy old bat, anyway?

She couldn't be right about Dad's blood pressure, could she?

"I'm quite capable of looking after myself," Merry told her father.

"Physically, sure," he agreed. "But, Merry, you're like me. You're not cut out to be alone. The best thing for my health is seeing you settled and happy with Lucas."

This time there was no mistaking Nurse Martin's pointed look.

As Merry left the hospital, she texted Lucas to ask his whereabouts.

The reply came a minute later: WITH HEATHER GUNN

Heather had been his girlfriend in his senior year in high school. These days, she was an optometrist, working with her dad at Gunn Optical, the only optometry practice in downtown New London.

Five minutes later, Merry pulled up outside the store.

She found Lucas in an examination room with Heather, whom she knew slightly. Although there was a station of sophisticated-looking test equipment, the two were sitting at a table, with several books between them. Heather hadn't changed; she was still blonde and busty. And her white coat made her look as brainy as her job suggested she was. She wasn't, Merry noticed as they said hello, wearing a ring.

"What are you doing here?" Lucas asked. Which was the most personal comment he'd directed to her since they'd had sex.

Ugh, she was trying not to think about that; doing so made it impossible to look him in the eye.

"We need to talk." Merry fixed her gaze on his left shoulder. "It's urgent." Her eyes flicked down, and she realized the books on the table in front of him were those Magic Eye 3D puzzle books. "But not if you're busy..."

Heather gave her an amused look as she stood. "I think we're done here. I'll see you next week, Lucas."

It wasn't until she left, closing the door behind her, that it occurred to Merry that she should have rehearsed what she wanted to say on the way here. She also realized this was the first time she'd been alone with him since their wedding night.

She hoped desperately that he didn't want to talk about it.

Lucas picked up a Magic Eye book, flicked to an image of multicolored, jumbled stars and handed it to Merry. "Tell me what you see."

She held the page to her nose, focused on looking "through" the image, then began moving the page away. When it was about eight inches from her face, she stopped. Waited. "There it is. A planet with rings around it—like Saturn."

"What? Let me see that." He grabbed the book, flipped to the back, presumably to the answers. "You're right. How did you do that?"

She shrugged. "I love those things. Why are you playing games with your old girlfriend?"

Lucas raised his eyebrows. "Heather says Magic Eye pictures might help improve my depth perception. I'll practice with these books, plus do some online tests, and she'll test me a couple of times a week until I resit my physical."

"You think that'll work?" It sounded too easy.

"It has to," he said, as if his eyesight would obey his command or else be court-martialed. "I was a borderline pass on the depth perception test Heather gave me just now."

"How is her test different from the navy's?" Merry asked.

"The navy test is harder," he admitted. "But I'll spend a chunk of each day on this for the next month, by which time I hope Dad will have made some calls on my behalf." Lucas grimaced. "He's probably as big a stumbling block as anything. Did you speak to him about supporting my resit?"

"I forgot," she admitted, "what with everything going on."

He nodded. "Understandable. So, how did your dad take the news of our divorce?"

"Ah." She picked up another of the Magic Eye books. It fell open at an image that looked like thousands of red and pink roses.

"I tried that one," Lucas said, disgusted. "Couldn't see a thing."

She held the page to her face and moved it away slowly.

"So what did your dad say?" Lucas leaned back so his chair tilted up on two legs.

Merry held the book still and focused. "His blood pressure is down. Still way too high, but the doctor hopes the new medication and a lack of stress might bring it down further."

"That's great. The divorce?"

"It's a heart," Merry said. "This picture." She turned the book in his direction. Of course, there was no way he could see the image just like that. "These things are genius."

"Merry," Lucas said suspiciously. "You did *tell* your dad, right?"

"Here's the thing." She put down the book, pulled out a chair and sagged into it. "I wondered if we could wait awhile."

"No way." His chair crashed back onto all four legs. "We got married because it was your dad's dying wish, remember? He's no longer dying—the doctor said he could live another twenty years."

"The doctor also said his blood pressure is the biggest risk to the new kidney. There's a good chance his lowered pressure is due to less stress—and it turns out I'm the major cause of his stress." At Lucas's blank look, she added, "His fears about my future. Dad says that worry has gone now that I'm married to you."

"We're not staying married twenty years for the sake of your dad's blood pressure," Lucas snapped.

When he put it like that...

But on the other hand... "If our divorce is going to affect his health, then I don't want to do it." It was that simple. She folded her arms across her chest.

Lucas's gaze dropped to her breasts.

She groaned inwardly. *Why did I sleep with him?* He looked as if he was wondering exactly the same thing about her.

"Waiting is a bad idea," he said, his voice clipped. "The longer we leave it, the harder it'll be to tell your father. It could have an even worse effect on his blood pressure, because he'll be more entrenched in his belief that we're happily married." His tone was detached, as if he was listing the pros and cons of a military engagement. And they were all cons.

She'd better do the pros.

"That's pure conjecture," she said. "Whereas I know for sure that right now, Dad's blood pressure is down, the doctor says it's a stress thing, and Dad says our marriage has got rid of his worries." *One and one and one make three.* "If we stay married for a while, it'll give his new medication regime a chance to kick in, and if necessary be tweaked. As soon as we're sure his BP is controlled, we can tell him the truth."

"What about my dad and Stephanie?" Lucas said. "I was going to tell them tonight."

"We'd have to keep up the pretense with them, too," she admitted. "I mean, maybe Dwight would agree to lie to Dad, but it's too risky." There was still enough of the old, hardheaded admiral in Lucas's father that she could imagine him snorting with disbelief at the idea of worry being the cause of John's hypertension. Dwight's almost religious regard for the truth would have him suggesting it was better to come clean now, rather than risk fallout later.

"See?" Lucas must have read the conflict in her face. "It's too complicated."

"Actually," she said, "it's simple, because it has a built-in expiration date. You said you'll need a month to fix your depth perception. Then you'll be back in the navy. Unless," she said with just the right amount of challenge, "you don't think you'll pass the retest."

He folded his arms, mirroring her pose. "Of course I'll pass."

Merry smiled encouragingly. There were some advantages to knowing him so well. "Great! So I'll have a few more weeks to make sure Dad's blood pressure is under control. As soon as you do the test, you'll be back in the Gulf. After a few months, we file for divorce and it'll be just like the good old days." And maybe one day, in about a million years, they'd forget they'd ever slept together.

"A month," he said, as if he was actually considering it.

She nodded. With Lucas, sometimes less was more.

"We could still file for the divorce now," he said. "It won't be final for ninety days."

"Every divorce petition in the county is listed in the legal notices in the *Day*. There's too much risk that one of our parents or one of their friends would see it."

He muttered something under his breath, not sounding particularly happy. "What about an annulment—did you look into that?"

Merry had spent a lot of time surfing the net from her phone over the past week. She busied herself stacking the Magic Eye books into a neat pile. "The only grounds for annulment are if the man is proved physically incapable of consummating the marriage."

That ship had well and truly sailed.

"The good thing is, we won't need to fake being happily married all the time, only when we're at your parents' house or with my dad." She moved quickly along from the issue of consummation. "We'd need to live together—we'd have Dad's place, while he's at your parents'. His house has two bedrooms, two beds."

She shouldn't have mentioned *beds* so close to *consummation*.

"I don't know." Lucas was looking wary again. She didn't blame him—she couldn't imagine anything worse than ending up back in bed with him.

She cast around for a new tack. "That conversation you want me to have with Dwight about the retest," she said.

"You can do that anytime, just give Dad a call."

"Maybe I'll hold off for a while," she said thoughtfully.

Lucas waited, correctly sensing there was more to this.

Merry sidelined her scruples. "How about you agree we can stay married until you go away. We'll wait a week or two to ensure Dad's recovery. Then I'll ask Dwight to help you get another physical."

Lucas leaned forward, elbows on the table. "And if I don't agree to stay married?" His tone was conversational, but silky menace lurked beneath the words.

She swallowed. "I won't talk to Dwight." She should have drunk some water before she left the hospital.

"You plan to blackmail me into pretending this marriage is for real," he said mildly.

"That's a simplistic way of looking at it. But there's more than one way to see it—just like these pictures." She touched the stack of books. "Behind the, uh, blackmail, it's about the two of us helping each other out. The way friends do."

"That sounds reasonable," he said.

"Really?"

"Of course not," he snapped. He stood, hands planted

on the table, glaring at her. "Your dad's doing fine, we're not moving in together, we're not staying married because you have some fantasy that it might keep his blood pressure down. This is the real world, we're all adults, we can handle the truth."

Panic squeezed her heart. "What if you're wrong?"

"I'm not," he said. "I'm giving you until midday tomorrow, Merry, to tell your dad. At twelve-oh-five—" stupid military timekeeping "—I'll tell my parents."

He whisked the Magic Eye books out from under her hand and left.

CHAPTER NINE

MERRY'S CLUMSY ATTEMPT at blackmail had done him a favor, Lucas thought as he floored the gas in his rented Ford Fusion the next morning.

She'd shown him that a plan to resit the physical that relied on her cooperation and his father's was a bad one. Even when they were kids, she'd had the knack of forcing him to rethink his ideas. Back then, he'd found it infuriating. Now he was grateful.

Lucas flicked the turn signal and hit the I-95 on-ramp. It was 7:00 a.m. He should be in Boston at nine. By ten, he should be free of his reliance on Merry and his dad, and on his way to Norfolk, Virginia, to stay with a buddy. Heather Gunn had been kind enough to set up an appointment with an optometrist there who would help him the way she had, so Lucas would have all the time he needed to focus on getting ready for the test.

He couldn't wait.

This whole marriage thing had spun out of control—*why did I have sex with her?*—and prolonging it would only make the situation worse. He liked Merry and her dad, and when the dust settled he didn't want to have created any lasting rifts. Best way to ensure that: let distance and days work their magic. While at the same time getting what he wanted.

He drove the rest of the way on autopilot, using the

solitude to rehearse the arguments he would present to Admiral Tremaine.

He reached the admiral's house at five to nine.

"Lucas, it's good to see you." Admiral Tremaine shook his hand. "It's been a while."

Tremaine had been a regular visitor at Dwight's house until the two admirals had fallen out over the Iraq war. Lucas was counting on the man's irritation garnering him some sympathy.

"Thanks for making time for me, sir." In the admiral's oak-paneled study, Lucas sat in the chair Tremaine indicated.

The older man inquired after Lucas's hand injury and made incidental talk for a minute as he pulled a pipe and a pack of tobacco from the top drawer of his desk. Then he said, "I'm sure you didn't come here to chew the fat. After you called last night, I did some checking. I understand you failed your physical. You can't fly."

"I'm hoping to retest," Lucas said.

Tremaine snorted. "Good luck with that." He stuffed a generous serving of tobacco into his pipe, struck a match and lit the tobacco. He tamped it down with a cylindrical brass tamper.

Lucas watched without saying anything.

Tremaine looked up. "Ah. That's why you're here. The retest."

"Yes, sir." Lucas found exploiting his connections as distasteful as his father did. But he'd been trained to make use of every available weapon. So he would.

"Your C.O. says you're his best pilot," Tremaine said. "And of course, I pinned that Navy Cross on you myself a couple of years ago."

Lucas didn't respond. He'd figured Tremaine wouldn't have forgotten giving him one of the navy's highest awards, earned when Lucas had risked his own life—though it hadn't felt like that at the time—to disable a mine that would have killed the entire crew of a gunboat whose escape routes had been cut off.

"A retest is rare, but not unheard of." Tremaine puffed thoughtfully on his pipe. "Waste of time if you can't pass it, though."

"I only failed the depth-perception test," Lucas said. The man probably knew that. "It's possible to improve with practice."

"We don't want people who can't see properly piloting our choppers," Tremaine pointed out.

"I'm asking for another chance to pass the test," Lucas said. "Not to be cleared with substandard vision. If I pass, it'll mean I meet the standard. If I was worried I couldn't pass, say, the running component, you wouldn't consider it cheating for me to practice and improve my times beforehand."

Admiral Tremaine nodded. "What does your father think about the retest idea?"

"He thinks I should stay home." Lucas quashed a twinge of disloyalty toward his father. Dwight's disapproval was the bait that would secure Tremaine's cooperation.

The admiral frowned. "You're currently on leave. How are you filling your days?"

"Practicing my depth perception, sir." Since the admiral seemed to know everything about him, he decided it was prudent to add, "I also got married recently."

Tremaine didn't look surprised. "Your wife's keeping you busy, then."

"She's doing her best, sir." Resorting to blackmail when necessary. Merry Wyatt had always been full of crazy ideas and romantic notions.

"Marriage is a wonderful thing," Tremaine said. "I like it so much I've done it three times."

Lucas smiled politely.

"Which puts me one step ahead of your father." Tremaine was joking, but it fell flat. "Stephanie is delightful, of course," he said hastily. "I see her every year at the admirals' dinner in Annapolis. And Michelle, your mother…lovely woman. Dwight has good taste."

"Thank you, sir," Lucas said stiffly. He didn't talk about his mother with anyone except Garrett and, oddly, Stephanie. Talking about Mom, like thinking about her, only served to rake up the question that had tortured him for years after she'd died of a sudden stroke in the grocery store. *If I'd been there, could I have saved her?*

It was a gross conceit, to imagine a twelve-year-old boy who'd recently learned CPR outperforming his older brother, then the bystander who'd stepped in, then the paramedics. But Garrett hadn't known CPR, not properly, and the other people hadn't loved the woman they were trying to save.

That made Lucas think of Merry and her immense love for her father. She was trying to do what Lucas had wanted to do: save her parent. Thankfully, in John's case, the outcome looked positive.

Unless Merry was right about John's hypertension being exacerbated by worry about her future. And her marriage to Lucas being, at this stage, the key to his health.

Lucas shook off sudden alarm, which was surely a reaction to thinking about his mother.

He tried to focus on what Admiral Tremaine was saying. Something about the retest. *Which is why I'm here.*

"I may be able to help you out," Tremaine said. "I need to talk to…"

Lucas's mind drifted away again. Back to New London.

What if John's blood pressure skyrocketed and he had some kind of attack that resulted in irreparable kidney damage? And Lucas could have stopped it?

It would be just like his mom, all over again.

His mouth dried.

John's not my father. Not my responsibility.

Which wouldn't matter a damn if he died, and Lucas could have saved him.

It wasn't that simple, Lucas knew. And yet it was.

"What I'd need from you," Admiral Tremaine said, "is—"

"Sir, could you excuse me while I make an urgent call?" Without waiting for a reply, Lucas stepped out of the room. He dialed Merry from his cell. Her phone was switched off, or out of range. He tried her home number—no answer.

Could she have told her father about the divorce already? Had he collapsed? *You're being stupid.*

Lucas glanced at his watch. Nine-thirty. John was due to leave the hospital at twelve. Knowing Merry, she wouldn't be in a rush to tell him the bad news; she'd wait until the last possible moment.

Lucas stuck his head back around the study door. "Admiral Tremaine, sir, I'm sorry, but I have to leave. Family emergency."

"Can it wait fifteen minutes?" Tremaine half stood. "I'm still not in a place where I can give unqualified support to your retest."

"Sir, I'm sorry, I need to go now. It's life-and-death." Lucas picked up his notebook. "I'll call you."

When he got into the car, he groaned. *I'll call you.* What kind of idiot talked to an admiral like that?

"DWIGHT WILL BE HERE IN HALF an hour," Merry told her father. Dwight's roomy Hummer was more suited to transporting a patient than Merry's Aveo. She just needed to explain that he could now come home with her, instead of needing to stay with his friend. Explain the divorce in such a way her dad wouldn't worry about her.

She scooted her chair back to allow Nurse Martin access to the patient. The nurse began changing his dressing, working with silent efficiency.

"Is Lucas picking you up, Merry-Berry?" John asked. "Or will Dwight take you home, too?" He smiled at Nurse Martin as she peeled back a piece of surgical tape. She didn't smile back.

Someone ought to complain about her.

Merry made a noncommittal sound. "Dad, I truly think the familiarity of your own home would be best for you. If we keep the door between the kitchen and the living room closed, we'll get rid of that draft…."

"I'm not going to play third wheel to you and Lucas," he said. "You need your privacy."

She sighed. "Not really." All roads led to confession

of pending divorce, but she couldn't quite bring herself to say it.

"And I need *my* privacy," he said, surprising her. "Merry, I've been giving this a lot of thought. I don't want life to go back to the way it was before the surgery."

"You don't?" Merry said, dismayed. She loved their old life.

"I was lonely," he stated.

"Dad, I'm sorry," she said. "I'd be happy to spend more—"

"So I plan to start dating."

For a long moment, the words hovered in the air between them, so foreign to Merry that she didn't comprehend them. Then they hit.

"You can't do that!" She grabbed his left hand, which was now completely unfettered. "You always said you could never look at another woman after Mom."

A clatter startled her. Nurse Martin had dropped a pair of scissors. She scowled as she bent to pick them up.

Merry realized she'd sounded a bit unreasonable. "I mean, it's too soon after your surgery," she said. "You're not physically healed yet. Besides, decisions made in the aftermath of a traumatic event are often unreliable." Such as deciding to sleep with Lucas when she'd been told her father was about to die.

"We'll talk about this later," he said. "Now, I didn't hear what you said about Lucas. Is he coming?"

Merry had racked her brain all morning for an explanation for their separation that would reassure her father, one that Lucas could live with and that held enough truth for Dwight not to feel compelled to set the record straight.

So far, she'd come up with big, fat nothing.

Guess it's going to have to be the truth.

"Lucas isn't coming, Dad." She felt the sharp gaze of the nurse on her. "Could my father and I have a few minutes alone, please?" Merry asked.

The woman didn't answer, just walked out.

It wasn't any easier without her. Merry clasped her hands in her lap. "Dad, Lucas and I—"

"Excuse me," Nurse Martin barked from the doorway.

"Yes?" Merry said shortly. What was her problem?

"Your husband is coming down the hallway."

Was it Merry's imagination, or did the nurse give the word *husband* an ironic inflection? *It doesn't matter what she thinks she knows.*

Merry darted to the door to see for herself. Yes, Lucas was here. Why?

He walked in as if he owned the place. "Hi, honeybun," he said, and planted a kiss on Merry's lips.

"Uh," she said. Her lips tingled.

Lucas moved to the bed. "Hi, John. You ready to get out of here?"

"You bet." Her father shook his hand.

"Thanks for letting us stay at your place," Lucas said. "We appreciate it. Boo will enjoy having a yard to run around in, too."

Merry felt herself sputtering as he slung an arm across her shoulders. When she tried to move away, his grip tightened.

Lucas had obviously changed his mind about wanting an instant divorce. Why? *There'll be time later to find out.* For now, all she had to do was grab his capitulation with both hands.

"Lucas…sweetheart," she said. "Is Dwight still coming to get Dad, or is that why you're here?"

"I'm here to take you home, honeybun, that's all." His fingers caressed her shoulders through her sweater. "And to tell John our idea."

Uh-oh. It would be typical Lucas behavior to declare himself in charge and start issuing orders.

"John, it occurred to me you're going to need some help when you first go back to work," Lucas said.

"There's a guy who sometimes helps out when I get busy," her dad said. "Thought I might hire him."

"No need," Lucas said. "I can help out for a few weeks, until you get back up to full strength."

"You?" Merry said. But why *not* Lucas? He'd worked there before.

"I appreciate that," John said gruffly. "Very much."

"But…*I* work at the boatyard," Merry said.

"What more could I want than to work with my wife?" he said with a grim relish that told her the prospect was as painful to him as it was to her. And yet, for whatever reason, he was determined to do it.

"We'd be together *all day*." She said it with a smile, trying to sound concerned rather than alarmed. "There can be too much of a good thing."

"There wasn't for me and your mother," John said happily.

"I plan to do this properly, Merry," Lucas said. "All or nothing."

What did he mean do this properly? When he said "all," he didn't mean… Of course not. They'd already both vowed they wouldn't have sex again. She planned to stick to that resolution like a leech to a blood vessel.

Her dad was nodding, hearing this conversation as innocuous.

This is what I wanted. For Dad. For his health. She'd been ready to blackmail Lucas for his cooperation, for Pete's sake.

Now, it appeared he was offering it freely. *Take it, before he changes his mind.*

Oblivious to the undercurrents, her father jabbered about the boat Lucas would be helping him build. Lucas was watching her, waiting for an answer. All or nothing?

Merry had the sense of stepping off a precipice as she said, "All."

CHAPTER TEN

"JOHN WYATT, I HAVEN'T SEEN you in here in more years than I can count." Merline, the waitress at Pete's Burger Shack, clutched the menus to her ample chest as if she wasn't about to let them go until she'd had a darned good look at John. And his date.

"Hi, Merline." He had chosen Pete's because there was enough going on there that he and Nurse Martin wouldn't be conscious of awkward pauses. John hadn't thought about the fact that people here knew him and now would know he was dating someone. *One date, it's just one date. No one cares, except me.*

So far, it had been bearable, if not enjoyable. John wasn't allowed to drive for at least four weeks after the operation, so Nurse Martin—*Cathy, I need to call her Cathy*—had picked him up, rather than the other way around. It didn't feel right, but they'd managed to chat enough on the way here for things not to seem too strained.

"You look awful," Merline said with the bluntness he'd forgotten. "Skinny as a scarecrow. You been sick?"

"A little," he said. Then, since she was eyeing his date with blatant curiosity, he said, "Merline, this is Cathy Martin."

Merline showed them to a booth against the left wall.

It was a little quieter on that side; maybe her policy was to put older customers there.

John looked around and realized he was at least ten years older than anyone else in the room. Ten years ago was probably the last time he'd been here, and that had been with Merry.

"This place is a New London institution," he told Nurse—Cathy, who was looking around curiously. "You haven't been here before?"

"No." Spoken with her usual conversation-killing brusqueness.

John picked up his menu.

"Pete does great burgers," he said. Maybe he should have taken her somewhere fancier. The Shack was looking a little worse for wear.

Cathy, on the other hand, looked…okay. At the hospital, her hair was always pulled back tightly. Now, loose around her shoulders, it looked softer. It was a blond-brown color, which he assumed wasn't natural, since she had to be in her mid-fifties. She wore makeup, which even to John's untrained eye looked inexpert— the lipstick was all right, but her eyes had too much… something. She wore black pants and an apricot-colored sweater. She had a curvier figure than he was used to.

Thankfully, he wasn't allowed to have sex until at least six weeks after the surgery. Even more thankfully, Nurse—Cathy would know that, so the subject wouldn't even come up.

She frowned as she scanned her menu, as if she couldn't see anything that met his description of "great burger."

I'm not trying to impress her, he reminded himself.

Quite the opposite. All he wanted to do was get through this, so he could move on from his idiotic resolution—to ask out the *first* woman he saw—to someone nicer.

By the time he'd been discharged from the hospital, John had realized Nurse Cathy Martin wasn't the right woman for him to date, not even once. But much to his surprise, she'd cornered him right before he left, and asked when he planned to take her to dinner. He'd entered her number into his cell phone and promised to call her.

John didn't go back on his word.

If the date doesn't go well—he was pretty sure it wouldn't—*I'll give it an hour, then say I'm feeling dizzy and I need to go home.* She would know dizziness was a side effect of his antirejection medication, which he was taking in high doses in these early days.

"You see something you like?" he asked. "I think I'll have the bacon double cheeseburger and a Coke." Cheese and cola had been forbidden foods before the transplant, when his phosphorous levels had been too high. The surgery had sent them too far the other way, so Dr. Randall was actively encouraging him to eat more of those foods.

"I'll try the chicken burger," she said. "I might have a glass of red wine with that."

John signaled Merline and placed their orders. If they were to get out of here within the hour, they'd better get started.

"So, uh, Cathy," he said, when Merline was gone, "what do you, uh… Why don't you tell me a bit about yourself?" He should have rehearsed some conversational gambits—he sounded like a twelve-year-old. Come to think of it, most of today's twelve-year-olds had probably had more girlfriends than he had.

"I came on staff at the hospital a few months back," she said. "I was previously at the pediatric hospital in Groton."

Groton and New London sat on opposite sides of the Thames River. Though they were only a mile apart, crossing the Goldstar, the steel bridge that linked them, could feel like a major excursion. John hardly ever went to Groton. He tried to imagine her being kind and gentle, nursing sick children. Turned out his imagination wasn't up to the task.

"Do you have kids?" he asked. He'd assumed from the start she wasn't currently married, since she wasn't wearing a ring.

She shook her head. "No kids. My husband and I tried for a long time. He left me for a more fertile woman twelve years ago and now has three."

"Uh…" John said. For his next date, he'd find someone less blunt.

She shrugged, as if it was no big deal. "Do you have just the one daughter?"

John felt his face soften at the mention of Merry. "Yeah. Sally, my wife, died when Merry was three years old. We were working on having another kid, but…"

"How did your wife die?" Cathy asked.

Merline arrived with their drinks; John waited until she'd gone again. He took a sip of his Coke. Man, he'd missed this stuff.

"Car accident," he said. "She'd been visiting a girlfriend. Some jerk ran a red light…."

"I'm so sorry." Cathy did actually sound sorry, and her face had gone pink with what might have been sympathy.

"It was a long time ago," John said. He didn't want

to talk about Sally, and was casting about for another topic of conversation when Cathy said, "What kind of work do you do?"

He could tell from her stilted tone that she'd rehearsed her questions. Not very well, but at least she was more prepared than he was.

"I build boats," he said gratefully. "Handcrafted wooden sailboats." He told her more about his business, then realized he was talking too much. He shut up.

"Sounds like hard physical work," Cathy said. "You won't be able to get back to that for a while."

That pessimistic streak might wear a guy down.

"I have orders to fill," he said. "I can't just ignore them. Lucas will help out with the heavy labor. There are some things I can do—painting, electrical work, maybe some sanding. But not for another week."

"How will you fill the time until then?" she asked.

Was she angling for another date?

"I used to like to paint watercolors," he said. "Haven't had much time for that, so maybe I'll start up again." Before she could interrogate him further, he asked, "Do you like nursing?"

"I love it," she said fiercely, surprising him.

"You don't seem that happy in your work," he said before he could censor himself.

She reddened. "I guess you think I'm a real grouch." She sounded a little hurt, which was unreasonable. If she didn't want to be thought a grouch, she should be less grouchy.

"Nursing must be stressful," he said.

Merline arrived with their food. They took some time

freeing knives and forks from the tightly wrapped paper napkins and seasoning their meals.

John used the seconds spent cutting his overflowing burger in half to sneak a glance at his watch. They'd been here twenty-five minutes.

Cathy caught him clock watching. She cleared her throat. "Nursing *is* stressful, but that's not…that doesn't matter. I lost someone last year. Actually, a year ago this month. I'm finding the anniversary hard."

"I'm sorry." John picked up half his burger. Did she mean a boyfriend? A partner, as they called them these days. *My partner.* No, he didn't like it.

"It was my sister," she said. "My twin."

John's irritation with her dissolved in a wave of sympathy. "I'm sorry," he said again, only this time it was heartfelt. "Were you identical?" He wasn't sure if that made a difference, but he sensed it might.

Cathy nodded. "Rue was fuller in the face and figure than I am, just a little. When we were together, you could tell us apart because of that, but if you met one of us on our own you might not be sure."

"What happened?" John asked.

Cathy drank some of her wine. "She was on vacation in the Bahamas with a couple of girlfriends and had a massive heart attack. Neither of us had a weak heart, far as we knew. I spoke to her on the phone, in the hospital, told her I was on my way. But she had another attack and died before I got there."

Her loss was so much more recent than his own, and equally significant, John realized. "It must have been agony."

Cathy looked taken aback at his emotive choice of

word, but she didn't dispute it. "My sister was like me—a nurse, couldn't have kids, and her husband left her. We moved in together five years ago. Now I feel as if half of me is missing."

She clamped her mouth shut, pushing a bite of burger around her plate with her fork.

"I can see how you would," John said.

"For months, I couldn't function," she said. "So I decided to make some changes. New job, new—"

She stopped so abruptly, John knew she'd been about to say *new man*. Sorry though he was for her loss, he didn't want to be that man.

He applied himself to his fries while Cathy ate her burger.

"Do you think you'll be lonely now that Merry is married?" she asked. "Is that why you asked me out?"

He hardly knew how to answer such a direct question. "Merry didn't live with me, so it doesn't make much difference. We'll still work together."

"But her focus will be on her husband."

"As it should be." He decided to come clean. "Getting a transplant made me realize I hadn't been living life to the fullest for a long time, and not just because of my health. Dating seemed an obvious area for improvement."

"So you're in the same place I am," she said thoughtfully.

That sounded a little too cozy for his liking. John pushed his plate away, his burger unfinished. "Cathy, I'm feeling a bit dizzy…."

She leaned forward, her eyes intent. "That'll be your medication. Is the dizziness severe? Do you need me to take you to the hospital?"

She sounded worried; guilt pricked John.

"It's no worse than I've had the past few days," he said. "I'll be fine if I go home to rest."

Next thing, she'd demanded the check from Merline, and John had to fight to stop her paying for the meal. "I'm dizzy, not broke," he growled.

She flashed him a sudden smile. "Sorry. I know I can be obnoxious sometimes."

"You're okay," he said gruffly. In fact, she was often obnoxious, but he could hardly agree with her.

She walked close beside him, watching him, as they left the restaurant. John was working on ways to convey *I'm not in the mood,* when she said, "You look steady on your feet and your color's good."

Her scrutiny was entirely medical. So much for his conceit.

"The dizziness has pretty much gone," he said. "Guess I overreacted."

"John, you just had major surgery. There's no such thing as overreaction."

Cathy took his arm, her motive clearly only to support him. They walked the hundred yards to her car, then drove back to Dwight and Stephanie's place in silence.

"I'm feeling fine now," John said. "No need for you to get out of the car." He'd been waiting on the porch for her when she arrived, so he hadn't introduced her to his friends. He didn't want to have to do that now.

Short of saying, *Goodbye, it's been nice knowing you,* which wouldn't even be true, he felt he'd made it clear he wouldn't be seeing her again.

"I had a nice time," she said with a kind of determined

cheer that didn't ring true. Reminding him this had been some sort of test for her, too. "Can we do it again?"

Unlike him, she didn't consider the test over.

John paused, one hand on the door handle. There was no chemistry between them, none of the magic he'd experienced on his first date with Sally, when he'd known instantly that she was The One. "Uh…"

"I'm working the afternoon shift the next three days," she said doggedly, "not finishing until ten. But I have a day off on Sunday. How about I choose something for us to do?"

Her face was calm, expressionless. But her eyes… dammit, her eyes looked soft and vulnerable. She'd told him she'd lost half of herself, and he'd bet she didn't tell a lot of people that. He knew how that felt, knew the pain.

"Sure," he said without any encouragement.

She nodded once, as if to say, *good enough*.

John got of the car. He held on to the door handle for a moment to steady himself. Because now he really did feel dizzy.

LUCAS HAD INVADED MERRY'S LIFE. Unlike when they were kids, she couldn't walk away and play with her girlfriends or her Barbie dolls, or anyone else equally unlikely to irritate.

She still didn't know why he'd changed his mind about keeping up the pretense of their marriage—he'd refused to answer her questions on the subject—and why he'd volunteered to work at the boatyard. She appreciated his commitment, whatever the reason.

But by the time she and Lucas—and Boo—had been in her dad's seafront cottage for ten days, she was ready to scream. And this was before they even started working together.

Merry had assumed their mutual inclination for avoidance would mean they'd barely see each other.

But no. Lucas, who should surely be practicing his depth perception, or working out at the gym to get fit for duty, or something—anything!—else, had thrown himself into his Temporary Husband role.

I should have guessed, Merry told herself, as she switched on her computer the Monday morning that her dad was due to start back at the workshop. Even as a kid, Lucas had meticulously mapped out his campaigns with success in mind. Which was why it had been so easy, and fun, to frustrate him by ignoring his plans and doing her own thing.

Her opportunities to do that now were limited. Because everything Lucas was doing made sense, and was for unarguably good reasons.

So while it drove her nuts that he'd put a chart on the fridge to record her dad's blood pressure when he reported in over the course of each day—information she usually kept in her head, and which was none of Lucas's business—she couldn't argue that if something went wrong, the doctors would be pleased to have that data written down.

And how could she refuse to have Lucas accompany her on visits to her father, when their entire marriage was for his benefit? When her dad was staying with Lucas's parents? They visited John every day, with Lucas acting like the ideal husband. No one but Merry seemed to notice the perfunctory nature of his caresses and endearments.

And that was another thing. Those caresses were having an unmistakable and unwelcome effect on her, perfunctory or not. But it was obvious only one person in this marriage was suffering from fluttery insides and hypersensitive skin, while the other was attacking the mission of Being Merry's Husband with military precision, and was thus unmoved by such pesky details as kisses.

Admittedly, she'd caught him eyeing her butt once or twice. Her chest, too. But on the whole, he showed a conspicuous lack of interest.

He was driving her nuts.

And now she had to work with him all day.

Over the past week, he'd been talking to John about how they might change things around at work to make them more manageable, and to share the load. Which was a great idea. Except Merry had assumed things could run pretty much as before, tweaked where necessary. She'd thought of today as the first day of life being back to normal.

It didn't seem that much to ask.

Instead, nothing felt right, and most of that was Lucas's fault.

He'd picked up her dad from Dwight's place at nine-thirty—Dad would put in short days for a few weeks—and brought him to the workshop. John was in good spirits, which improved Merry's mood. The boat he'd been working on when he collapsed—a twenty-eight footer commissioned by a merchant banker in Manhattan, who planned to keep it in the Hamptons—was awaiting finishing. It was a good project to start back with.

Lucas came into her office once or twice, issuing orders that she ignored. Instead, she caught up on the mail and supplier payments.

At ten-fifteen, she got up to put the kettle on for coffee. Her dad always had his morning cup at ten-thirty.

As she returned to her desk, she glanced out into the workshop. Dad wasn't in sight, but she could see Lucas's head over the top of the boat. As she watched, he came around to the near side.

He wasn't wearing a shirt.

Merry swallowed. Whatever might be wrong with Lucas's eyesight, his general fitness seemed excellent. Last time she'd seen his bare torso—their wedding night—they'd been in semidarkness. Now, with the sun's rays streaming through the high windows, he was captured in glorious daylight. Broad shoulders, arms and chest nicely muscled, flat stomach...

Merry wrenched her eyes away. Her thoughts took a few moments to follow.

Yet again Lucas was invading her life. And this time it was totally unnecessary.

He should be wearing a shirt.

Everyone knew boatbuilding was hot work, even at this time of year. But her dad managed to wear a T-shirt year-round.

Surely Lucas's state of undress was a safety and health issue. Wasn't there a manual around here somewhere?

She leaned to her left—causing Boo, who liked to lie beneath her feet, to twitch—and pulled open the bottom drawer of her desk.

She leafed through the hanging files. *Safety and health, safety and health...* Ah, there it was: *Keeping Your Marine Industry Business Safe and Healthy.* She pulled out the manual, still shrink-wrapped. Obviously long overdue a read. She sliced through the plastic with a thumbnail.

Out in the workshop, Lucas had stopped to take a call on his cell phone. Whoever the caller was made him smile. He was extremely good-looking when he smiled. Merry thwacked the manual open on her desk. The table of contents wasn't very detailed, so she turned to the index, looking under *C* for *Chest, bare*. Nothing. Come *on,* it had to be a hazard.

"Stephanie just called." Lucas's voice jerked her out of her reading. He stood in the doorway—still shirtless, damn him—one arm propped on the doorjamb. He could have posed for a sexy boatbuilders' calendar. If there was such a thing.

Boo scrambled out from beneath Merry's feet and trotted toward him. That was another thing Lucas had taken over. He'd suggested more exercise might help Boo's constipation, and had offered to take the dog on some of his runs. That was Lucas all over—if there was a problem, he would try to fix it. But in this case his logic made sense, so she'd agreed. But not only hadn't it worked, Boo was now slavishly devoted to Lucas.

"Stephanie and Dad invited us sailing on Friday—Dad has a day off," Lucas said. "They've already invited John, and Garrett and Rachel are coming up."

His brother, Garrett, two and a half years older than Lucas, had been outside Merry's sphere of interest when she was younger, and had left home at the earliest opportunity. He'd never gotten along with Dwight, unlike the uneasy truce Lucas had with his father. But he was excellent company when he made the effort, which he'd done increasingly often since he'd married Rachel. He'd met her at the Manhattan advertising agency where they'd both worked—though there was more to that than met the eye, apparently—and they'd married last December. Both Garrett and Rachel doted on Mia.

"Dad will love it." Merry kept her eyes on Lucas's face, away from that bare chest. "But I don't think we should go. Or at least, I shouldn't. It's just two more people to try to fool, and more explaining to do later."

"If your dad's going, we should keep an eye on him," Lucas said.

"Why are you taking such good care of him?" Merry asked, not for the first time.

"It's what we agreed," he said. Which wasn't entirely true, but she could hardly complain. "Having Garrett and Rachel there will take the focus off us," he added.

"I'll think about it." She looked back down at her manual. *Ah, found it. Clothing, protective.* Page 108. Behind her, the kettle whistled. Merry took the manual with her as she headed to the stove. "Can you tell Dad coffee's ready?"

When Lucas came back, he had a T-shirt slung over one shoulder. *Close, but no cigar.*

Her dad went to set up his blood pressure kit. He would measure his BP before he drank his coffee, which could skew the results.

"You need to put your shirt on," Merry told Lucas as she handed him a cup.

"Excuse me?"

She held up the safety manual and read aloud from page 108. "'Protective clothing must be worn when whenever conditions warrant.'"

"You think I'm going to spill hot coffee?" Lucas asked.

She snapped the book shut. "You need to wear a T-shirt at work. All the time."

She realized she was eyeballing his chest, and jerked her gaze upward.

Their eyes met in a long, charged moment. Merry was suddenly short of air. Gratifyingly, Lucas didn't seem all that comfortable, either.

Then he smiled slowly, speculatively. "Why, honeybun, am I causing you some anxiety?"

She glowered. "I don't want to get prosecuted for lax safety standards."

He handed his cup back to her and put on his T-shirt, which involved much stretching and flexing of muscles. Merry looked away, at her dad. He was yawning as he released the blood pressure cuff.

"You sleeping okay, Dad?"

"Sleep's not a problem, but I might have overdone it a bit yesterday," he admitted. "I went bowling."

"Dad, you might bust your wound open," Merry said.

"You should be careful," Lucas agreed.

A sidelong glance revealed he was now covered up.

"Relax," John said. "I only used a ten-pound ball. The doctor said I could lift up to fifteen pounds at this stage. Besides—" he cleared his throat "—my date was a nurse, so I had medical expertise right beside me."

Lucas went on the alert. "You're dating?"

He probably thought that was something else he needed to get involved in.

"Who is she?" Merry tried to sound interested, rather than disapproving. "Did you meet her at the hospital?"

"Yes, and so did you," her father said. "It's Nurse Martin. Cathy."

Merry's jaw dropped. "The *mean* one?"

"She's not so mean when you get to know her," John said. "She's had a tough time, that's all."

"Dad, she's horrible." Merry caught a warning look from Lucas. It was none of his business. Still, she spoke more moderately. "So, do you plan to see the nurse again?"

"Actually, bowling was our second date," John said. "We're going fishing next week."

Fishing! Fishing was special. Her father didn't do that with just anyone. "Dad, what about Mom?"

"I'm just dating this woman," John said, "and probably not for long. I'm not in love with her, and I'm not about to marry her. But if I want to live life to the full, I can't ignore my need for companionship."

Lucas's eyes met Merry's, clearly communicating that he didn't want to hear any more about her father's *needs*. That made two of them.

Merry didn't want to stop her dad having a fulfilling life—he'd been on his own for a long time. But he was the one who'd always declared he was a one-woman man. Period. That you didn't find a soul mate twice, and to settle for less would be a constant reminder of what he'd lost. Of how good love could be. Her dad might say his dating wasn't serious, but he wasn't the playboy type—before long, he'd reach a point where he either had to end it or take the next step. Merry didn't want him rushing into a relationship—with Nurse Martin, of all people—out of loneliness.

And if her dad did actually fall in love with someone,

would that make everything he'd said about soul mates and the existence of "one true love" a lie? Or at least wrong? Merry had been raised on her father's stories about that instant connection, that perfect unity between two people who'd never doubted they were destined for each other. Never even argued, if you believed her father. Not about anything serious.

"But while we're talking about marriage," John added, "Cathy said last night that she wondered if everything's okay with you two."

"She doesn't even know us," Merry said, outraged.

Lucas stepped closer and put an arm around her shoulders. His answer to every intimacy challenge, it seemed. "We're great, aren't we, honeybun?"

"Wonderful," she said firmly. "I couldn't be happier." Maybe she should have unclenched her teeth before she spoke.

Her dad didn't look reassured.

"John, how about you invite your, uh, nurse to have dinner with us so she can see for herself," Lucas said. "Does Thursday work for us, honeybun?"

No!

"You don't think that sounds too serious?" John said.

"Hmm, it might," Merry said.

"Strictly casual," Lucas assured him. "It'll be fun."

That was Lucas's idea of fun? Entertaining the nastiest nurse in town, possibly having to watch the woman flirt with Merry's father? It just went to show, Merry thought, she and Lucas were about as far from soul mates as two people could be.

CHAPTER ELEVEN

"I GO ON VACATION FOR TWO weeks—*two weeks*—and your dad almost dies, but gets a kidney transplant in the nick of time. Then Patrick dumps you, and you get *married*. To Lucas Calder, the guy *I* had a crush on in school and you couldn't stand? You have terrible sex with him, and now you're getting divorced?" Sarah Ford, Merry's best friend, bit into a slice of pepperoni pizza and chewed disgustedly. "Couldn't you have done some of this while I was here to live vicariously through you?"

"Sorry," Merry said, feeling better already for having shared her woes. She leaned back on her dad's couch. "Just to clarify, the divorce is a little way off. And I *could* stand Lucas in high school." Where did everyone get the idea she didn't like him?

"Meanwhile, the most exciting thing to happen to me was sunburn in an embarrassing anatomical location." Sarah grabbed a paper napkin from the stack on the coffee table in front of them and wiped a blob of tomato sauce from her chin.

"Much as I hate to trump your sunburn," Merry said, "Dad also got a girlfriend."

Sarah threw herself back against the sofa cushions theatrically, slopping her chardonnay over the edge of her glass. "Now I know you're making this up."

"It's true," Merry said glumly. "And she's awful.

Lucas invited her for dinner." She picked a slice of pepperoni off the last piece of pizza, which was still sitting
in the carton, both of them refusing to eat it out of polite-
ness. Merry popped the pepperoni in her mouth. "He's
driving me crazy. It's like he has a checklist in his head
that he's working through. All the things he needs to fix
before he leaves."

"And this is a problem why?" Sarah asked.

Merry huffed out a breath. "This isn't going to sound
reasonable."

"Try me."

"I don't like being on a checklist."

"You're right. Unreasonable."

"No, it's not," Merry countered. "Lucas and I have
been friends forever. In some ways we're like family.
But I don't get the impression he's done one single thing
the past few weeks because he cares. He does them because he can."

Sarah sipped her wine. "I'm not sure if the distinction
is worth worrying about if problems get solved."

"Sometimes he's more like a robot than a man," Merry
grumbled.

Her friend stared, then hooted with laughter. "You're
miffed because Lucas is getting you all hot and bothered, aren't you?"

"No," Merry said. "Yes."

Sarah snickered. "So, you're lusting after Lucas, while
he's being robotically practical."

"Most of the time." Because there had definitely been
looks.

Merry got up to choose a DVD. Sarah loved *Lassie*
almost as much as she did, and one of the movies usu-

ally formed a backdrop to their girls' nights in. She and Sarah were living proof that watching a G-rated movie in no way inhibited consumption of alcohol or salacious gossip. "Which version do you want? The 1994 or 2005?" One was set in the U.S.A. and the other in England.

Sarah thought for a moment. "Ninety-four. The dad's cuter."

"I can't agree, as you know." Merry preferred the 2005 movie on several levels, but she inserted Sarah's choice into the player.

A minute later, the opening credits were rolling. The sound was set on low; they would turn it up during the good bits.

"It's not like I even want anything with Lucas." Merry picked off another slice of pepperoni.

"Agreed," Sarah said. "Twice now you guys have failed to launch." She was the only person Merry had told about Baltimore.

"My brain is well aware that Lucas and I are incompatible on every level. Maybe I just don't like that the attraction is one-sided."

"He *is* hot," Sarah admitted. "I can't blame your hormones for getting confused. I always thought he'd be an amazing lover."

"Possibly our wedding night wasn't a fair test," Merry conceded, unsure what she thought about Sarah admitting to having considered Lucas's skills in bed. She sipped her wine.

Sarah shook her head. "If you're good, you're good. No matter what. Clearly, Lucas doesn't have what it takes."

Merry blinked. "You think?"

"Trust me," Sarah said, "he's bad in bed." She sighed. "What a waste of a hot guy. But, hey, I just gave you an excellent reason to stop feeling attracted to him."

"Just like that," Merry said doubtfully.

"Remind yourself he's bad in bed every time you look at him," Sarah advised. "After all, that's probably what he's thinking about you."

"Ouch!" Merry reached for yet another piece of pepperoni. "Following your logic, he's right."

"It works differently for women." Sarah started to laugh.

"Do you believe anything you just said?" Merry asked indignantly.

"I don't know," she said, still laughing. "But I think it would help *you* to believe it. Also, you should flirt with another guy to boost your ego."

"You should never get a job as an advice columnist," Merry told her.

Sarah shrugged one shoulder. "Okay, I won't. You'll just have to find some other way to stop thinking naughty thoughts about your hubby. Where is he tonight, by the way?"

"No idea. Probably doing eye exercises with Heather Gunn."

"The hot cheerleader-turned-optometrist?"

Merry nodded, aware of a surge of irritation. "Ooh, look, it's the part about the wolf." She pointed the remote control at the TV and raised the volume.

They concentrated on the movie for the next little while. This was the same version Merry had watched on her first date with Lucas. He'd pointed out that in real life, the wolf would definitely have killed Lassie.

Further on, he'd insisted there was no way Lassie could have rescued Matt from that waterfall, and so on. Over the years, they'd somehow got embroiled in several arguments about Lassie's capabilities.

Lucas came in with about twenty minutes of the movie left, Boo at his heels. He groaned when he saw what was playing, and left the room. But only, it turned out, to fetch a beer.

Merry tried looking at him through the eyes of someone who didn't have firsthand knowledge of all his imperfections. Someone like Sarah. Yep, definitely a waste of a hot guy.

"What kind of pizza is that?" he asked.

"Pepperoni," Merry said. "Help yourself."

Lucas picked up the last slice. "There's no pepperoni on it."

"I'll be sure to complain," she said.

He sat on the couch next to Merry, forcing her to move along or else be wedged up against him. She moved.

Boo slunk beneath the coffee table, lying with his nose on Lucas's feet.

"Keep quiet," Merry warned Lucas. "Lassie's about to save the day."

He yawned. Which, she supposed, was quiet.

Ten minutes later, the movie ended.

"That was great." Merry wiped her eyes.

"Lassie does it again," Sarah agreed.

Lucas snorted.

"She's a hero," Merry told him.

"She's not a hero. She's not even a she," he said. "All the dogs that have played Lassie have been male."

Merry gaped. "How do you know?"

"Internet."

"*Why* do you know?"

Lucas frowned. "I must have looked it up at some stage. Probably when you were waxing lyrical about what a hero Lassie is."

"Fascinating," Sarah said, bright-eyed. "Merry, hon, I think you might be wrong with your robot theory."

"What robot theory?" Lucas asked.

"Merry, can I use your cell?" Sarah said quickly. "I want to check that calorie-counting app of yours—see how much damage I did tonight."

Merry handed over her phone. "How's your depth-perception practice going?" she asked Lucas.

"Great," he said. "Tonight I could see three circles when I was supposed to."

She had no idea what that meant, but was vaguely relieved he'd been doing eye tests, as she'd guessed, rather than…something else.

I need to stop thinking about him. Period.

Merry's cell phone rang, and Sarah passed it to her.

"It's Patrick," Merry said in surprise.

Lucas straightened as she said hello.

"Merry, I got your text," Patrick said.

"My— Oh." She glared at Sarah. Who'd obviously decided to implement her own advice and find someone for Merry to flirt with. Merry hoped the text hadn't been too risqué.

"It's wonderful to hear from you," he was saying. "I've missed you so much."

Which admittedly was nice to hear. "Thanks," she murmured, aware of Lucas watching her from about three inches away. He might even be able to hear Patrick. She switched the phone to her other ear.

"I knew you were special, but I didn't realize how incredible you were until you were gone," Patrick continued dramatically.

Until you dumped me, she amended silently.

"Does he know you're married?" Lucas sounded annoyed.

She waved a hand to shush him. Because Sarah was right, there was no harm in getting an ego boost from an ex. But since Lucas looked as if he might grab the phone and enlighten Patrick himself, she said, "Patrick, that's so sweet, but I'm with some people at the moment. There are a few things you need to know—can I call you tomorrow?"

By the time she got him off the phone, Sarah had dashed out the door, trilling a goodbye over her shoulder.

"Why was he calling?" Lucas asked.

"Why did you invite Nurse Ratched for dinner?" Merry countered. She hadn't talked to him since then.

He laughed, and this close, she could see little lines crinkling around his eyes. "Why not? Dating a nurse makes a lot of sense for your dad."

"You think he should date her because he might need medical assistance?"

"Why not?"

"Which means I should date Patrick, a vet, because I own a dog."

"Not the same thing at all," Lucas said instantly.

She paused to let him elaborate.

Instead, he stared her down.

"What happened to dating someone on the basis of

attraction?" she said. "What happened to exploring the depths of human emotions? To love?"

He broke eye contact to take a swig of his beer. "Assuming that your father likes the nurse, which isn't a bad starting point, why not take practical considerations into account?"

"Because Dad will never be happy with less than what he had with Mom," Merry said.

"How do you know?"

The question flummoxed her for a moment. "Dad was blissfully happy with Mom. He says himself he won't find that again."

"Sometimes less is more," Lucas said. "The nurse is presumably keen, and she hasn't met her own *soul mate.*" He used the term mockingly. "She has medical skills. Most importantly, she's here."

"That's the worst rationale I ever heard," Merry said.

"Not everyone wants to 'explore the depths of human emotion,'" he returned. "Why should everyone have to do it the way you want? If, this time around, your dad's happy to find someone he likes, what's it to you?"

There didn't seem any point answering that. "I still don't want her here for dinner," Merry said.

"But you *need* her. You heard your dad—Cathy thinks our marriage is having problems. So if your theory about your marital happiness being key to lowering his blood pressure is right…"

Merry pressed her hand to her mouth. "I didn't think of that."

"It makes sense for us to invite them to dinner." Lucas's gaze alighted on her fingers. "To convince Cathy there's nothing wrong. Unless you think your father's condition is stable enough for us to tell the truth…"

She shook her head. "Not yet. His blood pressure's still volatile." She twisted around, which put her face very close to Lucas's. "Inviting Cathy was a good idea. I'm sorry for all the rude things I said to Sarah about you."

Lucas laughed. "While you're feeling contrite, which by the way I don't think I've seen in twenty-three years, it's about time you apologized for Date Number Three."

Lucas couldn't believe he'd brought that up. But in the past few days, each of their nine previous dates had crossed his mind. They'd all been disastrous—even Number Eight, with that incredibly hot kiss, which had led directly to the fiasco in Baltimore six months ago. But each had been disastrous in its own unique way. All of them had had that undercurrent of physical attraction that they could never quite pull together, which threatened to ruin a decent friendship. It made for a memorable dating history.

"No way," Merry said. "Dad would have had a heart attack if I'd gone bungee jumping with anyone else."

"I forgive you, anyway," Lucas said. "Specifically, for pretending your retina was detached." When she'd stumbled toward him after the jump, her hand covering her eye, Lucas had just about had a heart attack. He'd scooped her into his arms, ready to commandeer a chopper from the local airfield and fly her to the top eye specialist in New York City…. Then she'd dropped her hand and laughed, both perfectly healthy gray eyes brimming with amusement.

"If anyone needs to apologize," she said, "it's you.

Date Number Five. That restaurant on the beach in Mystic."

"You're the one who walked out halfway through dinner."

"Because you were ogling the redhead with the boobs at the next table," she agreed.

"I wasn't ogling her. She was arguing with her boyfriend, and the guy seemed like a jerk. I wasn't sure what he might do."

"I'm certain your interest was strictly protective."

"I didn't even notice her figure," he said virtuously.

Merry laughed, rightly disbelieving him.

"Okay, I behaved badly," he agreed, "but you punished me for it. I drove around for hours looking for you. Only to discover you'd *hitchhiked* home." He'd shouted at her over that. She'd stuffed in her iPod earbuds and ignored him.

"Just to clarify," she said, "did you apologize for your behavior on that date or not?"

She slipped her fingers into the back pockets of her jeans, which pushed her breasts forward. Lucas couldn't figure out why he always noticed her breasts when there was so little to see.

"No, I did not. Honeybun," he added. There was a subtle shift in the atmosphere. Did she notice it?

A part of him wanted to go with the shift, see where it led. But he knew where it led, as far as Merry was concerned. To complications neither of them needed. Without even the promise of great sex to make it worth the risk.

He downed the last of his beer, then stood and scooped

up the empty pizza box. "Guess I'll head upstairs. I have some Magic Eye books to work on."

He was putting a lot of time into making sure Merry's dad's blood pressure had every chance to settle down, which was fine, because that's what he'd decided to do. But he also needed to focus on getting back to the Gulf. He'd called Admiral Tremaine last week to apologize for the abrupt end to their meeting. The man hadn't agreed outright to push for a retest, but he'd asked Lucas to keep him informed of his progress with his eyesight, and hinted he might step in if it looked as if Lucas could achieve a pass. Lucas needed something more to report than the tiny, incremental gains he'd made with Heather.

He needed to stop thinking about Merry and her tantalizing curves and her tight butt. He needed to start thinking about what mattered.

MERRY COULDN'T CALL PATRICK from work the next day because she never knew when her dad or Lucas might walk into the office. The conversation was going to be difficult enough in private.

She did it the moment she arrived home, even though she should really be getting dinner ready for her father and Cathy. Merry had to tell Patrick she was married to Lucas. That the proposal he'd turned down had evolved from a temporary engagement to a temporary marriage, to a slightly longer marriage.

She expected him to be relieved he hadn't been sucked into all that. Instead, he blamed himself for abandoning her in her hour of need, and invited her out to dinner. "As friends," he added, when she pointed out that dating him while she was married might be a complication too far.

She turned him down, but by the time the call ended, she had less than an hour to prepare for their dinner guests.

Right away, she discovered she'd forgotten to buy pecorino cheese for the onion and pecorino tarts that she planned to serve with the beef fillet.

She called Lucas, and was lucky to catch him just as he was leaving the boatyard. She asked him to buy pecorino at Clark's Deli on the way home. It would delay his arrival, which was unfortunate, but only by ten minutes, tops.

Wrong.

Lucas arrived home twenty-five minutes late, only a minute before their guests were due.

"What's the problem?" he asked, as she snatched the pecorino from his hand.

"I'm running out of time, and I need this meal to be perfect." It was her mom's recipe; she wasn't about to ruin it in front of a woman who likely wanted to be the second Mrs. John Wyatt. Merry took a calming breath and said, "Thanks for the cheese. Was Clark's busy?"

"I didn't go to Clark's. It took me a while to find somewhere else that sold pecorino."

"If you'd just gone to Clark's..." she grumbled, as she started grating.

She registered Lucas's shuttered expression. And remembered. "Lucas, I'm sorry."

"It's fine," he said coolly.

"I didn't think." Clark's Deli was where his mom had suffered a sudden stroke and died when he was twelve years old.

"What needs doing around here?" He pushed up his sleeves.

Okay. Merry got the message. He didn't want to talk about it.

"You could trim those beans." She pulled a knife from the block and handed it to him, then took another to slice the onions. "I need to brief you about tonight."

His face lightened. "There's a briefing?"

"I thought you'd like that," she said. "I thought it sounded military."

"Depends on the briefing," he said.

She rolled her eyes. "Okay, if Nurse Cathy—"

"We probably shouldn't call her Nurse Cathy."

"—mentions she saw the text message about our divorce, we tell her it's a private joke. That we threaten to divorce each other, jokingly, whenever we disagree."

"This marriage sounds really unhealthy," Lucas said.

She lobbed an onion at him; he caught it and handed it back.

"As you said last night, *Nurse* Cathy needs to see us as a loving couple," she said. This conundrum had been on her mind all day. Having told Sarah she needed to stifle her physical attraction to Lucas, she'd signed on for extra challenges tonight.

"Loving couple," he said. "Check." Something— tension?—crackled in the air between them.

"But you and I will know that any PDAs between us mean nothing," she reminded him too emphatically.

"You mean public displays of affection, right? They mean nothing—check."

The doorbell rang. Boo started barking, which wasn't like him. The tension must be getting to everyone.

"I'll put him outside," Lucas said. "You get the door."

Her dad kissed her cheek as he entered. "Merry, you remember Cathy."

The nurse looked better out of her uniform, Merry conceded. Softer. But only a little.

"It's nice to meet you properly," Merry lied as she led the way to the living room. "Lucas, darling, could you get Dad and Cathy something to drink?"

Unfazed at the endearment, Lucas handed Cathy the white wine she asked for.

The nurse stared around John's living room. Merry tried to see it through fresh eyes, and realized just how quirky this place she took for granted was. She couldn't imagine Cathy liking quirky. Lucas was right; this dinner was a great idea.

"As you can see," Merry said, "Dad likes to collect stuff." This room spoke of John Wyatt's passion for the sea. A display of vintage oars on one wall, a lifebuoy above the fireplace and several ships in bottles on the mantel…

"It must be a nightmare to dust," Cathy said. If she was joking, it wasn't obvious.

John shifted on his feet. "I don't worry too much about that. A lot of these things I collected with Sally."

Cathy moved to the fireplace to inspect the ships in bottles.

"My mom gave those to Dad," Merry said. "One for each wedding anniversary." There were eight bottles on the mantelpiece. "They're his greatest treasures, aren't they, Dad?"

"Sure are," he said.

See, Cathy, my mom was Dad's greatest treasure.

Outside, Boo's barking had turned to howling.

"What's wrong with your dog?" Lucas asked.

"He sometimes howls when he has nightmares," Merry said, "but not usually at this time of night. Can you give him a couple of liver treats? Darling?"

Her father had moved to join Cathy, pointing out some of the ships' features to her in a low voice.

Merry ducked out to the kitchen to put her tarts in the oven. When she came back to the living room, Cathy was scrutinizing a watercolor on the wall. "It's the view from this window," she said, clearly surprised.

"Dad painted it," Merry said proudly.

"It's wonderful," Cathy said. "John, you're so talented."

Her eyes met Merry's and for a fraction of a second there was warmth between them.

"What do you like to do in your spare time?" Merry asked. "Are you artistic?" *Do you and my father have anything at all in common?*

"I don't have a creative bone in my body." Cathy darted a small, apologetic smile at John. "I like to garden, and I enjoy doing crosswords."

Nothing in common. Merry tried not to give her dad a significant look. "Dad met my mom when they were crewing in a yacht race," she said. "It was love at first sight."

Lucas came up behind her and wrapped his arms around her waist. She jolted. Whatever she'd been about to say, she lost her train of thought.

They sat down to eat in the formal dining room, a space used maybe once a year. Merry and Lucas sat on one side of the table, her dad and Cathy opposite. As far as Merry could see, there was no chemistry between the older couple. How could her father even contemplate such a relationship?

"How long did you two date before you married?" Cathy asked. Of course, she'd attended their wedding.

"Nine years, on and off," Lucas said.

Cathy smiled slightly. "Not love at first sight, then."

"Lucas wanted to marry me when he was ten years old," Merry said. "That's near enough."

Lucas slid his hand beneath her hair. His fingers found the sensitive nape of her neck. "This meal is delicious, honeybun," he said.

"It's one of Mom's recipes," Merry told Cathy.

"Honeybun, we need more wine," Lucas said. "Come help me choose one that matches the food. Excuse us, John, Cathy."

Out in the kitchen, he closed the door before he spoke. "What's going on out there, Merry?"

"We're acting happily married. You're doing a great job, thanks."

"That's not what I mean and you know it."

She pulled a corkscrew from a drawer. "The wine's in the laundry room. A sauvignon blanc would work for me, but the others might prefer red."

Lucas took the corkscrew. "You're showing Cathy up," he said. "Right now you look meaner than she does."

Merry couldn't stifle a gasp. "I just want Dad to see that she's not...Mom."

Lucas lifted a hand, as if he might caress her face, then dropped it again. "You think he doesn't know that? If you're not careful, you'll upset him."

"He doesn't even seem to like her that much."

"All the more reason for you to go easy." Lucas stepped into the laundry room and reappeared with a bottle of sauvignon. "And if John does like her, you don't want him stressing about how his daughter and his girlfriend are getting along."

"You're right," she muttered. "I just wish Dad would aim a bit higher."

"In the real world," Lucas said, as he deftly removed the cork from the bottle, "love is about compromise and practicality and hard work. Not an overflow of emotion that defies logic."

"You don't get to lecture me about logic over emotion," she said. "When was the last time you shopped at Clark's Deli?"

He stiffened.

"It occurred to me," she continued, "Date Number Seven—your ex-girlfriend's wedding. I needed to buy a stain remover pen to clean up that soda I spilled on my dress. You drove past Clark's, past the church, to a store three miles away. We were late for the ceremony."

"I wasn't worried about being late," he said. "So why should it bother you?"

"Have you been into Clark's since your mom died?"

Lucas glared.

Merry waited.

He leaned in and kissed her long and hard on the lips. When she tried to pull back, he clamped his hands on either side of her head. His fingers moved in her hair, mussing it.

"What was that for?" Merry gasped when he stopped.

"We've been out here awhile," he said calmly. "Best

for your dad and Cathy to think it's because we can't keep our hands off each other." He picked up the wine and strode to the dining room without a backward glance.

CHAPTER TWELVE

FRIDAY, THE DAY OF THE PLANNED sailing excursion, dawned sunny and with the kind of moderate breeze that made for pleasant yachting.

Lucas had hoped for a storm. Hoped for an excuse not to spend time with Merry, or a whole day in the presence of their parents, which would necessitate another demonstration of marital love. At least Cathy was working today, so they didn't have to prove anything more to her.

So far, on this marriage mission, he'd been doing just fine on the PDAs, as Merry called them. He'd managed the touches, the kisses, by thinking of them as part of the drill, nothing to do with his libido. Sure, once or twice his gaze had strayed in a way that was definitely libidinous—usually when Merry's was doing the same— but by and large he'd done pretty well.

Until last night. When she'd put the pieces together and realized the truth about Clark's Deli…realized what no one else in his family had. Lucas had panicked. Kissed her to…distract her or shut her up maybe. Whatever it was, he'd forgotten to do it out of his mission-focused side, and somehow another part of him had got involved. A deeper part.

A part she wasn't supposed to see. No one was.

It had rattled him sufficiently that he found himself

talking to the dog as they jogged along the promenade shortly before 7:00 a.m.

"I made a mistake," he told Boo. "But that's okay, I can fix it. Number one, we don't talk about Clark's. Not ever."

Boo's tongue lolled.

"We pull back on the PDAs," he said. "For today at least. Just so there's no confusion."

Boo was slowing down, which usually meant an imminent toilet attempt. Lucas slowed to a walk while Boo investigated various patches of grass.

"I'll keep things impersonal," he said as Boo squatted. Last night, after John and Cathy left, Merry had offered to talk to Dwight today about recommending Lucas's retest. He'd told her to forget it. He was pretty sure Admiral Tremaine would come up with the goods, and he didn't want to be beholden to Merry. He was also pretty sure she'd offered then only because she'd been thinking about the whole Clark's thing, and he didn't want her mulling over that. His personal stuff was beyond the scope of this mission.

Boo straightened up, having left a marble-size deposit for Lucas to pick up. "Useless," he muttered.

When they arrived back at the cottage, he gave the dog some water. "You're out of dog food," he said to Merry as he walked into the kitchen. Which was as impersonal a greeting as anyone could want.

"We can stop at the grocery store on our way home," she said.

Fine by him, so long as she didn't make any smart-ass suggestions as to which store that should be.

He registered that she looked fresh and pretty with

her hair pulled back in a ponytail and a slick of gloss on her lips. Her chunky, cable-knit cream sweater seemed cozy, touchable.

"I'll go shower," Lucas said.

THEY ARRIVED AT THE MARINA around ten, pulling up at the same time as Stephanie and Mia.

Dwight's boat, the *Aegis,* was moored near the end of the first pier. It was one of the biggest boats John Wyatt had built: forty-six feet of high-performance cruising yacht.

The casual observer would see a single hull, painted white and topped with a deck of strip planking cedar and a wooden cabin. Lucas, from his vacation work with John and his degree in marine engineering, knew that the hull was made with two cold-molded diagonal layers of mahogany treated with epoxy resins, that the cedar planking was finished with fiberglass and epoxy, and the internal structure was comprised of bulkheads and longitudinal girders. Despite the classic look of the outside and the almost cozy warmth of the teak cockpit, the yacht's underwater hull profile was modern as could be. It was that structural beauty that impressed Lucas the most.

Dwight and John had come on ahead to get the boat ready, which meant the rest of them had only to step on board.

Which they would do as soon as Garrett and Rachel arrived.

Garrett wasn't known for his punctuality, but Rachel must be good for him—they roared up in his black BMW M5 just ten minutes late. Not bad, considering they'd driven from Manhattan.

"Congratulations, both of you." Garrett clapped Lucas on the back, then kissed Merry's cheek. "Couldn't have happened to a nicer pair. Even if I didn't realize you were the marrying kind, Lucas." He grinned at Merry with the teasing of long acquaintance.

"About as much as you were," Lucas said. He still wasn't the marrying kind, but when his brother had fallen for Rachel, Garrett had lost the bundle of hang-ups he'd been carrying around. Putting a ring on Rachel's finger had become his all-consuming goal.

As Lucas understood it, she'd needed a bit of convincing that his brother was for real. But there was no sign of those doubts now. Garrett couldn't keep his eyes off her as she hugged Merry, and when she stepped back, she clasped his hand tightly.

"Good luck," she told Merry. "Given that Lucas is a Calder male, you'll need it."

"I'm way less of a jerk than Garrett," he said.

Merry didn't look convinced. But Rachel said, "That wouldn't be hard."

"Dammit, woman, I'm going to have to shut you up again." Garrett planted a firm kiss on her mouth, his hand sneaking around to caress her butt. Which, from where Lucas stood, wasn't half as cute as Merry's. He groaned inwardly. That unplanned kiss last night had left him fantasizing about her mouth, about that full lower lip. He already thought about her breasts way too much. He didn't need to add Merry's butt to the list.

Dwight cleared his throat. "You two, there are young eyes on you." He nodded toward Mia, who was clinging to his trouser leg.

Since Dwight took every opportunity to discreetly

grope Stephanie, regardless of their daughter's presence, Lucas didn't think his father had much of a case. Garrett obviously agreed, going by his grin. Lucas hadn't seen his brother this relaxed before, not in their dad's presence. But it seemed that what Stephanie had reported was true: Garrett and Dwight had bridged some of their differences when Mia was born, and now they were... not friends, but there was mutual respect and goodwill. And the promise of something warmer in the future.

John cast off, and Dwight motored out of the marina. As soon as they were clear of the bay, they rigged the mainsail. The light wind dictated that the other sail should be the genoa, rather than the jib.

While Garrett showed Rachel around the boat, taking a suspiciously long time in the bow stateroom, Lucas chatted with his father and John in the cockpit.

Stephanie called them to lunch at noon. Merry's dad insisted on manning the cockpit while the rest of them ate, but accepted Dwight's offer to swap halfway through.

They ate in the main cabin, some standing, some sitting. Dwight opened a bottle of sauvignon blanc, then went around filling glasses.

Rachel put a hand over her glass. "Not for me, thanks."

Stephanie's attention swiveled to Rachel, and her gaze sharpened. She cleared her throat significantly.

Garrett laughed. "We're going to have to tell them, Rach."

Stephanie didn't wait to hear the actual words. "You're having a baby! That's wonderful!"

She and Dwight pelted the expectant parents with questions. Grinning, Garrett held up his hands. "Rachel's three months pregnant, and no, we didn't plan it. It's a happy accident."

"Didn't Dad give you the birds-and-bees talk?" Lucas asked.

Dwight rubbed his chin. "You know, I'm not sure I did."

"I knew it all already." Garrett smirked. "Anyway, we're thrilled."

"It's great news," Merry said. "Congratulations. It'll be lovely for Mia to have a—a niece?"

There was a moment's silence while everyone contemplated that oddity.

"Or a nephew," Rachel agreed.

"If you and Merry get moving, there could be a cousin, too," Garrett suggested to Lucas.

"Lucas and Merry don't want to be thinking about a baby just yet," Stephanie said. "Next year is fine."

"Spoken like a true grandma-to-be," Garrett said.

Stephanie's eyes shone with tears, but she waved away Dwight's solicitous inquiry. Lucas guessed she was moved by Garrett's willingness to call her a grandma. For so many years, he'd refused to acknowledge she was part of the family at all.

Since Garrett and Rachel hadn't visited in a while, the conversation centered on their news. Dwight took a convincing interest in Garrett's work—he was chief creative officer at a top Madison Avenue advertising agency—which suggested their father no longer scorned it the way he used to.

Rachel sat next to Garrett on the sofa, and he held her hand on his knee. Lucas had noticed they held hands often. They seemed to have some kind of bizarre "chicken" game going, where one of them would grab the other's hand and they'd see who let go first. He found it irritating to watch.

The sound of Mia crying came from the aft cabin, where she'd been put to bed.

"That's a full diaper if I ever heard one," Stephanie said.

She went to change the baby. A couple minutes later she emerged from the cabin, Mia in her arms. "Lucas, just the man I need. Can you take your sister?" Without waiting for an answer, which would have been *no, I can't,* she thrust Mia at him.

He took the baby out of reflex. "What do you want me to do with her?"

"Just hold her," Stephanie said, "while I make her some lunch."

Lucas held Mia under her armpits, the rest of her dangling, which even he could tell wasn't quite right. But when he wrapped an arm around her, she let out a squawk.

"What'd I do?" he asked, alarmed.

Merry patted her hip. Right; Stephanie usually carried Mia on one hip. Lucas made the shift without dropping his sister, which he considered a victory. He wondered if he could put her down, but guessed she might not be steady enough on her feet in a moving boat.

Mia whimpered; he was doing something wrong again.

"Uh, hush little baby," he said, remembering a snatch of a lullaby from goodness knows where. He jiggled her a bit.

"Her name's Mia," Dwight said.

"I know her name, Dad."

"I've never heard you use it," he mused. "You don't take much interest in your sister."

"Actually, Dwight," Merry said, "Lucas talks about Mia all the time."

What was that about? Dwight looked gratified. He jerked a nod at Lucas that might have been halfway to an apology.

"Dwight, have you inquired about a retest for Lucas yet?" Merry asked. That's what it was about. Despite the fact that Lucas had told her not to, she was suddenly determined to get involved. Did that have anything to do with what she knew, or thought she knew, about Clark's Deli?

"I'm still thinking about it," Dwight admitted.

Lucas considered Admiral Tremaine a more likely ally, but if his father wanted to help, he wouldn't argue. He wouldn't beg, however.

"Don't you think Lucas needs more balance in his life?" Dwight asked Merry.

She snorted. "Lucas wouldn't be Lucas if he was more balanced. I like my men all or nothing."

Dwight liked that answer, Lucas could tell. All or nothing—that was the choice he'd given her when he'd agreed to stay on in this marriage. She'd chosen *all*. But he hadn't really been offering her that much. Couldn't imagine actually offering *all* to a woman.

Still, even though he knew it was just pretend—or maybe *because* he knew it was just pretend, so he didn't need to worry—having Merry go to bat for him with the same kind of unswerving loyalty he'd seen her show John over the years was strangely warming.

"Maybe you're right," Dwight said as Stephanie came to get Mia for her lunch. "Lucas, let's you and I talk some more about this."

THE REST OF THE DAY PASSED quickly; they moored back at the marina at four-thirty.

"We need dog food," Merry reminded Lucas as they pulled out into the traffic. She cupped her hands over her nose and mouth and puffed warm breath into them. The temperature had dropped significantly, and her nose was cold.

Today had been lovely. Dad had seemed his old self, and she'd been relieved not to have Cathy along. With Garrett and Rachel announcing their pregnancy, Lucas's prediction that they would divert attention from him and Merry had come true.

Things between her and Lucas had been…interesting. She'd seen a different side of him last night, one that intrigued her. Today, he'd started off distant and defensive, but now, as he pulled into the SaveMart parking lot, he grinned at her and said, "Your nose is red."

Okay, not the most flowery of comments. But his tone was friendly and didn't betray any intention of solving the problem of her cold nose. He seemed more relaxed, and she liked that.

Maybe she and Lucas really could get back to normal when all this was over.

In the entryway to the store, Lucas wrested a shopping cart out of the line. "Anything else we need besides dog food?"

"Apples," she said.

Fruit and vegetables were in the first aisle; Lucas put

a bag of Red Delicious apples in the cart. Merry grabbed a head of broccoli and some tomatoes in passing.

The next aisle was cereals. Lucas headed for the granola. Apricot Crunch was his favorite, she'd noticed, and they were out of it at home. She chose oatmeal for herself.

"What else?" he asked.

"Dog food is aisle eight," she said. "Then milk. Butter. Eggs, too."

Lucas's attempt to find a laxative-laced dog food failed—predictably—so Merry had him heft a large sack of Boo's regular brand into the cart.

In the dairy section, she pulled two bottles of two percent from the cooler and found a tub of butter.

Lucas swung the cart down the next aisle. Personal products.

"I need toothpaste," she said.

As she browsed the options for tartar control and whitening, she realized tampons were alongside. Better get some of those, too, since her period was due—

Six days ago.

Couldn't be. Merry calculated again. Same result.

No way. She was so regular you could set a clock by her.

Besides, she hadn't had sex in— Not since her wedding night.

We used a condom. There were parts of that night she didn't remember, but she definitely recalled the moment of panic when it had seemed Lucas wouldn't go through with it. Then her fortuitous recollection of those old condoms in her purse.

Just how old were they? And how old was too old?

I'm never late. Never.

"Merry?" Lucas grasped her arm. "You're white as a ghost. What's wrong?"

"I'm pregnant," she blurted.

CHAPTER THIRTEEN

MERRY WISHED INSTANTLY that she could take the words back.

There was still a faint chance she might be wrong.

"What do you mean?" Lucas asked. If she'd turned white, so had he. "We used protection."

She couldn't bring herself to mention the age of the condom. Maybe that wasn't even an issue. "I'm six days late. I'm never late. Never."

He glanced around, a hunted expression on his face. "Can something else cause that? A virus?"

She pressed her fingertips to her temples. "I think for some women...maybe stress has an effect." Never before for her, but there was a first time for everything.

"There you go." Relief raised his volume. "You've been under phenomenal stress the past few weeks. No way are you pregnant."

A woman choosing deodorant turned to look at them. Heck, it could be someone Merry knew.

It wasn't. "Can you talk more quietly?" Merry asked.

Could Lucas be right?

Next to the tampons sat the pregnancy test kits. She picked one up.

"We used protection," he said again.

She let out a slow breath. "Do condoms have an expiration date?"

Lucas swore. He snatched the kit from her hand and tossed it in the cart. "Let's go."

Neither of them spoke on the way home. All Merry could think was, *Pregnant. A baby. Pregnant.* If she was pregnant—and she just knew she was—what would she do? Keep it, of course. Anything else wasn't an option for her. But raise it…how?

At her dad's place, they carried the shopping inside. Lucas fed Boo while Merry put the groceries away. Finally, all that was left on the table was the pregnancy test.

Merry picked up the box and read the instructions. The process appeared as simple as she'd assumed it would be.

"Do it now," Lucas ordered.

She wished she could tell him to get lost. But the kit promised accurate results "any time of day." Great.

Without another word, Merry walked upstairs to the bathroom and did what she needed to do.

Paced to the door and leaned against it, out of sight of the stick, waiting.

Lucas knocked, making her jump. "Are you done?"

She unlocked the door and let him in. "I guess it must be ready by now." She picked up the stick.

A blue plus sign.

"You're pregnant," Lucas said, watching her face, not the test.

She nodded.

He took the stick from her, examined it. "How accurate is this thing?"

"Ninety-nine percent." She quoted the number off the pack. "Any error is more likely to be a false negative than a false positive."

He set the stick carefully back on the counter.

Feeling as if her legs might give way, Merry sat on the edge of the tub.

"I assume," he said, "it might be Patrick's."

Her head jerked up. "Patrick and I hadn't had sex in a few weeks. Not since before my last period."

"Why not?" Lucas asked.

Which was so not his business…and yet it was. "He was at a convention in Denver, then stayed on to spend some time with his parents," she said. "We were both busy when he got back, so…" She spread her fingers on her knees and stared down at them. Her engagement ring, which had also served as her wedding ring, was their only adornment. "Besides, we always used Patrick's condoms. Which were probably newer than mine." She lifted her head. "The other condom—there were two in my purse. We can check the expiration date."

Lucas jumped at the chance to do something, anything, that might take control of this situation.

He tossed the testing stick in the trash, which for some reason made Merry wince, then led the way downstairs.

Her purse was on the kitchen table. He went straight for the zip pocket, pulled out the single remaining condom. He peered at the expiration date embossed on the foil wrapper.

"A year ago," he said, disgusted. "And it's been in your purse, rather than somewhere cool and dry. Don't you *read instructions?*"

He was close to shouting. He consciously reined it in.

"What…" Her voice shook. "What difference does it make if it's expired?"

"It's more likely to break." Which hadn't happened

that night. Lucas tried to recall all the locker room horror stories he'd heard, and the cautionary tales from the navy's health professionals. "I think when the latex wears out, there can be microscopic holes." That sounded all too possible.

She pressed her hands to her face. "Lucas, I'm so sorry."

"It's my responsibility, too," he said. "I should have checked the date." Dammit, he should have. If he'd taken that simple step—which she'd been in no shape to do, regardless of her contrition now—they would have avoided this whole situation.

He ran a hand through his hair. "So, you're definitely pregnant, with my baby."

She nodded.

He drew a long breath. "I never thought I'd say this, but I guess it's a good thing we're married."

"Huh?" She gave two short, sharp head shakes. "I'm having trouble processing anything beyond *I'm pregnant*. What do you mean?"

"We're going to be parents," he said. "Raising a child together."

"*You* want to be involved?"

Lucas wasn't sure which one of them wasn't talking sense. He'd never felt so befuddled in his life. *Pregnant. A baby.*

"Of course I want to raise my child," he said. They were standing on opposite sides of the kitchen table, which didn't bode well for any discussion.

He walked around and pulled out a chair for Merry. "Take a seat."

"I can get it." She pulled out the chair next to the one he'd chosen, and sat.

Lucas had no idea what that gesture was intended to say. He settled next to her, forearms on the table, hands clasped. "When would the baby be due?" he asked.

"I don't know. I've never done this before." She glanced down at her stomach, as if there might be some clue.

"It's got to be nine months, give or take," he said. "So maybe August next year."

"You're getting ahead of yourself," she said with a visible effort. "Pregnancies often don't go the distance. I could miscarry."

What should have been a relief turned Lucas's insides cold. "We'll deal with that if it happens," he said gruffly. "For now, let's assume there's going to be a baby, and it needs two parents." *It.* Would it be a boy or a girl?

"Of course you could see as much of it as you want," she said.

"See as much—" He broke off with a curse. "Merry, I'm the father."

"Which is why I wouldn't make any major decisions without consulting you," she assured him. "But there's no reason we can't file for divorce when you're back with your unit, as we planned."

"My child won't be born illegitimate," he said.

Which was sufficient reason in itself.

Merry traced a groove in the pine table with her fingernail.

"I want my child to have a full-time father, married to its mother," Lucas said. He was making this up as he went along. He'd never thought about this stuff, beyond an instinctive decision that he hadn't wanted to be a sperm donor when that girlfriend had asked. An equally instinctive certainty backed him up now.

"Lucas, thousands of kids, millions of kids, are brought up by divorced parents."

"But not *my* kid," he said. "I take that responsibility seriously. I want to look after you and the baby."

He could see from her guarded expression he'd made a mistake, though he had no idea what it was.

"I don't want to be looked after," she said. "I want to be loved. I want my child to be loved."

"*Our* child," he said. "Are you suggesting I wouldn't love our child?" And why couldn't he do both—the looking after and the loving?

Her forehead creased. "I'm sorry, I didn't mean that. But you and I see love differently. Your idea of love is about protection and practicalities."

"And yours is about what? Fairy-tale happy endings?"

"My idea of love… If I love someone," she said, "I love them because of who they are, not because they have a position in my life that means I'm required to love them."

"I have no idea what you're talking about."

"You have a baby sister," she said, "whom you would probably say you love."

"Of course I love Mia," he replied.

He might have known that in Merry's world that would be the wrong answer. "Why?" she demanded, way more assertive than the question required.

"Because…because she's my sister."

"Exactly. You don't know her—don't love her for anything that's about *her*."

Mia was a year old! How was he supposed to *know* her? But Lucas realized that to ask that question would reinforce Merry's prejudice.

"Are you saying I shouldn't love my sister?" he said. "If, say, I knew her and didn't like her?"

"No." Merry's fists clenched on the table. "You should love Mia because she's your sister, naturally. But there should be another side to it as well, one that's all about the person she is, good and bad. I love Dad because he's my father, but I also love the way he gets halfway through the punch line of a joke and forgets the rest."

Sounded damn annoying to Lucas.

"I love that he sings Italian love songs when he cooks spaghetti. I love his artist's eye."

"Okay," Lucas said. "I get it. Of course there will be things that I love about our child."

"There's no 'of course' about it," Merry retorted. "I've known you a long time, and I've never seen you give yourself emotionally."

"That's garbage," he said. Whatever giving himself emotionally was, he'd done it.

She bit her lip off to the left side in that way of hers. "Lucas, obviously neither of us intended a baby to come from—from what was frankly the worst sex ever."

He winced. He hadn't thought about that aspect— they'd made a baby without a shred of enjoyment in the process. *We won't tell the kid that.*

"Two wrongs can't make this right," she continued. "I don't love you, you don't love me—we're getting a divorce."

Even though he'd sensed he wasn't making much headway, her words were a shock.

He stood, shoved his hands in his pockets. His voice was rough as he said, "I think you'll find a divorce isn't quite so simple once there's no mutual agreement, and once there's a baby involved."

Her eyes widened, and Lucas wondered if their child would have those same gray eyes. He shut off the thought, because sentimentality wasn't going to fix this.

"You say we're getting divorced, Merry, but I say we're staying married. We'll see who's right."

JOHN SKEWERED A PIECE of baitfish on the hook, then cast the line over the side of the *Sally Sue*. Nothing like the fancy yacht he'd designed and created for Dwight, it was the first boat he'd built. Despite sleek lines and a cedar trim, the *Sally Sue* was essentially just a motorized dinghy.

A labor of love, named for his one true love.

Cathy had noticed the name—how could she not?—as they approached the boat across the pebbled sand. She hadn't commented.

John liked that she was a woman of few words. Although she could be moody, she was undemanding. She didn't expect him to shower her with attention, but seemed comfortable just to be in his company. He was enjoying not doing everything on his own, and he liked that nothing about Cathy reminded him of Sally, from her closemouthed smile to her middle-aged buxomness to her sturdy ankles.

All that explained why he was still spending time with her, despite the absence of any romantic feelings. That, plus it wasn't so easy to tell her he didn't want to see her again.

"Here you go." He handed her the fishing rod. "Just hold it steady and enjoy the sunshine."

"How soon will I get a bite?" she asked.

She took everything seriously and she liked direct answers.

John shrugged. "Maybe five minutes, maybe never."

She pursed her lips, but didn't say anything. He baited his own hook, then cast his line the other side of the boat from hers. He sat in the stern facing Cathy, who occupied the center bench. They'd dropped anchor a hundred yards from the cluster of rocks locals called Jonkers Island, in a place where he'd had some good fishing a couple of months ago.

They fished in silence for a while. Sunlight filtered through high clouds to dapple the water with shades of blue and gray. John let himself be lulled by the lap of sea against the boat, the cry of the gulls. His mind drifted like a piece of flotsam on a slow tide.

"John, I love this," Cathy said, jerking him back to the moment.

"Love what?" He glanced around, looking for a source of such pleasure.

"Fishing. It's so restful. It's beautiful out here." Her cheeks had pinked up in the sun, and the light bouncing off the water seemed to brighten her brown eyes.

"The fish aren't biting yet," he reminded her.

That closemouthed smile made an appearance. "I don't mind. Can we do this another time?"

"Sure," he said, before he realized she'd done it again. Every time they went out, he'd planned to tell her this was the last. Every time, she somehow got him to commit to another date.

Ah, well. Hard to complain about a woman who didn't mind sitting in a boat fishing all afternoon.

"It *is* beautiful out today," he said, agreeing with her earlier comment. He slid his rod into one of the holders on the side of the boat. "I might just do me a little sketch."

His pencils and notebook were in a waterproof pouch in the backpack he'd stowed in the bow. He scrambled past Cathy to reach them, rocking the boat dangerously.

She gave a small gasp—a more excitable woman might have squealed—and clutched a fistful of his anorak. "Don't go overboard," she said.

"Not likely." Not impossible, though. "I'll be careful," he promised. He pulled the waterproof pouch from the pack and moved more carefully back to his seat.

Cathy didn't ask him what he was drawing, nor if she could see it, which he appreciated. He did a rough sketch of the seascape to get the proportions, then flipped to a new page to record a more detailed impression of the water and the play of light, and of the shore beyond. He would rely on this sketch, and his memory, when he started painting. It would be nice to start tonight, but most evenings he found he was tired early.

John turned the page in his notebook and began to sketch Cathy. He was no good at portraits, so he wouldn't paint her. But her stillness and quietness were a nice contrast with the perpetual noise and movement of the water.

"Would your sister have enjoyed this?" he asked, as he drew.

She darted him a smile, appreciating the chance to talk about her twin. "Rue was more sociable than I am. Her idea of a boat trip was a five-star cruise ship with plenty of friends and plenty of wine."

"So you weren't that similar."

"In a lot of ways we were," she insisted. "But we had— Oh!"

Her fishing rod jerked in her hands.

"You've got a live one." John stuffed his notebook and pencil back in the pouch. He stowed it away, then moved to help her. "Hang on tight."

"Of course I'm hanging on tight. Do you think I'm a moron?" she growled, and he chuckled.

"Okay, now you want to reel him in." It was easiest for John to reach around her from behind, placing his hands on hers so he could guide her movements. She softened against him for a moment, which wasn't altogether unpleasant. Then she focused on the business of reeling in her catch.

It was a snapper, about five pounds, John guessed. "Not bad," he said, as he removed the hook and dropped the fish into the cooler he'd filled with sea water.

"I like fishing even more now," Cathy said, and her smile widened slightly.

Briefly, he considered kissing her. No. Best not to complicate things.

They stayed out another hour. John caught a bluefish, just a three-pounder. He'd told Stephanie he hoped to bring home dinner. Luckily, she had some steaks in the refrigerator as backup.

After they motored in, Cathy said, "I don't think your daughter likes you seeing me."

"Merry likes the thought of me staying loyal to her mom's memory." He liked that thought himself, but he was tired of the loneliness, so was trying not to think too hard. "It might take a while, but she'll get used to me dating other women."

Cathy didn't look happy about his use of the plural. But she didn't try to pin him down, and they talked casually about his work at the boatyard as they drove to Dwight's place.

"Enjoy your snapper," he said, as he got out of her car.

"Why don't we swap?" she suggested. "I'll never get through such a big fish, but you and your friends will."

It was a kind offer.

It highlighted what a jerk John was being.

"Only if you join us," he said. "I should have spoken sooner, but it's not my house, so I didn't think to invite you." When she demurred, he insisted. "Stephanie and Dwight are great company." Well, Stephanie was. Fond though he was of Dwight, he knew his friend was an acquired taste.

In the end, Cathy came in, Stephanie cooked the fish and they had a perfectly pleasant evening. John caught Dwight looking at Cathy once or twice with slight puzzlement, as if he wasn't sure what John saw in her, compared with Sally. But John didn't need his friend's approval. Like Dwight, Cathy was an acquired taste.

She didn't outstay her welcome, rising to leave around eight o'clock. John was tired after the day, and he didn't try to detain her.

He accompanied her out to the porch.

"That was nice," she said. "The fishing and the meal. Thanks for inviting me."

"My pleasure." He meant it, he realized. "Good night, Cathy." He leaned in to kiss her cheek, but she turned her head so that he met her lips.

Surprise froze him in place for a fraction of a second. Then, well, it didn't make much sense not to finish the kiss, so he did. Her mouth was firm, but pleasant. The kiss was chaste—both mouths stayed closed—but curiously intimate. The connection sent a tingle through him that he hadn't felt in a long time.

She pulled away first. "Good night, John."

She seemed to step more lightly down the front walk. When she reached the car, she lifted a hand in a half wave. Then she was gone.

John ran his thumb and forefinger across his mouth, aware of the lingering sensation of her kiss.

An acquired taste, indeed.

CHAPTER FOURTEEN

THE DOORBELL OF JOHN'S COTTAGE rang at eight o'clock on Sunday morning. A full hour before Lucas had expected it, but he was ready.

He opened the door to Stephanie. With all the stuff piled around her on the porch, she looked as if she was moving in.

"I would have helped you get this out of the car," he said.

"No problem." She thrust Mia into his arms.

About to ignore his half sister, beyond the obvious requirement not to drop her, Lucas thought better of it. "Hi, Mia."

No answer. See, this was why they didn't have much of a relationship.

"This here's the travel crib." Stephanie pointed to an oblong of pink-and-gray nylon. "And that's her clip-on high chair, next to the stroller—it works with John's kitchen table. I brought the stair gate, if you'd rather not have the hassle of watching her around the staircase all day. Diaper bag and changing mat—" she indicated a brightly patterned satchel "—food, bottles. Drinking cup, if you can bear the mess. Toys, books. If you get desperate, there's an Elmo DVD."

"We won't get desperate, will we, Mia?" Lucas said heartily. The child gave him a doubtful look. "You'll be back tonight, right, Stephanie?" Because it looked as if his stepmother and Dwight were planning to skip the country, rather than drive to Old Saybrook to go sailing with friends.

Lucas picked up the travel crib with his free hand.

"No later than five," she promised. "You sure you'll be okay?" She followed him into the house, bringing a couple of the nursery items with her.

"Merry's still asleep," he warned her over his shoulder, keeping his voice down. He didn't know how soon pregnancy tiredness kicked in, but it was easy enough to see that arguing back and forth since Friday night, with neither of them budging from their respective positions, had been as exhausting for Merry as it had been for him.

Another couple of minutes and they had all of Mia's gear inside.

"Is there a schedule somewhere among all this?" Lucas asked.

"No, but it's pretty straightforward. She's already had breakfast. Give her a bottle at ten and put her down for a nap. Lunch around midday—a cheese sandwich or something will be fine, but use soft bread. Another bottle and a nap around three, and offer her water in her cup in between."

The naps sounded good. Lucas checked his watch. Eight-ten. "What does she do between now and the first nap?"

"She'll play with her toys or follow you around. Whatever. She can do her own thing, but of course you'll need to keep an eye on her. Toddlers can be inquisitive."

"I'm on it." He'd already identified a bunch of hazards and taken steps to eliminate them before Mia arrived.

"And…how does the diaper routine work?" Lucas recalled the stench his sister had managed to produce the day he'd arrived back in town.

"Change her before her naps, and whenever the diaper starts to seem heavy or smelly." Stephanie grinned. "You don't have to carry her, you know."

Gingerly, Lucas lowered Mia to the floor. For a moment she wobbled on her chubby legs, and he almost scooped her up again. Then she stabilized.

"Do you think you should wake Merry?" Stephanie seemed amused by his watchfulness. "She's looked after Mia before."

"I'll let her sleep a little longer," Lucas said.

"What a good husband you turned out to be." Stephanie patted his cheek. "Call me on my cell if you have any problems."

Maybe you could tell Merry the good husband bit. "Will do," he said.

The problem was, Merry didn't just want a *good* husband. She wanted a besotted husband. One who noticed what kind of songs she sang while she cooked spaghetti. To Lucas, that sounded like a guy who checked his brain at the door. Surely looking after a wife and family required a clear head. As well as all the emotional stuff.

Today, Merry would see the benefit of having a guy who could do both. If she was willing to look.

"Thank you," Stephanie said, "for offering to babysit Mia. Dwight and I haven't had a whole day without her since she was born. Much as I adore my daughter, I can't wait to have my husband to myself."

Stephanie set Mia up with some baby LEGOs; Lucas had had no idea they made the stuff in giant, pastel-colored pieces. A few minutes later, after prolonged goodbyes and smoochy kisses to Mia, Stephanie left. Watching her car disappear, Lucas knew a moment of panic. He quashed it. He was ready for this.

Ready to look after Mia, and ready to be a father to the baby he and Merry had made.

A baby. Thirty-six hours after he'd heard the news, the idea still had the power to rock him. It filled him with myriad feelings, some of which he couldn't name. Others...for sure they included anxiety, and a sense of challenge. Those two were fine: he liked challenge and he had a proven technique for managing anxiety. Namely, act quickly and firmly to prevent things going wrong.

"Okay, Mia," he said to his sister, who was absorbed in her LEGOs, "let's make sure we have everything under control."

It wouldn't hurt to write down those timings Stephanie had given him. He grabbed a pen, plunked himself on the couch and used the back of a takeout menu to record the schedule, starting with "0800—Arrival." Check. At the bottom of the page, he wrote "1700—Departure." In the space between, he filled in the times that Stephanie had given him. When he was done, the day still looked bare. Lots of white space. He added "Diaper Change" at 0955 and 1455, and designated from now until the first diaper change as "Free Play." That was better.

But today was about more than simply looking after Mia.

He scanned the schedule, then added "1430—Bonding (me/Mia)." Perfect.

"Hey, sis, according to this dandy list, you can just keep doing what you're doing." Lucas glanced at his sister—hell, she was gone. The door to the hallway was open; Lucas made a dash for it.

Mia hadn't made it far. She was on the staircase, third stair up.

"Hey, kid." Lucas kept his voice calm and quiet, so as not to disturb Merry. "Come back to your LEGOs."

Mia turned to look at him, and something about the jerky movement, or maybe it was her disproportionately large head, or her lack of coordination, but she tipped backward.

Lucas had no idea how he moved so fast, but a second later he'd caught her, just before the back of her head thudded onto the bottom stair. "Gotcha." His voice shook with relief. Imagine if he'd had to phone Stephanie already with questions about infant concussion. "Okay, kid, let's set up that gate."

He put Mia back with her LEGOs and closed the living-room door while he fixed the gate in place at the bottom of the stairs.

All right, that was better. Lucas checked his watch. Eight-thirty. Merry should wake soon. He wanted to look totally at ease when she came downstairs.

He opened the living room door carefully, in case Mia was behind it. No, she was over at the coffee table…tearing pages out of one of his Magic Eye books.

Damn. Lucas snatched the book away. Too suddenly; he gave her a fright. She whimpered.

"Hush, little baby," he soothed. "You don't want to wake Merry." The whimper seemed about to turn into a full-out wail. Hell. Lucas gave her back the book. "Try to stick to the first section," he said. "I'm only halfway through."

Not that he was making much progress. Those stupid pictures still never did what they were supposed to.

He retreated to the kitchen. As a military guy he wasn't comfortable with the concept of retreat, but he had to admit that's what he was doing. Just while he made a pot of coffee. He needed a cup, and Merry would, too. Whenever the hell she woke up.

The dog scratched at the back door; Lucas let him in. As he poured boiling water into the French press, he heard an exclamation from the hallway.

Merry.

Lucas had already figured his tactics from the night she'd taken the pregnancy test weren't going to work. He could say "We're going to stay married" until he was blue in the face, but that wouldn't make it happen.

He needed a new approach, a gentler approach. Hence Mia's presence today, and why Lucas stuck his head out the door to the hallway and called, "Morning, honeybun."

Friendly, casual, but acknowledging that no matter how little she liked it, they were no longer just friends.

She was halfway down the stairs, wearing a short— very short—terry robe, white with big black polka dots. Her hands were on hips.

"I don't believe it," she said. "I'm about five minutes pregnant, and already you're childproofing the house?"

She tried to push the stair gate out of the way, but of course he'd done an excellent job of fixing it in place.

"Let me get that for you." Lucas came to open it. "The gate's for Mia's benefit."

Halfway through a yawn, Merry stopped. Despite her sleep-in, she had dark circles beneath her eyes. "Your dad and Stephanie are here? I'd better get dressed."

"It's just Mia," he said. "I offered to babysit so Dad and Stephanie could have a day out."

"You're babysitting?" Merry asked incredulously.

"Yep. Though if you want to lend a hand, I won't say no."

Her eyes narrowed. "Ah, I get it. You're playing house, trying to show me what a caring guy you are."

He'd known she would see through him right away, but that didn't matter. "Yeah, I do have a point to make. Contrary to your belief, I do like Mia—" at least, he fully expected to soon, though it would help if she stopped destroying his stuff "—and having me as the father of your child isn't the worst thing in the world."

"I already know that," Merry said. "My point is, you're the father regardless of whether we're together or not."

They were headed back over old ground. Time for a diversion. "I made coffee," he said. "Come say hi to Mia and have a cup."

Merry couldn't logically refuse either of those, and she didn't. She walked through the kitchen, picking up her coffee on the way to the living room.

"Hey, Mia— Oh, no!" She perched her cup on the bookcase. "She's shredding one of your Magic Eye books."

"It's okay," he said. "That one doesn't work, anyway."

"That doesn't mean she can tear it up. She'll think she's allowed to demolish any book."

He hadn't thought of that.

Lucas watched while Merry gently scolded Mia, who accepted the confiscation of the book with guilty sheepishness. She didn't seem to mind being plunked back down with her LEGOs.

"You moved the furniture," Merry said, sounding confused.

"I covered up the electric sockets." He'd pushed the chairs and sofas against the walls.

"I don't think Stephanie worries too much about that stuff," Merry said.

"That's her choice, but Mia's not going to get electrocuted on my watch."

Merry shook her head—and caught sight of his schedule on the couch. She picked it up, started to read. "'Diaper Change—0955'?"

"It's just a rough guide." He sensed it would be a smart idea to deactivate the alarms he'd programmed into his cell phone for each of the items on his list. There was nothing wrong with being organized, but Merry would probably say it indicated a lack of *emotion*. "I'm totally flexible with all this," he said.

"You're completely out of your depth, aren't you?" she replied.

He started to deny it, then realized she was smiling. Which she hadn't done since they arrived at SaveMart on Friday night. And maybe he was a tiny bit out of his depth.

He swallowed his pride. "Yep," he said humbly.

But she was still reading his notes. "Don't pay any attention to that," he said quickly. Too late. He saw the moment she reached the place he didn't want her to go. Her brows drew together.

"*Bonding?* From two-thirty to two fifty-five?"

"It doesn't have to be those specific times." He cursed the impulse that had made him fill in the white spaces.

"How do you plan to achieve this bonding?"

She made it sound really dumb.

"I don't have a strategy yet, but—"

She groaned. "It's not a military exercise, Lucas, it's about letting your feelings develop. Without trying to package them or restrict them." She shook her head. "At least you're trying, I guess." She was still smiling, which was more than he'd expected.

"Are you around today?" he asked. "To spend time with me and Mia?"

"I'd arranged to meet Sarah for lunch, but I think I'd better cancel."

"Thanks, Merry."

"How about you cook me some eggs while I have a shower?"

At last, a job with a beginning and an end and clear measure of success or failure. "I can do that."

When Merry came down after her shower, Mia was in her high chair, which was clipped to the kitchen table, and Lucas was serving eggs and bacon.

"Impressive," Merry said. Not referring to his chest lovingly molded by a worn T-shirt, nor to his butt in faded jeans.

He saluted her. "I'm keeping her out of trouble. Do you think she could eat a piece of apple?"

"Sure." Merry pulled out a chair and sat. "You're good with the Heimlich maneuver, right?"

He paled. She laughed. "Mia will be fine with some apple—I've seen Stephanie give it to her. But you should keep an eye on her as she eats."

It wouldn't be long, Merry realized, before they would be having similar conversations about their own baby.

If Lucas was around. If he had his way and they some-how stayed together.

She realized Lucas had ceased all activity, too. He was watching her watch Mia.

His eyes met hers. "Is the reason you've gone quiet the same reason I've gone quiet?"

She nodded. "This is serious."

They both eyed Mia, pulverizing the apple slice by banging it on her tray, oblivious to the new reality she'd painted for them.

Right now, this felt cozy, Merry thought. But it was like a game: someone else's baby, someone else's house, a marriage that had been one long game of "let's pretend."

The real thing… Who knew how that would feel?

"Let's take Mia for a walk with Boo," she said louder than necessary.

"Great idea," Lucas said. "But we'd better eat first. You need to keep your strength up. So do I," he added quickly, as if she was about to call him on his protec-tive instincts.

After breakfast, they bundled Mia up until she resem-bled a powder puff. Lucas unfolded the stroller with ease and gave Merry a smirk.

"You want a medal for that?" she asked.

He grinned. "Nope. Got plenty of medals already. Are we good to go?"

"Just to let you know, Mia may fall asleep ahead of your schedule," Merry warned.

He swatted her behind. "I'm flexible. You'll see."

Out in the street, Lucas made sure the sun wasn't in Mia's eyes, adjusting the hood of her stroller. Merry didn't know what to make of his offer to babysit his sister. He'd admitted he wanted to impress Merry with his parenting skills…but he wasn't just paying lip service to the task. Of course, Lucas would apply himself with dedication to any job. That was his nature. But he'd recognized with that agenda item—"Bonding (me/Mia)"—that there was more to it. Whether he was capable of embracing that *more* in such a way that it was more than just an agenda item…

Where did duty stop and love start? The lines were blurred, Merry realized. There was no sign post that said Here.

They headed for the half-mile promenade that started to the left of her dad's place and led toward town. Lucas pushed the stroller, while Merry took Boo on his lead. It was mid-November, and already Christmas decorations hung from lamp posts. Would Lucas be gone by Christmas?

The thought chilled Merry. Probably because they were facing into the wind, which, though not strong, made it cold enough to huddle into their coats and not attempt conversation.

When they reached the restored city pier with its old-style streetlights and the historic, cone-topped building the locals called the Rocket Ship, the breeze dropped away and the sun seemed to try a bit harder.

"Let's sit down." Lucas pointed to one of the wooden benches that dotted the pier.

Merry turned her face to the sun, soaking up the wintry rays. After a minute she realized Lucas was watching a mom and dad with their two preschoolers, bundled up in coats, scarves and mittens, throwing bread crusts to a pack of greedy seagulls.

"Bad habit, feeding the gulls," he said.

"It only encourages them to grow more aggressive," she agreed. "And to foul the sidewalks."

Still, there was something in the kids' simple joy that captivated her.

"See how good that looks," Lucas said. "The mom and dad together? Look how the kids are loving it." They were; the girl kept looking to her mom for approval and the boy held his dad's hand.

As they watched, the man kissed his wife. It started off as a peck, then she kissed him back, and they prolonged it a little. Even when they broke apart, their gazes held.

"A mom and dad who *love each other,*" Merry agreed. "You can't beat it."

Lucas snorted. Then, after a moment, he said, "Perhaps I didn't make myself clear the other night. I'm not opposed to the idea of having feelings for you, Merry."

She burst out laughing. "Did you hear what you just said?"

He grimaced. "Let me try again. I admit I've never been someone who wants to get emotionally entangled with a woman."

"You mean, to fall in love," Merry said.

He rolled his eyes. "Call it what you like. But if that's what you want, then…maybe I could try it."

"Could try what?" she asked, confused.

"I could try…developing those feelings."

"Lucas, you can't just decide to fall in love."

"Okay, maybe I'm not talking about falling in love," he said. "Who's to say what that is, anyway? It's just words that people put around an attraction, to make it sound deeper."

"Says the guy with no depth perception," Merry pointed out.

"Leaving that aside…" It seemed he'd made a tactical decision to stop knocking one of the concepts she held dear. "Loving someone—no falling, no cataclysm, just a…a steady thing. That doesn't sound impossible. With you," he added quickly.

She didn't know whether to laugh or cry. He was putting so much thought into this, but missing the essence of what love was all about. "I imagine," she said, "that if you're really open to love, then you don't get to choose which way you fall or don't fall, and how the love ends up. Lucas, I don't want a man who has to train himself to love me. I don't see how that man would ever give me his heart."

"There's more to marriage than love, though," he said.

"And there's more to it than having a baby. The months spent with young babies go by quickly. If you and I stayed married, have you thought about what would take up the rest of the time? Day in, day out. Living together. Eating together." She paused. "Sleeping together."

He frowned, as if he hadn't considered all that. "I'm attracted to you," he said. "I know you feel the same."

"On one level," she admitted. She resisted the urge to look away, out to sea. With everything else that had happened, they might as well confront this particular reality. "But, Lucas, when it comes to practice rather than theory, I think we well and truly killed the physical attraction, don't you?" Even if the theoretical side was alive and kicking.

"You mean, our wedding night."

She nodded.

He ran a hand around the back of his neck. "Can I say in my defense I don't believe I'm usually awful in bed?" Ruefully, he added, "I'm sorry I let you down."

Could this conversation get any more awkward? "You don't have to take all the blame. I was just as bad, and, uh, I don't think I'm usually so terrible, either." She drew a breath and forced herself to continue. "Let's face it. Although there's been a spark between us over the years, the reality is we're not good together."

"I don't think you can make that judgment on the strength of one or two encounters." He leaned forward to adjust the angle of Mia's sunshade. "If I were to kiss you now, the way that guy over there just kissed his wife, things might be quite different."

As Lucas sat back, his eyes were on her mouth. Reflexively, Merry licked her lips.

"I doubt it," she said. Of course, the idea sounded tempting in theory.

"Wouldn't hurt to try," he said casually.

"It might."

His smile was quizzical. "We're in public, no chance of things getting out of hand."

She spurted a laugh. "No chance of that, anyway."

Something kindled in his eyes. A light she'd seen there ever since she was a kid—the light of challenge—but now with an added adult dimension.

"Not in front of the baby," she said, unsure if she was joking or not.

The darkening of Lucas's eyes said *he* was serious.

"No problem." He turned the stroller so Mia couldn't

see them. "Just pretend," he said, as he leaned in to Merry, "that we're a married couple."

"We *are* a married couple," she said, feeling slightly dizzy.

"I mean, like them." A tip of his head indicated the family with the seagulls. His mouth was so close, she felt the words as a breath of promise. "A couple who got married for better reasons than we did..."

He didn't say "let's pretend we're in love" of course, because by his own admission that was more than he would ever hope for.

His lips skimmed over hers and away again. "Let's pretend we like doing this."

His mouth settled in, and his kiss covered her.

Inside Merry, something clenched. Her lips responded, communicating the longing inside her.

Lucas drew back. "We like doing this a *lot*," he said huskily. Then his mouth met hers again in a slow-dance kiss that set off a rumble of desire inside her.

She parted her lips, he came in and—*whoosh*. The rumble had been a pilot light that set off the furnace. Since they were in public, Lucas wasn't all over her with his hands, which stayed at his sides. Though only their mouths touched, Merry felt stripped bare.

At last, from somewhere, she mustered the willpower to pull away. To *wrench* herself away, because that was what it took.

Her entire body tingled, crying out for him in hidden, secret places. How could she feel so attracted to a man who refused the emotional connection she cherished? How could she quash that attraction? She sat stiffly, staring out to the horizon, where sea met sky, trying to figure out what had just happened. What should happen next.

"Merry?" Lucas said.

"What?" Still, she didn't look at him.

When he spoke, his tone was…humble. "Will you give me a chance to work on the…the feelings side of this? To maybe *woo* you?"

She should say no. Because no matter how good his intentions—and his kisses—a man couldn't talk himself into falling into the kind of love she wanted. Lucas didn't want to, and she didn't want him to, either. She wanted a man who would love her unreservedly, and not just because she was having his baby.

But…there *was* a baby. And nothing was as simple as it should be.

Slowly, deliberately, she nodded.

CHAPTER FIFTEEN

JOHN HAD INVITED CATHY, AT HER suggestion, to go fishing again on Tuesday afternoon, her next day off. But by midday, it was raining fit to bust, and squally, too. He called her to postpone, but she somehow convinced him they should visit the Custom House Maritime Museum instead. She picked him up from the boatyard at two and they drove into town.

John had been to the museum several times over the years, though not in a while. It wasn't the most exciting place, but he didn't mind wandering through with her, reading the plaques that related the history of the U.S.A.'s longest-serving custom house.

At one stage, he took hold of Cathy's hand to move her on from a display of old ship's food containers that had caught her attention, and somehow he didn't let go. He liked the contact, and how young it made him feel.

Their kiss the other day had been entirely tame…but he'd been wondering what it would be like to take it up a notch. Or two. Maybe he should give it a try. There was no risk involved to his ego—he was certain Cathy wouldn't refuse—and none to his heart. Which wasn't to say he didn't like her. Her smile, never effusive, had a shy warmth today that he found attractive. But she wouldn't—couldn't—break his heart.

Upstairs, displays were spread throughout several

small rooms with sloping ceilings. The old attics. When John and Cathy came out of the map room, he opened the door of the next, only to find it was a storeroom.

"What's in there?" She was right behind him, and as he turned, his arm grazed her breast. He found her buxomness intriguing.

"Come," he said, leading her into the room and closing the door behind them. The overhead fluorescent fixture was off, but a dormer window admitted enough daylight that he could see her clearly.

Cathy didn't play dumb or act coy. Or even flirtatious, which relieved him, because he didn't think he was up to finding cute lines for what he wanted. He opened his arms; she walked into them.

Her mouth was eager in response to his, and this time, he parted her lips. So foreign, yet so familiar… He groaned as need took hold. With his hands, he scoped out her dimensions—plains, curves, hollows. Mostly curves.

He backed her up so she was leaning against the wall, and deepened the kiss.

She had none of Sally's exuberance, none of her poetry. But Cathy tasted sweet, her curves pressed against his chest, and one of her legs was tangled with his. He closed his eyes.

To his surprise, desire surged. He'd always known diminished libido was a possible side effect of blood pressure medication, but had never known if it applied to him. Now, he felt a twinge that suggested he still had something to offer.

"I want…" Cathy said against him, gasping a little and pressing closer. "I want to be yours."

That was what Sally used to say to him. "I'm yours."

He'd loved it, loved the giving and the taking and the greediness.

This isn't Sally. He didn't hunger for Cathy the way he'd hungered for his wife. If Cathy disappeared from his life tomorrow, he wouldn't think about her.

For her to offer herself so wholeheartedly to a man so lukewarm about the gift was wrong.

Just plain wrong.

As soon as he could, John pulled back. He tugged her sweater into place.

"Wow," she said, the comment unexpectedly youthful.

How should he respond to that? "Uh, yeah. Cathy, I don't think I'm ready for... The doctor said I should wait at least six weeks before..." Sure, blame it on the doctor.

"I wasn't expecting to make love right now, John," she said acerbically. "We're in a closet. At a museum."

"True," he said, relieved. "And those blood pressure medications are renowned for their effects on libido."

"You don't have to make excuses, John." Her forehead creased, and he resisted the urge to smooth it with his thumb.

"We have plenty of time," she continued. "And where there's a will, there's definitely a way."

She opened the storeroom door, flooding the place with light that revealed the strain in her features and made John feel about a hundred years old. As she bustled out, she said over her shoulder, "It's my birthday next week. Will you come to my place for dinner? Merry and Lucas, too, if they're free."

Tell her.

Tell her what? Tell her that he was lukewarm and therefore didn't think he should see her again...right before a birthday that also happened to be the birthday of her adored, dead identical twin?

"Sure," John said.

MERRY HAD BEEN ON TENTERHOOKS for days, ever since Lucas had said he planned to work on "the feelings." It was a good thing she wasn't literally holding her breath. A girl could die waiting for Lucas Calder to get in touch with his feelings, she thought as she updated the Wyatt Yachts budget spreadsheet to account for reduced downstream income as a result of her dad's illness.

As far as she could tell, nothing had changed with Lucas.

Was he waiting for some encouragement? She'd done her bit. She'd told him what she was looking for, and admitted she found him attractive. And after a solo first prenatal visit with her obstetrician, she'd invited Lucas to accompany her to the next one, which would be the eight-week sonogram. He'd seemed delighted.

Though not so delighted that he'd felt compelled to kiss her again.

Far from seeing more "action," they were talking more, at home and at work. Which she enjoyed. But she wouldn't call it romantic.

Romance and love weren't the same thing, of course. But for her, romance wasn't a generic gesture like a valentine or a bunch of red roses. It was the things a man and a woman did that were specially chosen with each other in mind. That wouldn't mean as much with anyone else.

Like the ships in a bottle that her mom had given Dad. Back then, he had been working for another boatbuilder, and starting his own business was a distant dream. Merry's mom had used the ships in a bottle to remind him to hold on to that dream. She'd rigged the boats herself, stitching numbers to each sail. Numbers starting with JWY, for John Wyatt Yachts. When John had finally started the business, a few years after Sally died, his first yacht had been JWY 1. Now, he was up to JWY 83.

To Merry, her mom's gesture with the sail numbers equaled both love and romance.

Merry sighed. She couldn't imagine Lucas doing anything like that in a million years. Though she was surprised he hadn't tried *something*.

Maybe he'd changed his mind about wanting to solve the problem of marriage and their baby. Maybe the kiss she'd considered bone-melting and meaningful had done nothing for him.

Merry didn't believe that.

More likely, he had no idea where to start.

She sighed as she looked at the new bottom line the spreadsheet had produced.

"We're not broke yet," her dad said from the table where he was testing his blood pressure.

"Nowhere near," she agreed. You wouldn't think it, to look at her dad's unostentatious lifestyle, but the business was highly profitable. "How's your BP?"

"It's 155 over 105," her dad said with excessive casualness.

Merry pushed her chair back from the desk. "Really?" It was the first time his systolic reading had dipped below 160.

"It'll probably be back up later," he warned, though he was grinning. His pressure tended to rise in the evening, though they'd had one day last week, the night he and Cathy had come to dinner, actually, where his blood pressure had remained more or less static from morning to evening.

"Are you still seeing Cathy?" Merry asked.

"Seems so."

She couldn't interpret his tone. "What is it you like about her, Dad?"

Her father squirmed on his seat as he rolled up the blood pressure cuff. "She's kind, quiet. She likes fishing."

"There must be a thousand women like that in New London," Merry pointed out.

"I haven't met all those women. I met Cathy."

"So…you're saying she's as good as anyone?"

Her shock must have sounded in her voice; her father winced. "I'm not looking for another love of my life, Merry. By definition, a man has only one of those."

Now that, she agreed with. "Do you think… Dad, would you get married again? Would you marry someone you didn't love the way you loved Mom?" Because that was effectively what Lucas was asking her to consider. For all his talk of "working on the feelings."

Her father stowed the blood pressure gauge on its shelf, next to the first aid kit. "If it was that or spend my life alone…I'd have to consider it. After all, Merry-Berry, you're married now, and who knows where you might end up with a husband in the navy."

"I'm not going anywhere in a hurry," she muttered.

"I don't mind if you do," John said. "You need to look forward, to build your own life."

Maybe so, but Lucas's suggestion that they stay married wasn't her last chance at finding someone to share her life with. Far from it, she hoped.

She heard the iron door opening—was it Lucas, back from Gunn Optical? He usually saw Heather after he'd finished work at the boatyard, by which time it was getting dark. She had suggested he come in to do the test in daylight hours, which could make a difference to his depth perception.

It wasn't Lucas; a courier driver came into the office. Merry signed for two packages. One was addressed to Wyatt Yachts, with their marine paint supplier listed as the sender.

"For you." She handed it to her father.

The other, a letter-size envelope, was addressed to her, with no sender's details. Merry tore off the plastic strip that opened it.

She pulled out a ticket wallet from the local indie cinema. Inside was a single ticket, not issued by a machine, but hand-designed. It was more an invitation than a ticket.

> You are invited to a private screening of
> *Lassie* (2005)
> Thursday, 7:00 p.m.
> A taxi will collect you from your home
> at 6:45 p.m.

Merry started to smile. And couldn't stop. She took back every uncharitable thought she'd just had about Lucas not understanding romance.

"Why are you smiling like the cat that got the cream?" her father asked.

She showed him the invitation. "I don't know if he remembers that the 2005 movie is my favorite, or if it's coincidence."

Predictably, her dad beamed. "You married a good man, Merry-Berry."

Maybe he was right. But was that enough?

MERRY HAD FELT A LITTLE extravagant, buying a slim-fitting new dress when she was about to get fat. But Lucas's grand gesture deserved some effort on her part. This felt like a new stage in their relationship…and she could always wear the dress again after the baby arrived, she reminded herself, as she checked her reflection in the full-length mirror that had been a present from her dad on her thirteenth birthday.

The baby… It still felt unreal that there was a new life growing inside her. She felt no different than she had a month ago. She looked no different, either. She still needed the dress's gathered bust to hide her lack of cleavage. On the plus side, she still had a narrow waist for the slinky red fabric to hug.

She blow-dried her hair with extra care and applied makeup, which she seldom bothered with during the day. Then she stepped into patent leather pumps and headed downstairs.

The taxi arrived right on time, at 6:45 p.m. Merry remembered she hadn't fed Boo yet, but the driver waited with good grace. They still managed to arrive at the theater by seven.

She felt a thrill of pleasure as she walked into the building, past the sign saying Closed for Private Function.

"You must be Merry." The woman who came to greet

her helped her out of her coat. "Upstairs, your prince awaits." She winked.

Merry did feel a bit like a fairy-tale princess as she walked up the red-carpeted staircase.

At the top, a round table was spread with a white linen cloth. On it sat a bottle of champagne in an ice bucket with two flutes next to it.

A little sigh escaped Merry. Incredible. For Lucas to reenact their first date—seeing *Lassie*—but to transform it into such a special night, was a stroke of genius. She could even forgive him for tempting her with champagne she couldn't drink.

"Merry," said a familiar deep voice behind her.

Not Lucas.

She spun, too fast on her heels and stumbled slightly. *"Patrick?"*

He stood there, wearing a tuxedo, hair stylishly slicked down, smiling that crooked, boyish smile.

"*You* invited me here?" she said.

Puzzlement flickered across his face, but he ignored her question, as if it wasn't part of the script. He took both her hands in his. "It's so good to see you. Forgive me."

"For—for what?" Her brain couldn't process what was going on.

"For being so stupid as to let you go. Five weeks without you have shown me I'm the biggest idiot in history."

Five weeks? Was that all it had been? It seemed a lifetime since he'd choked in Pete's Burger Shack. Since Lucas had saved him, then stepped forward as her fake fiancé when Patrick wouldn't.

Patrick tugged her closer; his hands moved to her hips, anchoring her.

"Patrick, I shouldn't be here." Merry wanted to cry. *Pregnancy hormones.* "I told you on the phone last week, I married Lucas."

He groaned. "Which is all my fault. I'm sorry, sweetheart, that I left you to that jerk."

"He's not…" She gave up. Patrick only heard what he wanted to hear. Besides, she wasn't sure what she'd call Lucas.

My husband.

That still didn't sound right.

The father of my baby.

No arguing with that.

"Merry, I can't say I like that you're married, either. But as you said, it's temporary." Patrick smiled ruefully. "Since I have only myself to blame, I can wait for your divorce to come through. I love you."

"I can't believe I have to listen to this again," Lucas said in a disgusted voice.

Merry whipped her head around to see him taking the last two stairs in one long stride. In faded work jeans and a copper-colored T-shirt, with the shadow of tomorrow's beard on his jaw, he seemed the essence of masculinity. Lucas made Patrick's tuxedo look like game playing. Like window dressing.

Patrick released her. "What the hell are you doing here?"

Lucas scanned Merry, clearly noting her sexy new dress, her styled hair. She couldn't tell if he liked them.

He addressed his answer to her. "You weren't home when I got back from my eye test, so I decided to take a toy that I bought for Mia over to Dad's place. When I got there, your father wanted to know why I wasn't at the theater." Lucas glared at Patrick. "I figured this goon was behind this dumb idea. Still after *my wife*."

"Your temporary wife," Patrick corrected.

"News flash," Lucas said, "things have changed." He glanced at Patrick's little feast. "Champagne, Merry?"

She should have realized Lucas wasn't behind this extravagance the moment she saw the bottle.

"Is that true?" Patrick asked her. "Your marriage isn't temporary anymore?"

Lucas tensed, his gaze fixed on her with the intensity of a heat-seeking missile.

"I—I'm not sure," she said. Aware that she'd just crossed a line.

Lucas hooked his thumbs in his jeans; he looked as if he owned the world. What had she done?

"Then why did you come tonight?" Patrick demanded.

"I thought Lucas organized it," Merry snapped. "As a grand, romantic gesture."

"Honeybun, you know I hate *Lassie*," Lucas said. Now that she'd implied the basis of their marriage had changed, he sounded laconic, supremely confident.

"Which would have made it all the more impressive if you'd done it for me," she snapped. "You said you were going to *woo* me."

Patrick issued a choked protest.

"I *have* been wooing you," Lucas said. "I've talked so much, I've just about lost my voice."

"*This* is wooing." She flung her arm wide to encompass the concept of the private movie screening…and managed to catch Patrick's champagne glass. Champagne sloshed over the sides onto his shoes.

"If you two want to have a marital spat," Patrick said sourly, "perhaps you could do it somewhere other than the theater I spent a small fortune hiring."

"Patrick, I'm sorry," Merry said.

And then there was nothing left to say. A minute later, she walked down the stairs—with Lucas—and out onto the street.

A streetlamp bathed her dad's old pickup truck in light. A far cry from the comfort of the cab she'd arrived in.

And yet, despite Patrick's attention to detail, she'd been so disappointed to see him, to realize he was the one behind the most romantic surprise she could have imagined.

Lucas opened her door for her, then got in the other side.

"For the record," he said, "you look great. That dress is fantastic."

"Thanks." She pulled her seat belt out and clipped it in place.

"So what Patrick just did, that's your idea of wooing?" he said. "Champagne and a sappy movie?"

"Patrick was doing something for me that he wouldn't have done for anyone else."

"Because no one else would be turned on by a *Lassie* extravaganza," he said, starting the engine.

"You need to raise your game, Lucas," she said.

LUCAS MADE MERRY'S COFFEE THE next morning, as usual, even though she'd made it plain how little value she gave that kind of gesture in the wooing stakes.

You need to raise your game. He muttered a curse as he ran along the seafront promenade, Boo alongside him.

"Nothing wrong with my game," he said to the dog.

Boo slowed down, looking for a comfort stop. Lucas headed for a grass strip on the other side of the street.

"Go ahead," he told him. He paced the grass in an attempt to keep his muscles warm while the canine squatted, straining but not achieving.

"You know what your big mistake was?" he asked Boo. "You got too close to your owner. Then you couldn't stop her dying, and now you're a loner who can't crap."

Lucas's cell phone rang. He fished it out of his pocket.

"Calder, this is Admiral Tremaine."

Lucas came to attention. "Good morning, sir."

"I've been thinking about our discussion," the man said. "I agree, you should get a resit. And I intend to make it happen."

"Thank you, sir. That's excellent news." Given his preoccupation with Merry's unreasonable attitude, he didn't sound as pleased as he should. "That's great," he added with more enthusiasm.

The admiral chuckled. "Thought you'd be pleased. You deserve it, Calder. The navy needs more men— more people," he corrected hastily, "like you. We should be trying to keep you, not tossing you overboard on the basis of a wonky eye test."

"Thank you, sir."

"You need to call Dr. Ziegler at Groton," Tremaine said. "I spoke to her yesterday, and she'll be doing your test. I'll have the paperwork squared away by then."

So it was definite. Great. *If I pass the test, I'll leave New London. Leave Merry. And the baby.*

"I'll call the doctor, sir." Next week. Maybe the week after. Now wasn't great timing, not at this sensitive point of negotiations with his wife.

"See that you do," the admiral said. "She's on vacation after the first week in December, so you'll need to do it by then."

Only a couple of weeks away. Had his depth perception improved sufficiently? Lucas wasn't sure.

"That's great, sir." Definitely on the hollow side. Lucas thanked the admiral again and ended the call.

Okay, he had ten days to get his depth perception up to standard. The retest was what he'd come to New London for. After all this effort, he couldn't blow it. He would put every spare minute into practicing.

If he passed, everything would change with Merry—for the worse. The best time to convince her to give their marriage a chance was now, before he got his job back.

He had the same two weeks to convince Merry their marriage should be real.

The rate he was going, he wouldn't achieve that in ten *years*. He *did* need to raise his game.

I need a plan.

CHAPTER SIXTEEN

"YOUR BABY IS DUE JULY 17," the obstetrician said. "Congratulations."

"Thank you." Merry beamed at him.

"Fantastic," Lucas said.

They'd known she was pregnant, but something about having a date…

"Hop up here," Dr. Fellowes said, "and we'll do the sonogram."

Merry lay on the bed while the doctor smeared a jellylike substance on her lower abdomen. He ran the ultrasound wand over it, pressing down firmly.

Merry watched the screen, and what looked like a bad static storm, intently.

"There we go," he said.

On the screen a jellybean-shaped patch of black appeared among the snow. "The gestational sac," the doctor murmured. He adjusted something, then moved the wand slowly. "There."

Inside the jellybean was an oblong of static. "Your baby," Dr. Fellowes said, with a hint of showmanship. He moved the wand to find a flicker of light. "And that's the heartbeat."

There was nothing to see…and yet there was everything. Merry's throat tightened. She was dimly aware that Lucas had grabbed her hand and was squeezing hard.

The doctor took some measurements on the screen. "All looking good," he announced. "How are you feeling, Merry? You're paler than the last time I saw you."

Probably because she was exhausted. Beyond the normal pregnancy fatigue, trying to figure out the best future for her baby, and exactly what role Lucas should play in both their lives, was draining. Even more so because a week after he'd been shown up by Patrick in the romance stakes, his efforts to woo her were still off the radar. He'd been preoccupied, away from home a lot.

Stephanie had told her he'd visited at least twice, and was spending time with Mia. He hadn't mentioned that to Merry, so she could only assume his commitment to his baby sister was genuine, not just an attempt to impress her.

Which was good. *But what about me?*

"Lucas, you might want to see if you can find ways to help out, maybe ease Merry's tiredness?" the doctor asked.

Lucas looked oddly hesitant. "We're having a night out of town tomorrow," he said.

"Since when?" Merry asked.

"It was going to be a surprise. We're staying at the Pelican Inn in Old Saybrook."

"The Pelican Inn," Merry breathed.

"Very nice," the doctor said.

It was more than very nice. "Lucas, that's where Dad took my mom on their honeymoon."

"You don't say," he replied drily.

"That's why you chose it?" She'd heard so much about the historic inn from her dad, and had always longed to go.

"Romantic enough for you?" Lucas asked.

The question was casual, but she sensed he cared about the answer.

"It's perfect," she said. Taking her to the place where her parents' marriage had started was exactly what she was looking for. The kind of thing a man who loved her might do.

LUCAS SET DOWN HIS AND MERRY'S overnight bag in front of the reception desk at the Pelican Inn.

The hotel clerk leaned over the counter to look at Boo. "You must be Mr. and Mrs. Calder," she said.

"That's right." Lucas put his credit card on the marble surface. Merry didn't like to leave Boo alone at night because he supposedly "had nightmares." The fact that the inn was dog-friendly was a good omen, Lucas figured.

The woman began the check-in process. "I have you in the honeymoon suite." She swiped Lucas's card. "Your private dinner will be served at seven o'clock on your terrace."

"Excellent," he said. Merry wouldn't be able to accuse him of not going all out on the romance front. He had everything planned…except how to tell her he had an eye test next week and might be shipping out. But he expected to have a plan for that soon.

The receptionist handed over an old-fashioned key. "Enjoy your stay, Mr. and Mrs. Calder."

"Suite" was an exaggeration when it came to their first-floor room. The king-size bed, with a ridiculous number of cushions piled on the snowy pillows, took up a fair chunk of the space.

Merry stopped just inside the doorway. It was obvious she hadn't considered the sleeping arrangements.

Lucas hadn't thought about much else.

"There's a sofa bed over there," he said, pointing.

On the far side of the bed, in front of the French doors to the terrace, was a couch in an expensive-looking striped fabric. "I thought I'd give you the choice as to whether we share a bed or not," he said. "Just to sleep, of course."

He couldn't see the point of sleeping separately. When they'd agreed to look hard at their marriage and see if it could work in the long term. The ability to share a bed was a big part of that.

He hoped she'd view things his way.

"Okay," she said. Which wasn't an answer.

Merry unzipped her bag. She pulled out a book and a toiletry bag and set them on the nightstand. Next, a ziplock bag of dog food and a bowl. Boo licked his lips. "Too early, boy," she said. She bent over to slip his provisions into the space at the bottom of the nightstand. Her jeans tightened across her shapely butt.

The clock radio on the nightstand showed 4:00 p.m. Three hours until dinner.

Merry was looking at the clock, too. "I'll take Boo for a walk, in case he needs to go."

"He always *needs* to go," Lucas said.

"You never know when the dam will break," she said.

Lucas winced at the resulting image. She grinned as she clipped the leash back onto Boo's collar. "I may be a while."

"I need to do some eye exercises," Lucas said. "Take your time."

The minutes passed with frustrating slowness. He had brought several Magic Eye books with him—more out of desperation than hope they would do any good—plus his laptop. At least with the online tests, he was improving bit by bit. But he had no idea if he could pass the navy's eye exam.

He was concentrating so hard he barely noticed Merry's return. She read for a while, then showered. She came out of the bathroom wrapped in a towel, and told him he needed to stop work and get cleaned up. So he did.

She was out on the terrace, admiring the view, when Lucas joined her. The inn staff had left a bottle of champagne and one of sparkling water in the ice bucket next to the candlelit table. They'd gone all out: white cloth, gleaming silverware, crystal, the works.

He poured their respective drinks, then raised his in a toast. "To your parents. And the memory of your mom."

Merry clinked her glass against his. "Thanks," she said softly. She sipped her water, drawing his attention to her mouth. Again.

"You look beautiful," he said.

She wore the same slinky red dress she'd bought for her big date with Patrick the other night. *She thought that date was with me,* he reminded himself.

A waiter arrived with their appetizer, some kind of smoked salmon dish. Merry sat down. Lucas took the chair opposite, while Boo parked himself next to him, head on his paws.

Beyond the terrace, the sea was purple-blue in the dusk. Scattered clouds floated across the fading sky, ringed with the glow of the setting sun.

"How did your eye exercises go?" Merry asked.

"Not worth the paper they're printed on," he grumbled. This could be an opportunity to tell her he had a resit arranged. *Too soon.*

"This salmon is great," he said, tasting a mouthful.

"This is certainly an improvement on our other dates," she joked. "A step up from Pete's."

"Hey, I took you to Pete's because it was the coolest place in town," Lucas said. "Besides, expensive dates were wasted on you. Remember Date Number Six?"

"The French restaurant," she said appreciatively. "That was good."

"That was annoying," he corrected. Lucas had settled the bill for their dinner while she was in the bathroom. She'd meticulously counted out her share and stuffed it in his jacket pocket when he wouldn't take it. "For a woman who wants to be wooed, you're no good at accepting wooing when it comes your way."

"You wanted to pay because you thought it was the right thing to do. Not because you thought I was worth every last penny."

"Of course you were." He ate some more salmon.

She grinned. "Liar. We both know those dates happened because our dads wanted them to."

"That's why you wouldn't let me pay? Because you didn't like my motives?"

"Yep." Merry dredged some salmon through a pool of dill dressing. "But I plan to let you pay for tonight."

Which in her book was some weird vote of confidence.

"Thanks," Lucas said, and meant it. He drank some champagne. "You know, Merry, those dates might have been our dads' idea, but it's not like I dreaded them or anything."

She pressed a hand to her chest, drawing his attention to her curves. "Be still my heart."

"I even looked forward to seeing you each year," he said generously.

"Yeah, right," she said.

"Admittedly, that usually only lasted about half an hour, until you drove me nuts. But you are one of my oldest friends, Merry."

She gave him a quizzical look. "Funny, I had the impression that for most of our childhood you tolerated me, but didn't particularly like me."

"Why would you say that?" He set down his glass. "Of course I liked you. And still do." But her saying that cast a new light on some of their past arguments. "What did I do," he said curiously, "that made you decide you would never play the game my way? You'd never let me rescue you, you'd never need me. What did I do to ensure that you would never trust me, not even in a *game,* let alone in real life?" He hadn't planned to ask that. Was surprised that he had. But now, he wanted to know the answer.

She opened her mouth. Closed it again. "Of course I trust you. I'd trust you with my life."

"So what was the problem?" he asked.

"What we had was never friendship," she said. "Friends do things together."

"Exactly," he replied. "I spent more time with you than with any other single person."

"Those games we played as kids," she said, "always involved me being held captive somewhere, and you charging in to be the hero. They were never about the two of us trekking through enemy territory, fighting danger together."

"So what?" He had no idea what she meant. Besides, she'd always managed to change the agenda in their games, anyway.

"You're not about the shared journey, Lucas. You're about swooping in, saving the day, then swooping out."

"Someone has to save the day," he said, confused. "Why shouldn't it be me?"

"Maybe you would have saved it better if you'd had some help," she said. "My help."

"Okay, this is way too deep for me." They were talking about imaginary crises, for Pete's sake.

"Your depth perception issues," she murmured.

He snorted. "Seems to me you're the one with issues. I really valued you as a friend—I wanted to marry you when I was ten, remember? Even though you were the biggest pain in the butt I knew, I kept coming back for more."

"Wanting to marry me lasted exactly one day, as you pointed out," she said.

"You really think I hung out with you all those years because I had no other choice? That I had no other friends?"

She knew damn well he'd been one of the popular kids, though that had never mattered to him.

"I guess not." She sounded uncertain.

"All those years, you never truly believed I was your friend," he said with disgust. "And you're determined not to believe that I care for you now."

"It's not that…"

But the way she fidgeted with her water glass told

Lucas it was that. He'd forced her to confront her own attitude and now she was rattled. Good.

Before Lucas could press his case, the waiter appeared with their next course: filet mignon, cooked perfectly, medium rare. A baked apricot cheesecake followed. Throughout the rest of the meal, the conversation stayed on safe topics. Merry was an expert at keeping it that way.

It was only nine-thirty when they finished dinner, but she was visibly exhausted. "I'm pretty tired," she said. "I think I'll get to bed." She nudged Boo with her shoe. "Up, boy. Time for your constitutional."

"I'll take him," Lucas offered.

"Thanks."

They walked back into the room through the French doors.

That king-size bed beckoned. This was the moment of truth.

"What did you decide about the sleeping arrangements?" Lucas kept the words innocuous, his tone casual. She clasped her hands behind her head and stretched. It had the effect of pushing out her breasts. She looked from him to the bed.

He held his breath. *Pick me. Pick me.*

"I'd rather we had separate beds," she said.

Disappointment gushed through him. It must have shown, because she said, "Look what happened the last time we slept together." She put a hand to her stomach, and he thought of the sonogram, of that tiny heartbeat.

"I was only talking about sleep. Besides, you can't get pregnant again," he said.

"I mean, we didn't enjoy it," she said. "It could have wrecked our friendship."

"What friendship?" Disappointment made him rude. "From what you said tonight, you never thought we had a friendship at all."

He clipped the lead to Boo's collar and left.

CHAPTER SEVENTEEN

LUCAS TOOK BOO FOR A WALK along the beach. In the end, after much effort, the dog produced three marbles of poop, rock-hard when Lucas scooped them up with a bag. "Good job, buddy," he said encouragingly as he dropped the output in a trash can. "Your life is going better than mine."

When they got back to the room, the sofa bed had been made up. Merry was already in the real bed, covers drawn to her chin, eyes closed. Boo turned around a couple of times, then lay at her feet.

Lucas didn't think she was asleep, but he had no desire to talk. He grabbed his toiletry kit and headed for the bathroom. When he came out, the room was dark. She'd been awake, then. He groped his way to the sofa. A snuffling snore came from Merry's bed, suggesting she wasn't awake any longer. As he slid between crisply laundered sheets, the one good thing about hotels, he hoped her snoring wouldn't keep him awake.

He must have fallen instantly asleep, because soon he was dreaming. He was in his mom's car outside Clark's Deli. He and Garrett were arguing over which radio station to listen to, when he saw a face pressed against the store window, mouthing something. His dream self, twelve years old, scrambled out of the car, pushing Garrett aside. In the next moment, he was in the store, kneeling beside his mom, doing chest compressions. His hands were slippery, wet with tears he couldn't stop, which rained down as he counted out fifteen compressions. Then two breaths, into her mouth, then back to the compressions. Hands reached out, trying to pull him away, but he hunched over and doggedly kept going. And then he felt it. The merest whisper, flicker of life. "Yes," he shouted, triumphant, and redoubled his efforts. "Mom, yes."

Behind him, someone howled.

Lucas sat bolt upright.

A dream. He hadn't been there. Hadn't saved her.

The howl, though, was real. It came again. And again.

"What the hell?" *The damn dog.* Lucas shook his head to throw off the fog of sleep as he groped for a light switch. He vaguely remembered a lamp next to his sofa, but couldn't find it. A clattering from across the room suggested Merry had the same problem. She said something that he didn't hear over the howling.

Lucas's arm knocked into something that felt suspiciously like a lamp. It crashed to the floor. He swore and pushed his covers back, got out of bed and tripped over Boo—damn animal had moved. As Lucas went flying forward, Merry's lamp snapped on. A second later he landed on top of her.

At least now he could see where he was. Which turned out to be half off, half on her bed, facedown on her thighs. He'd been worse places.

He registered silence. Or, more precisely, the absence of howling. He could hear two sets of breaths: short puffs from Merry and panting from the dog.

Now that she was partway out from under the covers,

he saw she was wearing a cherry-red camisole. One strap had slid off her right shoulder, baring the line of her collarbone and the gentle swell of her breast.

Then she said, "Are you planning on lying there all night?" and she sounded like Merry, not like some seductress.

"My apologies, Mrs. Calder."

Lucas braced himself with a hand either side of her and pushed himself upright. He was annoyed to feel not entirely steady. "What's wrong with your damn dog?"

The animal was now sound asleep at Lucas's feet, as if he'd never made that racket.

"Just one of his nightmares," Merry said. She shuffled up against her pillows. "Patrick says dogs do dream, and Boo's done it before.... I think he's missing Ruby, his owner."

Boo's ears twitched at the name.

"Maybe I should tie him up out on the terrace," Lucas said. "You need your rest."

"Actually, you're the one who woke me, before Boo started," she said. "You were talking in your sleep."

"I wasn't." He realized his heart was still thumping with the adrenaline of performing CPR on his mother.

"You were dreaming," she said. "Shouting. You said *Mom*."

"I don't think so."

She wriggled higher up the pillows. "Do you dream about her often?"

"Nope." This was the first time in a long time. He wondered why it had come back now. "Good night," he said.

"I remember when she died." She rubbed her eyes. "You were twelve, going on thirteen."

Lucas grunted.

"It was in April or May? It must have been around five in the evening. Garrett had gone shopping with her."

"It was April 19. Garrett's fifteenth birthday," Lucas said.

His elaboration of the details surprised Merry. That dream, whatever it was, must have unsettled him. She'd forgotten that his mother had died on Garrett's birthday. Poor Garrett.

"Mom told him she was going to buy milk, but really she needed candles for his cake. They were only supposed to be gone ten minutes."

"You stayed at home."

"It was just a stupid errand." He tipped his head back. "I should have been there."

He sounded so bleak, Merry caught her breath. "You think you could have saved her?"

He gave a barely discernible shrug. "For years afterward, I used to lie awake imagining how things might have been different if I'd been there. I was in the sea cadets. I'd had training in CPR." He lowered his gaze to hers. "Someone, a guy in the store, did give Mom CPR. Garrett tried, too, after they called him in. But in my head I used to picture myself shoving that bystander guy out of the way and taking over. Doing it better than he did. Better than Garrett did, too."

Merry couldn't stop herself from touching Lucas's hand on the duvet.

He didn't seem to notice. "In the dream, I keep trying,

long after the other dude would have given up, long after it was possible to save her. And in the dream, she…lives."

"You don't… Lucas, you don't feel guilty that you weren't there, do you?" Merry asked.

He started, as if he'd forgotten her presence. He slid his hand out from beneath hers. "Of course not." His face closed up. "Go to bed, Merry."

Realization dawned.

"That's why you decided to stay married to me," she said. "You were afraid that if we filed for divorce, and then my dad died…"

"I wasn't *afraid*," he said.

"You didn't want it on your conscience, then." No, that wasn't right, either. "You didn't want to miss a chance to save him," she said. *That* was it.

Lucas's expression turned stony. Every rigid inch of him telegraphed that he didn't want to have this conversation.

"Lucas, I'm so sorry I put that burden on you." Though she couldn't say she wouldn't have done it, even if she'd known. Her dad's survival was paramount. But she might have found a way to make it easier for Lucas.

"There's no burden," he said coldly.

She leaned forward. "Lucas…"

He looked blatantly down at her camisole, which had slipped forward.

"Another half inch, honeybun, and things might start to get interesting," he said, his voice deeper than it had been a moment ago.

It was such a flagrant attempt at distraction, she laughed.

He hooked the front of her camisole with his finger.

"Lucas! I'm trying to talk to you."

"I don't want to talk." He held her gaze. "Did you know your hair has gold glints in this lamplight?"

She swallowed. "That's very poetic."

"I'm a romantic kind of guy." His gaze settled on her mouth. "I just realized I forgot to kiss my wife goodnight."

"I'm not that kind of wife," she reminded him breathlessly.

"I think it would help settle Boo down. Give him a feel of being with family."

"You're not thinking at all," she said.

"Maybe you're right. Maybe that's a good thing." His lips met hers in a kiss that was there one moment, gone the next.

Yet when he pulled back, she was trembling.

"You should go back to your bed now," she said shakily.

He shook his head. "I'd like to try something different." The heat in his eyes drew her in.

"What's that?" she breathed.

"I'd like to make love to you when someone isn't about to die."

She stared. "You think that's the problem?"

"I'm sure of it," he said.

"You don't think it's that you're bad in bed? Sarah said you are."

He huffed a laugh, which she thought was pretty generous, given the subject. "And Sarah knows this how?"

"Just a good guess."

"Or a not so good guess," he said. "Trust me, honeybun, the problem isn't that either of us is bad in bed."

"Oh." She considered that. "It could be that you're not sufficiently attracted to me."

"That is the stupidest thing you've said in all the years I've known you. And that's saying a lot."

She laughed.

He stopped the laugh with his mouth on hers.

Hot, questing. No hesitation.

A kiss wouldn't hurt. When Lucas probed the seam of her lips with his tongue, she opened for him.

"I love your mouth," he murmured. "So good."

"It's just a mouth," she said against his, enjoying the vibration of the words.

He pulled back, traced her lips with one finger. "I'm considering this mouth for the title of Merry's Greatest Asset." Before she could guess what he'd do next, both hands went to the bottom of her camisole. He peeled it up and stared. "On second thought, honeybun…"

She laughed, self-conscious but pleased. Her breasts were so unimpressive…yet no way was he faking the reverence with which he gazed at them.

"Make love to me, Lucas," she murmured.

There was a moment of suspended tension…and then a rush of tugging and undressing, a tangle of limbs and lips.

When they were both lying completely naked, he paused.

Oh, no, not again.

This time, she would say it first. "Maybe we should—"

"Quiet, Petty Officer Wyatt," he ordered. "No talking during inspection."

She sighed, feigning exasperation. "Aye, aye, Captain."

He grinned. "That's the first time you've ever said that to me." He propped himself up one elbow and perused her body from head to toe. She'd never felt so exposed in her life…and yet she'd never felt so wanted.

"Did I pass inspection?" she murmured.

"With flying colors," he said.

Then he moved down and kissed her stomach.

From that moment, things turned serious.

Lucas made love with passion, intensity, determination. Like a hero.

Merry was powerless. She was powerful. She adored every second. And when they were both deliciously, exhaustedly complete, she knew things would never be the same again.

CHAPTER EIGHTEEN

LUCAS WOKE TO THE GLARE OF sunshine through an imperfectly closed curtain, and the sound of waves. It took him a moment to remember.

The Pelican Inn.

Merry.

Incredible. Finally, they'd made love and got it right.

More than right. Lucas had never experienced anything like last night. If this was married sex, no wonder the institution was so popular.

He turned his head to the right so he could see her. Still asleep, facing him, one hand tucked beneath her cheek, a half smile on her lips.

He wanted her all over again.

We get to have sex like that for the rest of our lives.

Because if last night had achieved anything besides sublime pleasure, it had brought them together in a way he hadn't suspected was possible. Not even Merry could deny that they had the ingredients to make their marriage work.

It dawned on him he'd be one of those navy guys with a wife and kid, a family either back home or on a navy base, depending where he was deployed.

In the past, he'd imagined that being a distraction at best, a burden at worst. He'd never "got" the sentimentality that made men carry letters from wives and messy drawings from kids in their chest pocket, over their heart. The photos taped inside lockers, the playing over and over again of "our song" on iPods...

Now those things seemed...still kitsch. But kind of cool.

Beside Lucas, Merry stirred, opened her eyes.

"Hi." Her smile widened. "Wow."

"Yeah." He suspected his grin was sappy, but he didn't care. He kissed her, slowly and tenderly, with the sensual leisure of a man who had all the time in the world to please his wife.

Boo woofed next to the bed, jerking them apart.

Lucas cursed.

Merry laughed. "He's probably hungry. I know I'm starving."

"You're the great romantic in this marriage. Shouldn't you be surviving on passion?"

"Passion plus breakfast," she said. "Do they do room service?"

He pushed the covers aside and got out of bed, aware she was watching his nakedness.

While he ordered a hearty breakfast, she disappeared into the bathroom. A minute later, he heard the shower running. When she came out, she was dressed in skinny black velvet jeans and that cream cable-knit sweater she'd worn on the boat. She looked *touchable*.

"I'll take Boo out while you're in the shower," she said.

She came back just as their breakfast arrived, and they sat down to pancakes with a side order of scrambled eggs. Merry took one look at her plate and shuddered.

"I just lost my appetite. I've been queasy the past couple of mornings and it just got worse."

He pushed his chair back. "What can I get you?"

"Stay where you are," she said. "It's morning sickness—it happens to almost everyone. I'll drink some orange juice for the vitamin C, and maybe try a dry pancake."

Lucas thought about suggesting a doctor, but Merry was a woman who knew her own mind. Reluctantly, he returned to his meal. She seemed okay, sipping her freshly squeezed orange juice.

"So, honeybun," Lucas said, "we need to map out where to go from here. We can't keep living at your dad's place."

"As I see it, we have a few other things to cover before we get to where we live. Shouldn't we figure out the state of our relationship first?"

He poured syrup over his pancakes. "The state is pretty obvious, honeybun."

She set down her glass. "Go ahead, enlighten me."

Lucas paused. There was an edge to her tone that made him think he might have just walked into a minefield. Without a mine detector. But, hey, he was an expert on minefields. And after last night, how dangerous could this conversation be?

He chewed his mouthful and swallowed before answering. "First up, I'd say last night debunked the 'we're incompatible' myth."

"True," she said with a saucy smile that turned him on all over again.

Beneath the table, he captured her foot between his. "In fact, that was the best sex of my life."

She laughed, blushed. "Mine, too," she admitted.

"Which is a damn good thing for a marriage," he pointed out.

She tore a piece off one of her pancakes and put it in her mouth. "True."

This was all going nicely. Time to move her along. "I believe," he said, "that if you and I are prepared to work at it—which I know I am—we could make this marriage great. We could have a strong partnership." An inspired choice of words, after what she'd said last night about those games they'd played back in the day.

Incredible that for all those years, she'd had it wrong.

"Plus, I think we can be great parents to our child," he said. "We can be great parents separately, but I think we'll be better together."

There. He'd laid his cards on the table.

He inclined his head to her. *Show us what you've got.*

"Here's where I'm coming from." Merry wiped her fingers on her napkin with a deliberation that didn't bode well.

Dammit, did she always have to come from somewhere other than where he was? She'd accused him of doing his own thing without involving her, but when had she ever tried to bring him along with her?

"Last night was amazing," she said. "In fact, I didn't know—"

"It could be so good," he agreed. Their eyes met, and there was a moment of almost shocking intimacy as her mind and his went to the same place.

Maybe they could take the rest of the conversation as a given and go back to bed.

Merry swallowed. "Last night was a beginning, not an end."

"Absolutely," he said.

"A step that brought us closer to one day being able to say yes, this is it, this is forever."

It took Lucas a moment to process that. "Wait a minute," he said. "Last night was the beginning of the rest of our lives." Which sounded so much like a bad greeting card, he almost gagged.

Merry did gag. She clamped a hand over her mouth and ran for the bathroom.

"Sorry," she said when she came back a minute later. "And no, I don't need a doctor." She sat down again. "This isn't quite how I imagined this conversation going," she said ruefully.

"Me, neither." Lucas wasn't sure what he'd imagined, but it hadn't been this feeling that Merry was calling the shots. He was pretty sure bed would have featured at the end of it.

"One thing I've learned in the past few weeks," she said, "is that all those ideals I have in my head, about how love works, and how family works…they only go so far."

"You mean, real life is messier?" Lucas suggested. He knew that, but was surprised to hear her say it. It was, he thought, a good sign.

"Messier," she agreed. "But also potentially more rewarding. If you're prepared to work at it. I've accepted that a relationship—a marriage—isn't always going to be the romantic idyll my parents were blessed with. I've even decided that compromising doesn't have to mean settling for less than wonderful."

"So, you're saying more or less what I'm saying." That sounded too good to be true.

"Not really," she said.

There you go.

"Lucas…" She shredded some pancake between her fingers. "What exactly do you feel for me?"

Merry watched the play of expressions across Lucas's face: distaste, dismay, resolution.

The question needed to be asked. Otherwise, a girl might make important decisions based on the euphoria of last night's lovemaking, only to discover she'd made some wrong assumptions.

Lucas put down his knife and fork, his gaze fixed on the rim of his plate, where a blob of maple syrup had landed. "I guess I should have seen that one coming," he said lightly.

She waited for him to sift through his thoughts. As she'd told him, she'd come a long way in the past few weeks. She wanted to believe he had, too. If it took him some time to figure that out…

He lifted his head. "I love you, Merry."

Her heart leaped in her chest; her brain said, *Don't get excited, not just yet.*

"I do," he said, sounding stunned. "I really do love you."

Merry crumpled her linen napkin and set it on the table. Now for the hard question. "What do you love about me?"

He blinked. Raked a hand through his hair. "Am I supposed to answer that? I only now realized how I feel."

"Just tell me what's on your mind," she said lightly. "And then I'll tell you."

Because the realization she'd had in the night would burst out of her heart if she didn't say it soon.

Please, let him love me the way I love him.

He puffed out a breath and flexed his fingers on the table, as if she'd asked him to lift a two-hundred-pound weight.

"I feel differently about you than I have about any other woman," he said.

Good start. She smiled in encouragement.

"The fact that we're already friends makes it easy to love you," he said. "I know you're going to be a wonderful mom, just like you're great with Mia. I love making love to you, and I want us to do that forever. You're cute, and pretty and loyal." He stopped, as if even he could hear how scrappy his answer was.

Merry swallowed her hurt. Lucas was new to the idea of emotional commitment; she couldn't expect miracles. Best to lead by example.

"Let me tell you what I love about you," she said.

Surprise and pleasure flared in his eyes. "Really? You love me, too?"

She nodded.

He leaned back in his chair, his face alight with anticipation, his posture wide open as if to say, *Lay it on me.*

"Let me start with the obvious. I love making love to you," she said. "I love your hands and your mouth, and the things you do with them."

"Duly noted," he said.

"I love that you have so much physical strength, but your touch can be gentle and coaxing. I love that you use your strength to protect others. That you care what happens to the people around you, and you take it upon yourself to get involved…even when you're misguided."

"Thanks, I think."

"I love that you make decisions based on a skewed view of what you can do and what you're responsible for. I love that you jumped into this marriage because you were too kind to disappoint my dad, even though I forced you into it. And then you stuck around because you have this crazy idea that you can't let anyone die on your watch."

"That's not—"

"I love that beneath your swoop-in, swoop-out attitude, there's a man who loves for a long time, who honors the people who've shaped his life. Your dad has been a jerk for as long as I can remember, but you've always respected him—and you offered my dad a kidney out of respect for the connection between our families. And when I called you on your attitude to Mia, you made a real effort with her, even though you couldn't see the point of getting to know a one-year-old."

His smile had turned uncertain.

"And your mom," she said. "I love that it still hurts you to think of her. I love that you're too stubborn to talk about her, but you keep her in your dreams. I love that you have this inflated view of your own abilities that lets you think you might have saved her."

"That's enough," he said sharply.

"I love your bossiness, your integrity, your unreasonable conviction that your way is always the right way. I love how you're fearless in the face of death, but petrified in the face of love."

She stopped. Lucas wasn't smiling anymore.

His expression was a mix of shock, pity, confusion. And understanding of what she'd been trying to tell him: that when he said I love you and she said I love you, they were talking about two different things.

"I love you, Lucas," she said. "Not as a good husband or a great father, though I'm sure you'll be those things. I love that you need me—"

He recoiled.

"—even though you don't know it. I don't want a hero, Lucas. I don't need you to rescue me, and I won't stop loving you if you fail. I love *you,* for better or for worse, no matter what."

She stopped, her heart completely bared.

THERE WAS A LONG SILENCE.

Lucas poured himself a cup of coffee from the pot on the table between them. It saved him having to speak for another moment or two.

He didn't know what to say. He'd been happy—proud, even—to lay out the feelings he had for her. Believing they would, what—impress her? Move her into staying married to him?

His offering had been a carefully measured teaspoonful. Hers was an overflowing bowl, an extravagant mix of words that made no sense and truths that pinged somewhere deep inside him, thoughts spoken in a language he only half understood.

One thing he did understand: her feelings were in a different league from his.

He sipped the coffee, which was almost cold.

He had two choices. Accept the vast gap between

them—and its implications—or step up into her league. Pulling her down to his wasn't an option.

"Merry, I'm honored by your feelings," he said. "But we want different things. I do love you, please believe that."

She bit her lip.

"But you have a picture of me as this vulnerable person who... And I guess there is some of that in me," he conceded. "But that's not the person I want to be. I don't want to be open to—to all that. I want to be back in the Gulf, doing what I do best."

She nodded. "I understand."

His laugh was shaky. Tomorrow, he would be his old self again, he promised silently. "You're doing better than I am, then," he said. "I'm in way over my head."

"Poor Lucas." Her smile was sympathetic, not teasing.

"When the baby comes," he said, "you'll help me to be a good dad, right? Even though we won't be together." He understood that now, though acceptance might take a while. "You'll tell me when I screw up."

"I tell you that now. Why would things change?"

He laughed, reassured that she sounded like the old Merry. Despite all that had happened, they might still be friends. "I know you don't want my help," he said. "But you're going to have to accept it as far as our child is concerned. Financial help, help with finding a house, making those big decisions..."

"Performing the Heimlich maneuver," she interjected.

"Definitely." He rubbed his palms down his face. "And I'll put in a leave request so I can come back when the baby's due. I want to be here."

She touched her stomach briefly. "You think you'll get a retest, then? Did your father say something?"

"I already heard from Admiral Tremaine," Lucas said, feeling embarrassed. "I have a new physical scheduled next Friday."

She absorbed that fact, and the fact that he hadn't told her. Her face gave nothing away. "If you pass, you'll go back to the Gulf right away?"

"Yeah."

"If you're leaving, we need to tell our parents the truth," she said.

"What about your dad's blood pressure?" Lucas asked.

"Keeping up this marriage act was always a temporary thing while you waited for a retest," she reminded him. "Dad's had a few weeks of more stable blood pressure, and Cathy will be monitoring him."

Lucas folded his napkin. "I suppose you'll want to file for divorce before I go."

"Actually…I was thinking we could wait until after the baby's born," she said. "That way there'll be no confusion about your parental rights."

"Thanks, Merry." He touched her hand across the table. "I wish we'd been able to work this out better."

"It was never going to work," she said.

"How would you know?" he asked, annoyed. She sounded like the smart-aleck Merry who liked to foil his plans.

"Ask yourself this question." Her smile was sweet, but sad. "If I wasn't pregnant, would you want to stay married to me?"

Why hadn't he asked himself that question before? Because he didn't like the answer.

CHAPTER NINETEEN

"WHERE'S LUCAS?" MERRY'S father asked when she arrived at Cathy's town house alone that evening.

"Long story. I'll tell you tomorrow." She and Lucas had agreed they would give their parents the news of their divorce the following day. She'd declined his offer to come with her this evening. Why bother with another night of pretense? Besides, she needed some time away from him. "I need a drink," she told her dad. Then she remembered. "Of orange juice," she said without enthusiasm.

Cathy's place was cozier than Merry might have expected for a woman who acted so aloof. Her dad had said she'd lost her twin sister recently. Maybe that was why she was so moody.

She certainly didn't seem bad-tempered tonight. She wasn't effusive—Merry suspected she didn't have that in her—but she smiled and made easy conversation. When she looked at John, she seemed to glow with pleasure.

Did the nurse love him? In the way that he deserved to be loved? If so, then who was Merry to say they shouldn't be together? She'd learned that compromise was not only possible, but desirable in her own life; it might prove key to her father's happiness, too.

As they chatted over a predinner drink, Merry's resentment lessened. If Cathy and her dad could work out a way to be happy, then Merry shouldn't hold him to his undying love for her mother. Of course, that old love didn't have to die, even if he found happiness again.

"Is this you with your sister?" Merry asked Cathy, crossing to a framed photograph on the living-room wall. Silly question, since the two women in the photo were identical. Even though the clothing suggested the picture had been taken in the eighties, there was enough of today's Cathy in the women to make it clear who they were.

"Yes." She seemed glad to be asked. "That was taken on vacation in the Florida Keys. Rue loved the sun."

In a spirit of conciliation, Merry examined a couple more photos and asked enough questions not only to please Cathy, but to limit opportunities for her dad to quiz her about Lucas's absence.

"Unfortunately, I don't have any photos of the two of us that are less than ten years old," Cathy said when they reached the end of the collection. "I kept hundreds of them on my digital camera, but Rue took it on vacation with her. It got lost in the confusion after her heart attack, and never turned up among her belongings."

She went very quiet at that. Merry cast around for another topic of conversation. She found it on the wall: a cross-stitched sampler that read "The more people I meet, the more I like my dog."

"This is cute," Merry said. "Did you make it?"

Cathy nodded. "For Rue's birthday, a few years ago now. She loved dogs, but I was never a dog person, I must admit. I gave her dog away when she died. I didn't think I could look after him with my shift work." She pressed her lips together. "Sometimes I wish I'd kept him." She looked tearful, and Merry winced. It seemed all roads led to her twin sister.

"Maybe you should get a dog of your own," John said. "For companionship."

"I have enough companionship." Cathy smiled warmly at him.

Merry saw her father's ever-so-slight withdrawal. Uh-oh. She hoped she hadn't been so negative about the nurse that she'd put him off.

When her father excused himself to go the bathroom, Merry said, "Cathy, tell me honestly, how do you rate Dad's health at the moment? His blood pressure?"

She switched into efficient nurse mode. "He's doing great. His BP is consistently around the 150 over 100 mark. I'm hopeful it will go lower—the doctor is still tweaking the dosage and mix of drugs."

"So you think it's the drug that's helping," Merry said. "Rather than the fact that he's not worrying about me."

"Everything helps," Cathy said. She hesitated. "I know this is none of my business, but are you asking if a change in your marital situation—a separation or divorce, for example—would send your father's blood pressure up?"

Merry grimaced. "I knew you saw that message on my phone."

"I don't want to know any details," Cathy said. "My concern has only ever been your father's health."

"Lucas and I plan to tell our parents tomorrow that we're splitting," Merry said. "I'm worried how Dad will react.

"Truthfully, it's not helpful," Cathy said. "But over-all, your father's health is much better than it was before. Bad news of the kind you're talking about might cause a short-term spike, but that can be taken into account by the doctor monitoring the efficacy of his meds. Plus," she added carefully, "your father has someone in his life to share the stresses."

She meant herself, of course.

"I'm sorry I was rude to you when you came to my place for dinner," Merry said. "I behaved like a spoiled brat."

She guessed she shouldn't be surprised when Cathy nodded, rather than uttering platitudes about how Merry hadn't been that bad.

"Is there any other news you'll be telling your father?" Cathy's gaze flickered in the direction of Merry's stomach.

"What makes you think…"

"You're drinking orange juice while looking long-ingly at my wineglass, and I've noticed you scratching your palms once or twice." She took Merry's right hand and turned it over. "Palmar erythema—often starts in the second month of pregnancy. Your palms will be pink and itchy probably right through the birth." In response to Merry's questioning look, she said, "I've done my share of obstetric nursing."

Somewhere down the hallway, the toilet flushed. Her father would return any moment.

"I don't want Dad to know before twelve weeks," Merry said. "It would be devastating if something went wrong."

"He won't hear it from me," Cathy said.

John returned from the bathroom to find his daughter and his girlfriend—after half a dozen dates, Cathy probably qualified for that title—getting along just fine.

"Let's eat," Cathy said in a tone that almost qualified as bright.

John had brought a birthday cake as his contribution to the meal, along with a birthday present for Cathy. Merry had brought flowers, which she'd handed over when she arrived. He should have given his gift then, but he'd missed the moment. It sat on the sideboard, wrapped in red paper, tied with a gold ribbon, as they ate chicken casserole, then sang "Happy Birthday" and cut the cake.

He'd spent hours, days, deciding how personal this present should be. Yes, he and Cathy were dating. But they weren't intimate, and he still had that sense that if she walked out of his life tomorrow, he wouldn't miss her.

Now he worried that his present had been sitting there so long, she'd be thinking it was something really significant.

He went to get it from the sideboard. "You'd better open this." He wished the store hadn't used such fancy wrapping, but it had been easier to accept their offer of free giftwrap than do it himself.

"Thank you, John." She met his eyes, smiled.

"It's nothing much," he warned, but he could tell by the careful way she undid the ribbon and slid a fingernail under the tape that she wasn't listening.

Merry was watching as if it was a big deal, too. John felt suddenly hot. Maybe if he said he wasn't feeling well… Come to think of it, he was a bit achy….

Too late. Cathy pulled away the last of the red paper and opened the plain white box. She pulled out his gift.

A coffee mug. Emblazoned with the slogan Nurses are IV Leaguers. It had seemed funny in the shop.

Cathy turned the mug around in her hands, as if to check there wasn't more to it. She turned it upside down.

"It's bone china," John said. "Dishwasher safe." Ugh, he was trying to sell her on a gift that looked cheap and thoughtless. It hadn't been that cheap—in his book, twenty-five bucks was a lot for a cup—but now it looked tacky.

"I'm pretty tired. I think I might get going." Merry jumped to her feet. "Cathy, that dinner was delicious, and I so enjoyed talking to you."

John stayed sitting while Cathy saw Merry to the door. Cathy hadn't said a word about the mug yet, not even the neutral thank-you he'd expected.

She came back, sat down. Still saying nothing.

"I'm sorry it's not a very special gift," John said. "I couldn't think of anything." Which wasn't true. He'd discarded earrings, a journal and a scarf as too personal.

"No problem," Cathy said. "After all, it's not like you're serious about me."

John blushed. "We haven't known each other long." *I should have got the damn earrings.*

"And you have no intention of loving anyone the way you loved your wife," she said helpfully.

"It's a big jump between a few dates and falling in love," he said in his own defense. "I don't know if you and I might end up together in the longer term. But I'm not ruling it out." He stopped, appalled. He sounded like an arrogant jerk.

"I *am* ruling it out," she said, so calmly that it took a moment for her meaning to sink in.

"What?" he said.

"I admire the fact that you still love your wife and still

miss her," she said. "I understand that it's not easy to date again. It certainly hasn't been easy for me."

He hadn't thought much about her side of their relationship.

"It's been worth pushing myself through the hard parts," Cathy said, "because I like you. A lot. The fact is, John, I could love you."

His heart started beating faster. "Cathy, I—"

"Quiet," she barked, in what Merry would call her Nurse Ratched manner. John shut up. "Perhaps at my age I should be lowering my expectations," she said. "But I don't believe I'm such a bad bargain that the best I can hope for is a man who's settling."

"It's not like that," he said, the back of his neck burning.

"Are you offering more than that, John?" she asked. "Can I expect ever to be more than a runner-up to Sally? A consolation prize?"

Her brown eyes fixed on his with that steady intensity he was getting used to. He owed her honesty.

"No," he said. "You can't."

CHAPTER TWENTY

MERRY WASN'T SURPRISED to hear the next day, Sunday, that her dad and Cathy had broken up.

That mug had been a terrible gift.

Her father seemed quiet, but not depressed, so she and Lucas went ahead and told him, along with Dwight and Stephanie, that the marriage they'd rushed into for John's benefit wasn't working. That they would separate immediately and "at some stage in the next few months" they would divorce.

Handling the questions and "helpful" suggestions from their fathers took a couple of hours, but at last they convinced everyone that no one had a broken heart (not entirely true) and that they were still friends. Which, oddly enough, *was* true. Even without the fact they were having a baby, something about having known Lucas forever made it impossible for Merry to contemplate cutting him out of her life in order to allow her heart to heal.

John planned to move back into his cottage the following day, so Merry and Lucas went there to pack.

"Dad will probably be pleased to be home," Merry said as they walked into the house.

"Will you stay with him?" Lucas asked.

She shook her head. "I've missed my apartment. So you could stay on here if you'd rather not be with your parents."

"I'll think about it." He let Boo in from the backyard. In keeping with his new preferences, Boo ignored Merry and spent his time getting under Lucas's feet.

"He'll miss you," Merry said.

Lucas nudged the dog with his knee. "He's not a bad mutt. But he'd be losing me to the Gulf soon, anyway."

Merry felt that potential loss far more keenly than Boo, but she said nothing. They both packed up their possessions and replaced the furnishings where John had had them.

By lunchtime, they'd unraveled the brief life they'd built together.

"That's it, then," Lucas said, as Merry pulled the front door shut behind them.

She headed to her Aveo, Lucas to Stephanie's BMW, which he'd borrowed.

Merry opened her car door. "Good luck with your eye test."

"Thanks. But I'll probably see you before that."

"Probably," she agreed. *Not if I can help it.* Lucas wouldn't be at work this week, since he planned to spend as much time as possible preparing for his physical. It would be best if she didn't see him at all.

She loved Lucas, far more than he loved her, and it hurt. That wouldn't be so easily unraveled.

IN THE SUN PORCH THAT SERVED as an occasional studio, John looked at the sketches he'd drawn the day he and Cathy went fishing. He still hadn't had a chance to paint any of them. The good news, since she had dumped him and he was back in his own home, was that he had all the time in the world.

It was Wednesday, four days after her birthday dinner and the mug fiasco.

Four days in which he'd felt relieved to be rid of a relationship he hadn't wanted in the first place.

Four days in which he'd felt out of sorts and niggled.

He'd tested his blood pressure several times. There was a slight rise. Any change in routine or environment could impact the reading, and over the past few weeks he'd gotten used to having Cathy—

He didn't want to think about her, and, yes, some of that was due to a sense of guilt. He'd known she cared more about him than he did about her. She was the one who'd done all the asking out, after that initial date. But he wasn't obliged to love her, just because she "could love" him, was he?

The vulnerability of that admission still haunted him.

John rubbed his temples. It didn't help that he was coming down with the flu. He'd thought it was embarrassment heating him up that night at Cathy's place, but since then his limbs had been aching, and when he felt his forehead he thought he could detect a mild fever.

He looked at his sketches again, holding them up to the early-afternoon light. The seascape with Jonkers Island... He'd paint that.

He hoped Cathy was all right. He'd called her home and her cell phone a few times, wanting to reassure himself, and with the idea of preserving some kind of platonic link. She hadn't picked up.

He pottered around, setting up his easel, then paints, brushes, water, rags. He found the swivel stool he liked to sit on when he was painting in the kitchen; the kids must have moved it. He carried it back to the sunporch, as easily as he would have done twenty years ago. The marvels of modern medicine. And hospitals. And nurses.

John planted himself on the stool. He gripped the edge for balance as he closed his eyes, and tried to picture the sea that day, the dappling effect of the sky on the waves. Jonkers Island, harsh and gray, breaking out of the water.

He was having trouble building the image in his head. Instead, he saw Cathy, sitting in the middle of the boat, her face by turns serious and animated. She'd been talking about her sister, Rue.

He wondered what she was up to right now. If she was lonely. John had had twenty-three years to get used to being alone, while Cathy had only had a year without Rue.

She should get a dog. That'd cheer her up.

Maybe I'll get her a dog. It would make up for that dreadful mug.

Cathy had mentioned Rue's dog a few times, and been fiercely adamant—too adamant?—that she would have struggled to look after it. But John had heard the wistfulness in her voice. He wondered what sort of dog Rue had owned. Wondered if Cathy would prefer one of those big, protective breeds—a husky or the like—or a miniature something-or-other that she could take anywhere. Her town house had only a small garden, but if Merry could manage Boo in her apartment with just that tiny terrace… Mind you, it helped that Merry didn't have to worry about getting Boo to a toilet area. Who ever heard of a dog mourning its owner for this long?

Wait a minute. Didn't Boo's owner…? Could it be…? Nah. Not a chance.

Maybe.

John picked up the phone and called Merry.

"What did you say the name of Boo's owner was?" he asked.

"Ruby. Ruby Kramer. Why?"

Ruby. Rue. More than possible. Cathy's sister had been married, so he wouldn't expect to recognize her surname.

"You said she died on vacation overseas, right?" he asked. "About a year ago? Of a heart attack?" New London had a population of about twenty thousand people. How likely was it that *two* women from the town had died from a heart attack while on vacation overseas late last year?

"She was on a cruise," Merry confirmed. "In the Caribbean."

Rue had died in a hospital in the Bahamas.

"Brace yourself, Merry-Berry," John said. "I have news."

THE DOCTOR HAD CLEARED JOHN for driving on Monday, but he hadn't yet gotten behind the wheel. He felt shaky and odd as he drove to Merry's apartment at about twenty miles an hour. She brought Boo downstairs. As a sign of faith, she'd packed up all the dog's belongings. She put them in the bed of the pickup truck, while Boo got in the cab.

After another slow, nerve-racking drive, John pulled up outside Cathy's house. She didn't know he was coming, since she still wasn't taking his calls.

He got out of the pickup and went around to open the passenger door. Boo squeezed out while the door was still half-closed, and proceeded to go berserk.

Barking, leaping, chasing his tail.

John didn't need to put him on the lead; Boo raced ahead of him to the front door. Just as well, since John wasn't strong enough to control fifty pounds of overactive dog.

He didn't need to ring the doorbell, either, since Boo set up a frantic barking that only a dead person wouldn't hear.

Then Cathy opened the door, and it was hard to say who made the most noise, her with her shrieking or Boo with his excited yelps.

"I take it this is Rue's dog?" John shouted over the frenzy.

"Yes." Her whole face was alight in a way John hadn't ever seen it. She dropped to her knees, her arms around the dog's neck. "Boo, darling, welcome home." She buried her face in his fur and laughed as the dog twisted his head to lick her.

John was pathetic enough to feel jealous of the damn dog.

"Where did you find him?" Cathy asked. "I asked the vet for the details of his new owner, and he refused to give them out."

"Because the new owner was his girlfriend." John told her the whole story.

"But Boo is yours now," he concluded. "Merry wants you to have him."

Cathy didn't utter a word of protest. She opened the front door wide. Boo gave one sharp bark, then streaked for the kitchen. When Cathy and John followed, they found him waiting by the back door, tail thumping against the floor.

"I know what you want." She opened the door, tutting indulgently.

Boo raced past her, heading unswervingly to a patch of ivy in the bottom right-hand corner of the yard. He made his way into the middle, squatted.

"No way," John said, flabbergasted

At Cathy's querying look, he explained the dog's bowel problems.

She laughed, a full-throated laugh he hadn't heard from her before. "This is where Boo always goes."

Sure enough, the dog was having the time of his life. The dump of his life.

When Boo came back inside, John would swear he was grinning.

It dawned on John that he had no further reason to hang around. To stand side by side with Cathy, beaming down at the dog like a proud parent.

He shoved his hand in his pocket, jiggled his keys. "Guess I should hit the road." She didn't argue, so he added, "This was my first time driving."

At last she dragged her gaze away from the dog and paid him some attention. Even if it was only professional courtesy.

"John, you look flushed," she said.

He was grateful for even that crumb of concern. "I think I'm getting the flu," he said, making his voice just a little feeble.

She pressed the back of her hand to his forehead, and he realized he'd missed her touch. *That's probably more about my loneliness than about Cathy.*

"What are your symptoms?" she asked.

"Aching limbs, a bit of nausea."

"Lift your pant legs," she ordered, as brusquely as if they were back to "Mr. Wyatt" and "Nurse Martin."

He obeyed.

She gasped, and he looked down and saw what she did.

His ankles and calves were swollen. Uh-oh.

"John, you're having a rejection episode." Her calm words struck a chill into his heart. "It's quite common and possibly not at all serious—" in which case, why had her voice started shaking? "—but we need to get you to the hospital."

Two minutes later, they were in her car, reversing out of her garage.

John knew it was psychological, but he felt sicker already. "I thought I had the flu," he said, as Cathy swung out into the road.

"You're an idiot," she said.

"I know."

"DAD'S FINE," MERRY TOLD Lucas the moment he opened the door at Dwight's house. She could have phoned, but she'd annoyed him, possibly even upset him, so she wanted to explain in person.

"I ought to toss you out on your butt." He stood aside to let her in. "I've been calling the hospital. As John's family I'm entitled to updates about his condition…but apparently you instructed them not to tell me anything."

"Sorry," she lied.

He didn't sound as angry as she expected. Which suggested that he trusted there might be method in her madness.

"Dad and Stephanie are on their way to the hospital," Lucas said. "Apparently, *they* are allowed to visit."

She widened her eyes innocently.

He tsked. "When you say your dad's fine, what exactly do you mean?"

She followed him into the dining room. "Seventy percent of transplant patients have a rejection episode, according to Cathy. Most don't lose their new kidney. The doctors are feeding Dad some stronger drugs for a couple of days, and keeping him in the hospital for observation, since he lives alone." And since Cathy had insisted on it. Merry would happily have stayed with her dad at his home, but she preferred knowing he was in the hospital.

Lucas had obviously been working in the dining room. His laptop was open, and a number of Magic Eye books were spread across the table.

He leaned against the edge of the table, arms folded across his chest. "So what was all that about? One vastly inadequate text message, then telling the hospital I wasn't allowed to visit or receive information over the phone."

"How did it make you feel?" she asked.

"How do think?" he growled. "Powerless. Useless. Desperately worried." His voice cracked, revealing a raw vulnerability that filled her with contrition.

"I'm sorry," she said, meaning it this time. "But, Lucas, there was nothing you could do, and if it had turned out to be more serious, if Dad had died or something, I didn't want you to have a single thing to hang your overdeveloped sense of responsibility on."

It took Lucas a moment to process that. "Are you saying you kept me out of it so that *I* wouldn't get hurt?"

"I guess you could put it like that," she said.

"But I wanted to be there. To support you. To do what I could for your dad." He hadn't slept last night for worrying about her, and it was all because of some crazy whim?

"I would have loved to have you there in support," she admitted. "No one's better at that than you are."

"Don't pander to me now," he grumbled. Though he did feel somewhat mollified.

"But you couldn't do anything for Dad," she said. "Not a thing. And I know you, Lucas. If he'd died last night, you'd be torturing yourself for goodness knows how long about what you might have done differently."

He wanted to yell at her that he wasn't that stupid. But…she was right. He was conscious of feeling enormous relief that he would have been spared that burden. But at the same time…

"I can't just not show up at *life,* so that I don't have to feel bad afterward," he said. "What if that had been our child?"

"Then of course you'd have been there," she said quickly. "And I won't do this to you again. I just wanted to, I guess, teach you something." She bit her lip on the left side. "Did it work?"

"You are such a pain," he said, half laughing, half wanting to shake her.

"It did, didn't it?" she said, adorably pleased with herself. "Go on, tell me what you're thinking."

He rolled his eyes. But she'd earned the right to an answer. "I'm thinking," he said slowly, "I might have to accept that even if I'd been there with Mom that day, it wouldn't have changed anything." The admission left him with an ache in his throat. "It's not like I didn't know that in my head already," he said severely.

"I realize that," she said. "But maybe you had trouble accepting it—" he thought she would say *in your heart* "—deep down."

Deep down. That was better. He nodded. "But I think…I think just now I've accepted it."

Merry blinked rapidly. "Okay. Good."

Feeling himself flush, he turned away.

"How are your eye exercises going?" she asked, a change of subject that was clunky but welcome.

"I'm going nuts," he said. "When I do the online tests, I feel like I'm improving, but I still can't see a damn thing with those Magic Eye books. And neither of them is comparable to the navy test, so I have no idea if I'm going to pass."

She made what he considered a moderately sympathetic sound. Insufficient.

"My test is tomorrow," he reminded her.

She grinned. "Okay, okay, poor Hero Chopper Pilot, how awful, et cetera."

"Thanks a lot," he said, but he couldn't hold in a grin.

"Maybe I can help," Merry said. "Let's take a look at one of these Magic Eye books."

"What's the point?" he said.

She snickered at his petulance. "Come on, I'm good at these. Maybe I can coach you through it."

They sat at the table, and she opened the nearest book. Sitting this close to her was as disturbing as Lucas remembered. She smelled of wild strawberries and her lips were a crushed pink. He loved her mouth.

"Have you been holding the book right up to your face?" she asked.

"Uh-huh." Her nose was pretty cute, too.

"Okay, let me take a look at a couple of these, and then we'll do them together." They tried four pictures, all of which Merry found instantly. But when she talked Lucas through it, he always lost focus before the hidden image showed up.

"Maybe you're not looking through the front picture properly," she said.

"It's a book—it's impossible to look through," he said.

"Ah, I think we have our problem." She thought for a moment, her forehead creased.

Lucas sat on his hand so he wouldn't reach out and smooth that crease.

"I know!" she said. "Pull your chair out from the table and turn it around."

Since she'd already proved rather smart this morning, he obeyed without question.

"Now hold the book at the height you normally would." She appraised his posture. "That's about right. I'm going to stand in front of you, so the book is between us." She moved into position. "Now, bring the book closer to your face and try to look through the image."

"I already I told you, I *can't* look through— Merry, *what* are you doing?" He started to lower the book, but she grabbed his wrists, held them in place. His pulse thudded beneath her fingers.

"Now you're going to have to start over," she scolded. "It's very important to keep the book at eye level."

"That would be easier to do," he said, "if you weren't *taking your shirt off*." What on earth was she up to?

And why was he complaining?

She gave him a saucy grin. "Here's the deal. If you hold the book up and try very hard to look through the image, I'll take off my shirt. And by the way, I'm not wearing a bra."

He groaned.

"And when I believe you're trying as hard as you possibly can," she said, "I might just give you a reward."

"*Might just* isn't much of a promise," he complained.

"Take it or leave it."

Lucas took it, of course. He held the book to his eyes.

"Okay, I'll tell you when to start. You need to know I'm undoing the second button. Now the third." From the corner of his eye, he could see small movements. "Now look right through the picture, trying to see my breasts as you slowly move the book away."

"You're insane," he said. "And this is getting painful." He didn't mean for his eyes.

"You do look like you're trying *very* hard," she said admiringly. "For that, I'm undoing another button."

He cursed. "It was going fuzzy, then I lost it."

"Fuzzy's good," she said. "Now, look hard *through* the image, Lucas, because I'm undoing the last button." A moment later she murmured, "Now I'm holding on to my lapels. You need to start moving the book away."

Slowly, he did so. If it was possible to actually see through this page, he was looking hard enough to do it.

"Now—keep looking through—I'm pulling my blouse open."

"I got it!" Lucas yelled. "I can see a snowman. With

a hat and a pipe." He shifted the book. "It's still there, even when I move."

"Congratulations," Merry said. "I'm so proud of you."

He lowered the book and there she was, her blouse wide open, no bra.

"My breasts are getting bigger, don't you think?" she said.

"I don't know," he croaked. "But they're incredible."

She grinned. "I suppose I did promise you a reward." She slipped the blouse off her shoulders and let it drop to the floor.

Lucas was with her in one stride. "Merry, honey-bun—"

"What's going on?" said a voice from the doorway.

His father.

Merry screeched and crossed her arms across her breasts. Lucas, moving faster than he would have thought possible, dived for her blouse, tossed it to her then stood in front of her to shield her from his parents, who were standing in the dining-room doorway.

"What are you doing?" Dwight asked.

Stephanie doubled over next to him, in paroxysms of laughter. "What do you think they're doing?" She tugged on his arm. "Dwight, we need to leave."

"I thought they were getting a divorce," he said.

Behind Lucas, Merry whimpered.

"Dad..." Lucas's voice wobbled, and he knew she'd make him pay for that later. "Listen to your wife. You need to leave."

Ten seconds later, they were alone. Lucas burst out laughing and couldn't stop. Merry was half laughing, half crying, fumbling with the buttons of her blouse.

"Here, let me." He took over the buttons, reminded of when he'd helped her with that wedding dress.

"Your father saw me naked," she moaned.

"Not quite, honeybun. And he's old—in another ten years or so he won't remember a thing."

"Lucas, I'm so mortified."

"Don't be, honeybun. Dad and Stephanie are probably in the living room, so we'll sneak you out the back door, like a respectable stripper."

She groaned.

"But first, I just need to…" His mouth found hers. She melted against him, rising to his kiss. After a few minutes, he had to stop, because next thing, his dad and Stephanie would be walking in on something far more embarrassing.

Reluctantly, he pulled away. He tucked a strand of hair behind her left ear. "Thanks, honeybun. You might have just saved my bacon with that Magic Eye trick. I couldn't have done it without you."

"Happy to help. Even if I can never face your parents again." She planted a quick kiss on his mouth. "This is kind of ironic," she said. "If you pass the test, and I'm in some way responsible, then I just helped you leave me and our baby."

She was gone, out the door, before he could respond.

CHAPTER TWENTY-ONE

LUCAS'S EYE TEST WAS SCHEDULED for eleven o'clock on Friday morning. He'd found he performed better in the mornings, presumably because his eyes hadn't had time to get tired.

On this Friday, he woke at seven, and did something he often meant to do, but seldom did. He called his brother.

Garrett was still at home. Unlike Lucas, he wasn't a morning person, so didn't usually get to his Madison Avenue office before nine.

"What's the problem?" Garrett asked, after they'd exchanged greetings.

Which was an indication of how infrequently they spoke. There had to be a problem for one of them to pick up the phone. *We should probably work on that,* Lucas thought.

"How did you know you were in love with Rachel?" he asked, then grinned, as he could almost hear his brother thinking, *Whoa.*

But Garrett took the question seriously. "Mainly, I found myself fantasizing about putting a ring on her finger. Scary stuff, I tell you."

"Merry's already got a ring on her finger," Lucas grumbled.

"She's your wife," Garrett said, sounding confused. "You're supposed to know you love her by now."

Another good reason to call his brother more often. To fill him in on such trivia as his upcoming divorce.

"It's not that simple." Lucas gave a concise version of the saga to date, from forced wedding to separation. Then he waited for…he wasn't sure what. Advice?

"Sorry, little brother, but you're in trouble," Garrett said.

"How do you figure that?" Lucas demanded, irritated. He realized now he'd wanted his brother to say there were plenty more fish in the sea, or something else typically blasé.

"You're in that denial stage where you think you can get the girl without having to change a thing about yourself," Garrett said.

"And why not?" Lucas asked, though he didn't agree with the assessment. "What happened to loving someone as they are?" Merry had said herself, when she'd laid her cards on the table and trumped him with the scale of her love, it was for better or for worse.

"That works for about five minutes," Garrett said. "Then you realize love changes you and it changes her, and you have to keep adjusting."

It sounded complicated. And risky.

"I'm going back to the Gulf," Lucas said, unsure if he was changing the subject or not. "As soon as I pass my retest."

"That'll screw things up on the home front," Garrett observed.

"Merry's pregnant," Lucas blurted.

His brother started to laugh.

"What's so funny?"

"I find it amusing that the favorite son can make such a mess of his life," Garrett said cheerfully.

"Shut up," Lucas said. Then he realized why he'd called.

"What's up?" Garrett must have sensed a change in the quality of the silence.

"When Mom died," Lucas said. "When you were there, at Clark's."

"What about it?" His voice had cooled.

As kids, they'd talked about their mother all the time. As adults, not so much.

"I'm not sure if I'm trying to confess or apologize," Lucas admitted.

"If this is about you thinking I didn't do a good enough job of trying to save Mom…" Garrett sounded weary.

Hell. "You knew I thought that?" Lucas said, appalled.

"You weren't exactly subtle at twelve," Garrett said. "It wasn't hard to figure out why you kept asking me for a blow-by-blow description of every breath, every compression that I and the paramedic and that other guy did."

Lucas groaned. "I'm sorry."

"I just didn't realize you still thought that way," Garrett said.

"I don't," Lucas said. "For the last dozen years or more, it's been myself that I've blamed, not you."

His brother snorted. "Stupid."

"Yeah. But not anymore. It was one of those things, Garrett. It happened."

"Yeah," he said. "It happened."

Silence fell, a comfortable one. Then Garrett said, "I

better get off the phone before all this touchy-feely crap wrecks my Real Man Ale campaign."

"Seriously, there's a beer called Real Man Ale?" Lucas asked.

"You don't need to tell me you don't drink it," Garrett assured him.

Lucas hung up the phone, feeling drained but invigorated. Catharsis had its pluses.

Why stop now? He checked his watch. Eight o'clock. Plenty of time before his eye test, and Merry wouldn't have left for work yet. He picked up the phone again and called his wife.

FIVE MINUTES AFTER HE PULLED into the parking lot at Clark's Deli, Lucas still hadn't let go of the steering wheel of Stephanie's car.

Merry tapped on the window, startling him.

He unwrapped the fingers of his left hand from the wheel, rolled the window down.

"Why am I here?" she asked. It was cold out. She chafed her arms as she spoke, and her breath came in visible puffs.

"Because I don't want to go in on my own," he said.

"We're going in?" She smiled and put her hand over his on the wheel. "Thanks. I'm honored."

"Yeah, well, you've been so great at pointing out my insecurities," he said. "It's only right you should live with the consequences."

Maybe because he had Merry at his side, walking into the store didn't prove as difficult as he'd feared.

Clark's didn't appear to have changed in all these years. The store was long and narrow, with four aisles of shelves, coolers and freezers holding a mix of fancy deli food and grocery staples. Clark's was convenient and quick to get around, but not cheap. When Lucas's mom was alive, she'd done her main shopping at the big supermarket a mile away. But there were enough emergencies and incidentals that she'd stopped here frequently, and Lucas had often come with her.

Had they played Muzak back then? Lucas couldn't remember, but right now, something jazzy was playing through the speakers.

"I take it we're not here to buy beer," Merry said.

He couldn't quite smile. "It happened... Mom was at the checkout."

The store still had just two checkout counters, with a wide aisle between. Right now, there was no one at either register.

"Can I help you?" asked the clerk on the right, a girl with a pale face and dyed-black hair.

Lucas rubbed the back of his neck. "Uh, is there anyone around who used to work here seventeen, eighteen years ago?"

"Only Mr. Clark, but he's not in today."

"In that case, we're just looking," Lucas told her. To Merry, he said, "Mom always used to go to the checkout on the left, even if the line was longer. The clerk on that side was way more efficient."

"So you think she would have been in that line that day?" Merry asked.

"She was at the front of it. The clerk was scanning her items when Mom collapsed. The store delivered the groceries the next morning." He frowned. "I don't know if anyone ever paid for them."

Merry touched his arm, as if to tell him it was okay to be quiet. He didn't need to entertain her.

He stared down at the speckled linoleum floor, picturing the scene, the way he had so many times. His throat clogged.

Merry leaned in close. He let go of her hand and put his arm around her, pulling her closer still.

His vision blurred. "I couldn't have brought her back," he murmured.

"No," Merry agreed.

He lifted his head, scanned the checkout area. Then higher, gazing at the ceiling, with its acoustic tiles and fluorescent lighting.

"She's not here," he said. The words just fell out of his mouth. Thanks to his lack of thought, it was about the stupidest thing he'd ever said. *Quite clearly, my dead mother isn't here.*

"You don't need this place to be some kind of—of shrine to her." Merry got right to the essence of what it was he'd meant. "Your mom's in your heart. She always will be."

He drew a deep breath, suspiciously shuddery.

Then a customer pushed past him. She hadn't bothered with a basket, and had her arms full with two cartons of milk and a pack of eggs. A loaf of bread dangled in its plastic bag from between two fingers. She shifted her burden, trying to put something down without dropping the rest. Just as Lucas stepped forward to help, she lost the battle. The eggs fell to the floor; the carton burst open. The very spot that Lucas had been regarding, as Merry said, almost as a shrine, was now smeared with egg: yolks, whites, shells.

As the checkout girl came out from behind her counter with a roll of paper towels, Lucas started to laugh.

"What on earth...?" Merry said. Then, laughing too, she wrapped her arms around him, went up on tiptoe and kissed him.

The initiative was all hers—demanding lips, seeking tongue—and she set Lucas alight. His hands moved down to her butt as he kissed her back, ferociously. Voraciously.

"Excuse me." The woman who'd dropped the eggs paused in her assistance with the cleanup. "This is a public place, and that's inappropriate."

Lucas pulled away from Merry, still snickering.

"You were amazing," Merry said. "I don't mean the kiss, though that was amazing, too. I mean coming here, doing this."

"It's not that big a deal," he lied.

"I hate to scare you," she said, "but you're evolving into a man who's in touch with his emotions, right before my eyes."

"Garbage," Lucas said. He recalled his brother's words from earlier. *You think you can get the girl without having to change a thing about yourself.*

Dealing with a couple of his outstanding issues wasn't changing or evolving. He wasn't trying to get the girl; he wasn't even in the running. He couldn't be.

"We're done here," he told Merry. "I have an eye test to get to."

WHITE LIGHT. SO BRIGHT, JOHN could see it with his eyes closed.

This was what he disliked most about being in the

hospital, having no choice about when lights went on and off when he ate.

Small complaints, given that the doctors were committed to saving his life once again. The life he'd "started over" six weeks ago today.

Not such a big deal, saving it this time. This was his third day in the hospital, three days of heavy-duty medication with side effects like vomiting and headaches. Unpleasant, but he was going to be fine.

Noises filtered into his consciousness. The occasional clank of metal penetrated first, then distant voices. Last time, at a moment just like this, he'd decided to ask the first woman he saw on a date. And had ended up with a sharp-tongued, shy-smiled, full-breasted nurse.

He missed her. A complete life wasn't lived alone.

I need someone. No, not *someone.* He didn't want to date the first woman he saw, or any woman. Except Cathy, who hadn't been out of his head for more than five minutes since she'd had the good sense to dump him nearly a week ago.

He heard footsteps next to his bed. With a surge of excitement that made him feel twenty years old, he opened his eyes, already smiling.

"We're in a happy mood, Mr. Wyatt, aren't we?" Nurse Barbara Kay was sweet, jolly, patient and always cheerful.

He didn't want her. "Is Cathy Martin working today?" he asked.

She shook her head good-naturedly over his lack of a greeting. "I believe she is, Mr. Wyatt, but you know how it is."

He knew. Cathy had asked not to work with him. The news had hurt him, even though he'd understood why.

He'd been a jerk.

"This has gone on too long," he told Nurse Kay as she flashed a thermometer into his ear.

"How about I get you some nice breakfast?" Nurse Kay thought everything was "nice."

"How about you get me Nurse Martin," he said. "Tell her I have something for her... No." Inspiration struck. "Tell her I have something of her sister's."

Nurse Kay looked skeptical.

"Tell her now," John said. Meekly, he added, "Please."

While he waited, he brushed his teeth—you never knew when you might need fresh breath—and replaced his pajama top with a T-shirt. He looked at himself in the bathroom mirror. Was this all he had to offer? He must be joking.

He did have something else to offer, he reminded himself. The art folio that Merry had brought in at his request, along with his paints and brushes, was propped against the wall. He unzipped it, retrieved the watercolor he'd spent most of the past two days on. The conditions hadn't been ideal—harsh hospital lighting, a drawing board propped against his knees, and even Nurse Kay's endless patience tried by the clutter. But the picture had been so clear in his head, it hadn't mattered.

John climbed back into bed.

Just in time, because Cathy arrived a minute later, brisk and snappish, in pale pink scrubs. Someone should tell her it wasn't her color; she looked much nicer in the lilac.

"Barbara said you have something of my sister's." She stood, hands on hips, scowling.

He knew that scowl, knew that it masked pain, that it held her defenses in place so she could get through the day.

"How are you, Cathy?" he asked. She wasn't close enough. He wanted to touch her.

She blinked. "I'm fine."

"And Boo?"

"He's fine." Then, belatedly, truculently, she asked, "How are you?"

"All the better for seeing you," he said.

Naturally, she didn't think much of that. "What is it you have of Rue's?" she demanded.

"Ah. I lied."

She turned on her heel.

"Tell me this," he said loudly, "how does a sixty-one-year-old man who hasn't been with a woman in over twenty years fix things when he screws up with a woman he cares for?"

A young nurse walking past the doorway burst into giggles, a clue that he might have overdone the volume.

But at least Cathy had stopped. She turned around. "He doesn't," she said stonily. "If he doesn't care enough, nothing's going to fix it."

"What if he's been blind and stupid, and hadn't realized how much he cared?" John asked.

Her shoulders trembled. "How much *does* he care?"

That was his Cathy. Straight to the point, wanting a specific, quantifiable answer.

"I painted this for you." He turned over the portrait on his knees, held it out to her.

It wasn't large, about the size of two sheets of printer paper. She took it in both hands.

"Oh," she said, and tears spurted in her eyes.

"You said you didn't have any recent pictures of Rue," he reminded her. "I'm not great with portraits, but I thought…this might do."

For the first time in his life, he'd painted a scene that was equal parts fantasy and reality. Reality was Cathy, sitting on the middle bench of the *Sally Sue,* straight-backed, fishing rod in hand, smiling closemouthed. Fantasy was that, alongside Cathy, was another woman, almost a mirror image, but fuller in the face and figure. Not holding a rod, but raising a cocktail glass to the viewer, her smile wider than Cathy's.

"It's her," she said. "It's exactly her." Carefully, she set the painting down on his tray table. She pressed her fingertips to her eyes, dabbing at moisture. "Better than a mug," she said.

He cringed. "I'm sorry about the mug. I hate the mug."

At last she came close enough for him to touch, and he took her hands in his. "You wouldn't believe how happy I am to see you."

Her dubious expression suggested he was right, she wouldn't believe it.

"I've missed you, Cathy."

"You've missed having the company," she said uncertainly.

"I've missed *you*." He squeezed her fingers. "I don't want anyone else, any other company. When I think about you, you're not runner-up. To anyone."

Her lips parted and her brow furrowed, as if she couldn't be certain of his meaning.

"I could—" John cleared his throat "—I could love you."

CHAPTER TWENTY-TWO

"THAT WAS THE LAST OF THE activity tests, Lieutenant Commander Calder." Dr. Ruth Ziegler smiled at Lucas. "So far, you've passed with flying colors. You may just want to rub yourself down with that towel before we move on to the eye test. Wouldn't want sweat in your eyes."

He'd had to sit the entire physical again, not just the component he'd failed last time. Which meant pretending his hand didn't hurt, but that was okay.

"Will you be doing the eye test in here?" Lucas asked, looking around Dr. Ziegler's large office, which held several fitness machines. She worked here at the submarine base in Groton, and was apparently one of the navy's top medics.

"I will. The equipment pulls out of this cupboard." She crossed to a floor-to-ceiling unit and opened it. "Any last requests?" she asked, as she wheeled the familiar optometric testing station out.

"Can you open the blinds, please?" Lucas asked.

"Someone's been reading up on how to pass the eye test," she said. But she raised the venetian blinds so the window was bare. The office was much brighter. "Let's have you sitting on this stool, please."

The first part of the test, for short- or long-sightedness, astigmatism and other eye problems Lucas didn't have, went fine. At least, he assumed none of those things had changed in the two months since his last test.

"Now for the biggie, depth perception. You've obviously been practicing," Dr. Ziegler said with interest. "What have you found most useful?"

Outside, a cloud chose that very moment to cover the sun, lowering the light level in the office.

Lucas stifled a curse.

"It's not too bad," the doctor sympathized. She handed him a device, a kind of "black box."

"What's this?" Lucas asked.

"It's a Verhoeff stereopter. It tests your depth perception."

"I didn't use this last time." Hell, had he been practicing the wrong kind of test?

"It's one of several tests approved by the navy," Dr. Ziegler said. "It's the one I prefer."

They started the test. Lucas pretended Merry was standing beyond the machine, topless, and did his best to look through the various combinations of three bars whose distance he was required to judge.

He felt as if the exam was easier than last time…but last time he'd had no clue that he was missing half of what he was supposed to see, so who knew?

Dr. Ziegler read his results. "Hmm," she said.

What did that mean?

Lucas forced himself to breathe. If he'd failed…he'd just have to stick around and help Merry when the baby came along.

The office brightened, as that damn cloud moved away.

"We're going to run through it twice more, Lucas," Dr.

Ziegler said. She moved swiftly to set him back up again. "Try sitting ramrod-straight with your heels against the back of the chair's footrest. It improves the blood flow to the optic nerve."

The stereopter used a randomizing process, so the test wasn't at all the same as the one he'd just completed. When he was done, the doctor viewed the new results.

"Interesting," she said. "The first test, you were three points short of a pass. Second and third time around, with better lighting, you were right on the pass mark."

"Which score do you plan to record in my test results?" Lucas asked.

"I'm going to pass you." She beamed. "You're back in. Congratulations."

Not quite back in; he still needed to get the discharge officially revoked. But now that he'd passed the eye test, that was a mere formality. If he wanted it to be.

He could be back in the Gulf with his unit, back in his chopper, doing the work he was made for, in a matter of days. The guy who'd been flying his chopper temporarily would doubtless be miffed. But Lucas was the best man for the job.

He wouldn't see Merry again until the baby came. Then he'd be back to work, before the kid even learned to smile.

"Lieutenant Commander, would you like a tissue?" Dr. Ziegler proffered a Kleenex box.

Hell. Lucas pulled out a couple of tissues, mashed them against his eyes. "Those eye tests," he muttered. "They're quite a strain."

MERRY TOOK A WALK ON THE BEACH during her lunch break, hoping the breeze might blow away the nausea that came on around ten o'clock most mornings and disappeared around three.

Actually, this wasn't so much a lunch break as the end of a shortened day. With Dad in the hospital, there was a limit to how much she could do in the office. She grinned as she remembered the phone call she'd had from her father a few hours ago. He'd patched things up with Cathy, and he'd sounded happier than Merry could remember.

It was strange walking on the beach without Boo, but he was ecstatic to be back in his old home. She wondered if he knew Cathy wasn't Ruby, or if he just didn't care.

Next July, she'd be walking with her baby strapped to her chest, so she wouldn't need to wrestle a stroller across the pebbles and sand.

Merry patted her still-flat stomach. *Grow, little baby, grow.*

Lucas would probably want to take the baby for walks, too, when he was on leave. She wondered if he'd finished his eye test, and what the outcome was. For his sake, she hoped he passed.

I'll miss him so much.

As if her longing had transported him here, she heard him call her name. She looked up to see him striding along the beach, into the wind. It was amazing that she'd heard him at all.

He wore a khaki uniform under his leather flight jacket, so he must have come straight from the test. As he drew closer, she could see he was grinning.

He'd passed.

Merry's stomach dropped like a rock and fresh nausea roiled through her. She dredged up a smile, pinned it on.

"You passed," she said, when he reached her. "Congratulations."

"Thanks." He hauled her into his arms and kissed her with a sweetness that made her want to cry. *Baby hormones. And a northerly wind.*

Sniffing, she pulled back. "So, now what? You appeal the discharge?"

Maybe he would say no, he'd changed his mind.

"Already did," he announced. "I spoke to my C.O., and he said it'll be revoked in a day or two."

It was stupid to be surprised, Merry knew. This was who Lucas was, the guy always looking for the next rescue mission.

Lucas pulled a rolled-up sheet of paper from the inside pocket of his leather jacket. "I got you something."

She took it, unrolled it. "A Magic Eye picture? Haven't you seen enough of those?"

He grinned. "This is a custom picture, made to order. For you. I sat on the phone to the Magic Eye people until they agreed to do it right away."

Merry examined the jumbled pattern of rings and hearts in blues, white and yellow. "I don't get it."

"That's because you haven't looked at it yet, honeybun." He touched her cheek, and something in his face—a tenderness—made her heart stutter. "You need to hold it up to your face. Would it help if I take my shirt off while you look at it?"

Yes, please. And more.

"It's December in Connecticut," she said. "I'd rather have you alive." *And with me.* But he'd already said that wasn't going to happen.

She held the picture up to her eyes, then moved it

back. The hidden image came into focus, two words standing out, clear as anything: *Rescue Me*.

She stared at it for long seconds.

"Can't you see it?" he asked anxiously.

"I see it." Merry bit her lip. "I'm not sure I understand it." She knew what she wanted it to mean, but she wasn't about to lay her heart on the line again.

He took the picture from her, rerolled it and slipped it into his jacket. "When I asked for my discharge to be revoked, I requested that it be a temporary measure."

"But…you're going back to the Gulf?"

"Yes and no."

Her heart started to race. "What does that mean?" She shivered.

"Honeybun, you're cold." Lucas unzipped his jacket. He tugged her into his arms, then pulled the jacket around both of them. "That better?"

Much. She nodded.

"You may not know this, but I'm the best guy in my unit at mine detection."

"I do know that, Hero Chopper Pilot." Dwight had told her dad, who'd told her.

Lucas kissed the tip of her nose. "So, naturally, I need to be back there to make sure not too many people die, that kind of thing."

"If you say so," she said. Had she been dumb enough to think that Lucas might have learned something recently?

"Wrong," he said. "I need to do my bit, but I can't take full responsibility for every man we have in the Gulf."

Okay, maybe he *had* learned something.

"I'm going back over there to pass on my knowledge

and experience to the other guys," he said. "To bring them up to standard. When I've done that, my responsibility will have been discharged. Though I might need you to remind me of that sometimes."

Especially, she thought, if they heard reports of mine-related fatalities. Her heart swelled with pride in him. "So, will you be somewhere nearby, that I'll get to tell you these things?" she asked.

"I'll be back before the baby arrives," he said, "and from then on I'll be very close by. About as close as I am now." He took a break from explaining to kiss her thoroughly. "I love you, Merry."

For some reason, her brain didn't issue the caution it had the last time he'd said that. Her heart went a bit crazy, though.

"I know you're going to ask me why I love you," he said. "So here it is. You're stubborn, your standards are too high, you never let me get away with anything."

He stopped.

"That's *it?*" she said.

"Nope, that's just the worse part of '*for better or for worse.*'"

"Can I hear the better?" she asked.

"You see right into the heart of me," he said, "and I don't know why, but you love me anyway. You have faith in me to be a better person, and you make me want to be that person. I don't laugh as much with anyone else as I do with you. I know that whatever plan I come up with next, you'll point out all the holes, but you'll be with me every step of the way."

He stopped again.

"Uh…" Merry said.

"That's the short version," he said. "I hope to have the rest of my life to tell you the rest."

Even as she blinked away tears, she couldn't contain her smile. "That sounds like a plan," she said.

"And by the way, the answer to your question? Yes. If you weren't pregnant, I'd still want to stay married to you. I love you, Merry," he said. "You may not need me, but I need you. Say you'll be my wife, now and always."

She put a hand to his cheek, cupped it. "I'll be your wife, now and always."

His joyous laugh rang on the breeze.

"I love you so much," she said. "And I do need you, but don't let that go to your head."

"I won't," he said solemnly. "Well, I probably will, but again, I'll rely on you to set me straight. We're in this together, honeybun, you and me, side by side, each for the other."

Merry sighed happily. "There's nothing wrong with your depth perception at all," she said. And kissed him.

EPILOGUE

Christmas, one year later

"IT'S OFFICIAL," LUCAS SAID as he taped his daughter's diaper. "You're stinkier than your aunt Mia."

Rose Michelle Calder gave him one of her smiles that grabbed him by the heart and squeezed every time. At nearly six months old, she'd recently started laughing—great, fat chortles that made Lucas and Merry chortle back.

Lucas picked Rose up from her changing table and carried her back to the living room of the Victorian house he and Merry had bought. They'd moved in last February, and since Lucas had arrived back from the Gulf in June, he'd been renovating the place full-time. Turning it into a home for his family.

Today, Christmas Day, was the first time they'd had everyone here. A traditional Christmas dinner had left them all replete, and a contented hum of conversation filled the living room.

Though Lucas's entry with Rose caused a bit of a stir.

"I'll take her." John held out his arms for his granddaughter, beating Cathy, Dwight and Stephanie to the punch. Rose had more adoring grandparents in her life than was good for a young girl. But they would come in handy later, when Lucas and Merry wanted more private time for themselves.

When he was sure John had Rose safely in hand, Lucas headed for his seat on the couch next to Merry. To get to her, he had to dodge the LEGOS castle that Mia had built. Maddie, Garrett and Rachel's nine-month-old daughter, watched Mia from her father's lap, fascinated.

At last, Lucas dropped into his space next to Merry. She turned to kiss him, as if he'd been gone five hours, not five minutes. Naturally, one touch of her lips and he wanted to drag her upstairs and make love to her. Something he'd been doing at every opportunity since he got home. Something he'd never grow sick of. In the interest of decency, he settled for caressing the nape of her neck.

A languorous half hour later, John spoke up. "Cathy and I should probably get home for a rest. I'm still a bit tired from the surgery."

His claim produced good-natured hoots from the assembled company. John had been back at full strength for months now. He'd had no more rejection episodes and was in excellent health, his blood pressure high, but controlled by medication. Still, he trotted out that "tired from surgery" excuse every time he wanted to rush home and make love to his new wife. As he'd once confided to Lucas, in a moment Lucas would rather forget, "I have a lot of catching up to do."

Cathy's cheeks had turned pink. "And we do need to get home to Boo," she said, which was her equivalent of the surgery excuse.

No one could be bothered getting up to see them out, so John and Cathy said their goodbyes right there, then walked out hand in hand. "See you at work," John called over his shoulder to Lucas.

After much thought, Lucas had decided to put his marine engineering degree to use by going into business with John. It wasn't about Lucas coming to the rescue; it was more about finding something that interested him deeply. John had welcomed Lucas's knowledge of new materials and new technologies that could be absorbed into the business without losing the handmade, craftsman flair that made Wyatt Yachts so popular. Lucas would have his first day there on Monday.

Dwight and Stephanie gathered up Mia's paraphernalia—diminishing in volume as she grew older—and left, after they'd secured a commitment for drinks on New Year's Eve.

An hour later, Garrett and Rachel headed upstairs "for a nap." They were staying a few days, and Lucas had relished the time spent with his brother. Merry and Rachel were getting along like a house on fire. They'd been talking this week about going into business together, starting something that would fit with the time they wanted to spend with their families. Lucas didn't doubt that with Rachel's marketing skills and Merry's imagination and organizational genius, they would pull off something exceptional.

At last, Lucas was alone with his wife. Her eyes were closed, betraying her tiredness after the long day. But when his finger traced the neckline of her low-cut sweater, she smiled.

"Does Rose look ready for a nap?" she asked without opening her eyes.

"Definitely." He slipped his hand into the sweater and cupped one perfect, small breast.

She gasped.

Now Lucas had a dilemma. He wanted to take their daughter to her crib, but not let go of his wife.

"Rose first," Merry said, reading his mind, still with her eyes closed. "I'm not going anywhere."

But when Lucas got back from the nursery, she was stretched out on the sofa, sound asleep. Though disappointed that he wouldn't be making love to her in the next few minutes, Lucas couldn't imagine a prettier sight.

He turned out the light, put another log on the fire, tossed in a couple of pinecones and sat looking into the flames, Merry's feet in his lap.

A hero to no one but his wife. Happy as a man could be.

* * * * *

COMING NEXT MONTH
from Harlequin® SuperRomance®
AVAILABLE NOVEMBER 27, 2012

#1818 THE SPIRIT OF CHRISTMAS
Liz Talley

When Mary Paige Gentry helps a homeless man, she never imagines the gesture would give her the windfall of a lifetime! The catch? Having to deal with the miserly—but gorgeous—Brennan Henry, who clearly doesn't know the meaning of the season.

#1819 THE TIME OF HER LIFE
Jeanie London

New job, new town...new man? Now that Susanna Adams's kids are out of the house, she's ready for a little *me* time. But is she ready to fall for Jay Canady, her irresistible—and younger—coworker? The attraction could be too strong to ignore!

#1820 THE LONG WAY HOME
Cathryn Parry

Bruce Cole has made avoidance a way of life. But when he goes home for the first time in ten years, he has to face the past he's been running from. And Natalie Kimball, the only person who knows his secret....

#1821 CROSSING NEVADA
Jeannie Watt

All Tess O'Neil wants is to be alone. After a brutal attack ends her modeling career, she retreats to a Nevada ranch to find solitude. Which isn't easy with a neighbor like Zach Nolan. The single father and his kids manage to get past her defenses when she least expects it.

#1822 WISH UPON A CHRISTMAS STAR
Darlene Gardner

Her brother might still be alive? Private investigator Maria DiMarco has to track down this lead, even if it's a long shot. Little does she imagine her search will reunite her with her old flame Logan Collier. It could be that miracles do happen!

#1823 ESPRESSO IN THE MORNING
Dorie Graham

Lucas Williams recognizes the signs. When single mom Claire Murphy starts coming into his coffee shop, he sees a troubled soul he's sure he can help—if she'll let him. First, he'll have to fight his attraction to be the friend she needs.

You can find more information on upcoming Harlequin® titles, free excerpts and more at www.Harlequin.com.

HSRCNM1112

REQUEST YOUR FREE BOOKS!
2 FREE NOVELS PLUS 2 FREE GIFTS!

Harlequin®

Super Romance®

Exciting, emotional, unexpected!

YES! Please send me 2 FREE Harlequin® Superromance® novels and my 2 FREE gifts (gifts are worth about $10). After receiving them, if I don't wish to receive any more books, I can return the shipping statement marked "cancel." If I don't cancel, I will receive 6 brand-new novels every month and be billed just $4.69 per book in the U.S. or $5.24 per book in Canada. That's a saving of at least 15% off the cover price! It's quite a bargain! Shipping and handling is just 50¢ per book in the U.S. and 75¢ per book in Canada.* I understand that accepting the 2 free books and gifts places me under no obligation to buy anything. I can always return a shipment and cancel at any time. Even if I never buy another book, the two free books and gifts are mine to keep forever.

135/336 HDN FC6T

Name	(PLEASE PRINT)	

Address		Apt. #

City	State/Prov.	Zip/Postal Code

Signature (if under 18, a parent or guardian must sign)

Mail to the **Reader Service:**
IN U.S.A.: P.O. Box 1867, Buffalo, NY 14240-1867
IN CANADA: P.O. Box 609, Fort Erie, Ontario L2A 5X3

Not valid for current subscribers to Harlequin Superromance books.
**Are you a current subscriber to Harlequin Superromance books
and want to receive the larger-print edition?
Call 1-800-873-8635 or visit www.ReaderService.com.**

* Terms and prices subject to change without notice. Prices do not include applicable taxes. Sales tax applicable in N.Y. Canadian residents will be charged applicable taxes. Offer not valid in Quebec. This offer is limited to one order per household. All orders subject to credit approval. Credit or debit balances in a customer's account(s) may be offset by any other outstanding balance owed by or to the customer. Please allow 4 to 6 weeks for delivery. Offer available while quantities last.

Your Privacy—The Reader Service is committed to protecting your privacy. Our Privacy Policy is available online at www.ReaderService.com or upon request from the Reader Service.

We make a portion of our mailing list available to reputable third parties that offer products we believe may interest you. If you prefer that we not exchange your name with third parties, or if you wish to clarify or modify your communication preferences, please visit us at www.ReaderService.com/consumerschoice or write to us at Reader Service Preference Service, P.O. Box 9062, Buffalo, NY 14269. Include your complete name and address.

Turn the page for a preview of
THE OTHER SIDE OF US
by
Sarah Mayberry,
coming January 2013
from Harlequin® Superromance®.

PLUS, exciting changes are in the works!
Enjoy the same great stories in a longer format
and new look—beginning January 2013!

THE OTHER SIDE OF US
A brand-new novel
from Harlequin® Superromance® author
Sarah Mayberry

Oliver Garrett was only trying to introduce himself to his new—and very attractive—neighbor, Mackenzie Williams. Nothing wrong with being friendly, right? But then she shut the door in his face! Read on for an exciting excerpt from THE OTHER SIDE OF US by Sarah Mayberry.

OLIVER STARED AT THE DOOR in shock. He was pretty sure no one had ever slammed a door in his face before. Not once.

He walked to his place.

Clearly, Mackenzie Williams was not interested in being friendly. From the second she'd laid eyes on him she'd been willing him gone. Well. He wouldn't make the mistake of doing the right thing again. She could take her rude self and—

He paused, aware of the hostility in his thoughts. Perhaps too high a level given his brief acquaintance with Mackenzie. They'd been talking, what? For a handful of minutes?

Six months ago this incident would have made him laugh and worry about her blood pressure. Today he had the urge to do something childish to let her know that he wasn't interested in her anyway.

But that wasn't entirely true.

HSREXP1112R

Because he *was* interested. When he'd gotten that first glimpse of her, had seen her gorgeous toned body, he'd lost track of his thoughts. And it had taken a second or two to remember what he'd intended to say.

So, yeah. He did want to know his new neighbor. He wanted to think there was a good explanation for her rudeness, that it wasn't a reaction to the sight of him.

Guess that means another trip next door.

Next time, however, he'd be prepared. Next time he would give her a strong reason *not* to close the door.

What will Oliver's plan to win over Mackenzie be?
Stay tuned next month for a continuing excerpt from
THE OTHER SIDE OF US by Sarah Mayberry,
available January 2013 from Harlequin® Superromance®.

Copyright © 2013 by Small Cow Productions PTY Ltd.

ROMANTIC
SUSPENSE

Get your heart racing this holiday season with double the pulse-pounding action.

Christmas Confidential

Featuring

Holiday Protector by **Marilyn Pappano**

Miri Duncan doesn't care that it's almost Christmas. She's got bigger worries on her mind. But surviving the trip to Georgia from Texas is going to be her biggest challenge. Days in a car with the man who broke her heart and helped send her to prison—private investigator Dean Montgomery.

A Chance Reunion by **Linda Conrad**

When the husband Elana Novak left behind five years ago shows up in her new California home she knows danger is coming her way. To protect the man she is quickly falling for Elana must convince private investigator Gage Chance that she is a different person. But Gage isn't about to let her walk away…even with the bad guys right on their heels.

Available December 2012 wherever books are sold!